Mr. K and the Super

A FICTIONALIZED ACCOUNT OF A STUDENT-SUPER IN NEW YORK CITY IN THE EARLY 1950S

Frank W. Dressler

outskirtspress
DENVER, COLORADO

Mr. K and the Super
A fictionalized account of a student-super in New York City in the early 1950s

Outskirts Press, Inc.
http://www.outskirtspress.com

ISBN: 978-1-4787-0969-5

Outskirts Press and the "OP" logo are trademarks belonging to Outskirts Press, Inc.

PRINTED IN THE UNITED STATES OF AMERICA

FOR OUR GRANDCHILDREN

Foreword

I completed this manuscript some 30 years ago, or at least 25 years after serving as Superintendent of 6 and 8 West 90th Street in New York City in the years 1951-1953. Even then my memories of some tenants and events were hazy. What is not hazy is my memory of Mr. K's efforts to blend his limited English with what I am sure was his excellent Polish. I can't and haven't tried to replicate this in the manuscript, however to my surprise, by watching Mr. K. carefully while he spoke, I was usually able to accurately translate what my boss was trying to tell me.

But all of the events and conversations herein took place more than 60 years ago. I kept no notes or letters or other documents of our eventful two years and have only recently lost touch with the last of the former tenants with whom we exchanged Christmas cards. In short, this is not a memoir but a fictionalized account of the Dresslers' wonderful two years in residence at 6 and 8 West 90th Street.

After completing the manuscript, I sent the required brief description plus a few chapters of the manuscript to a number of publishers and quickly received rejection notices from one and all. That did it. I placed two copies of the manuscript in brown paper bags, over-wrapped them in duct tape and placed them in a filing cabinet.

Now in my eighties, I recently noticed the bundles. I finally found the courage to open one and re-read the manuscript. Was it something our kids and grandkids would enjoy? Wini (think Cindy) and I (aka Franklin) weren't sure, but finally decided to have copies made for family members. Why? Because in our case the start of our marriage, combined with preparing for and launching our professional careers, was one of the most exhilarating, maturing, and satisfying periods of our young lives. Hopefully this will resonate in the lives of our kids and grandkids – especially our grandkids.

Are any of the residents of 6 and 8 West 90th Street still alive? After 60 years our guess is there would be precious few since we were the youngest tenants at the time I was Super. Our hope is that our remarkable landlords, the Karbowskis (a fictitious name), lived to see their beloved Poland regain its freedom.

Frank Dressler

Table of Contents

CHAPTER 1

Poisoning Pigeons in the Park,

The voice on the phone was distraught. "Franklin, Franklin," it shouted. "Get down here! There are pickets outside blocking the entrance to the apartments. Donna and Uncle Louie are afraid to enter the building!"

The voice belonged to Jack Ripon, normally one of the most composed people I knew.

Pickets? Why would anyone picket 6 and 8 West 90th Street in New York? More to the point, what could I do about them? No one ever told me that confronting picketers was a building superintendent's duty!

I ran downstairs to the inner door of 8 West and looked out. Sure enough, there was a small crowd of about 20 people, well-dressed, well-behaved, but obviously angry, and they were moving in a circle outside in front of me. They were carrying signs, and what I read on them made me shudder.

THOU SHALT NOT KILL!

STOP THE KILLING!

PIGEON POISONERS DESERVE DEATH!

Pigeon poisoners? Was poisoning pigeons what these stern people were so upset about? And what did that have to do with anyone living here?

I went out through the foyer and slowly edged my way across the sidewalk and asked an onlooker what the picketing was all about.

"Don't quite know, son," the old man said. "Judging from the signs, they're members of the local Audubon Society. And judging from their clothes and their binoculars, I'd guess they're all rich birdwatchers."

He stressed 'they' as if 'they' were a strange breed of bird themselves.

"Do you know why they're angry?" I asked.

He shifted his weight. "Appears they've found someone who's been poisoning the pigeons in Central Park."

I frowned. "Any idea who?"

He turned to look me full in the face, puzzled by my continued questions. Seeing I really wanted to know, he decided to share the rest of what he knew. "The leader – that guy with the megaphone – said it was some sort of foreigner, probably a Communist out to destroy our way of life," he said.

I frowned again. Foreigner? Communist? To be sure, this was 1951, and Joe McCarthy, the junior senator from Wisconsin, had many people suspecting there were Communists everywhere. But at 6 and 8 West 90th Street, New York City, which were owned by a Pole whose beloved homeland was ruled by Communists?

The whole thing was nuts. But the question remained: What should I do? Call Mr. K, the landlord? Call the police?

I decided that calling in "outsiders" would only make the picketers more upset. The man with the megaphone, whom I hoped was the leader, looked like a well-to-do lawyer or businessman who was not likely to be violent, so I moved towards him and caught his arm.

"Sir, I'm the Super of these two buildings," I said by way of introduction. "Can you tell me what this is all about?"

He shrugged. "Can't hear you."

I repeated what I had said. "And the tenants are getting frightened," I went on. "How long do you plan to keep this up?"

"What's your name, son?" he asked, ignoring my questions.

"Noyes, sir. Franklin Noyes. I'm the Super here." I made a sweeping motion to indicate both buildings.

"My name is VanderCork," he announced. "Joshua VanderCork. And you are the superintendent here?"

Once more I indicated that I was. "Only part-time, though. I'm also a full-time student at Columbia. I've only been the Super here a month."

"Hmmm," was Mr. VanderCork's response. "Who's the landlord?"

I was getting ruffled. Here I was answering all of his questions, but he hadn't answered any of mine.

"How long do you plan to keep this up?" I tried again.

He seemed not to hear me. "Who's the landlord?" he repeated.

I was getting nowhere fast. "Mr. Karbowski," I told him. "He and his wife live there in 6 West, in apartment four."

"Is Karbowski a short, gray-haired man, built like a tank, thick accent?" VanderCork shot at me.

I sighed. "Yes, that's him."

Mr., or rather Reverend Mr. VanderCork (only then did I notice his clerical collar), suddenly raised both his hands above his head and brought the circling picketers to a halt.

"The man we seek lives here!" he shouted. "He owns these buildings! We must keep picketing until he comes down here and repents his sins. There must be no more poisoning of pigeons in Central Park!"

Mr. K? Repent his sins? What sins? And how did I get into this crazy mess? More to the point, how would I get out?

I prayed that Mr. K could answer the questions.

I worked my way through the picketers and onlookers into the entrance foyer of 6 West and let myself in with my passkey. Mrs. K, two floors up, was bewildered when, opening the door to see who was knocking so hard, found it was me.

"What's the story with the pigeons?" I pleaded. "That's an angry crowd out there."

She and Mr. K, standing behind her, both shrugged. They had no idea what I was talking about.

Taking a deep breath, I plunged into a direct confrontation with Mr. K and asked the big question: "Have you been poisoning pigeons in the Park?"

He reacted as though I had stabbed him. Then his look suggested that he thought I had gone crazy. In a moment he stopped, shifted his eyes, then walked into the kitchen and opened the refrigerator, taking out something I couldn't see and putting it in his pocket, he asked me to accompany him outside.

"I will talk to these people and make them go away," was all he would say.

We waited in the downstairs front hall until I spotted Rev. VanderCork, then I grabbed Mr. K and pulled him outside with me. We quickly confronted Rev. VanderCork who just as quickly threw up his arms again and stopped his encircling troops.

"Here is our pigeon killer," he boomed. "What have you to say for yourself, sir? Why do you do this terrible thing?"

Mumbles of "terrible" and "atrocious" filtered from the crowd.

Mr. K was unruffled. "I do not kill birds," he said quietly. "I love birds."

"Do you deny feeding them THIS?" Rev. VanderCork challenged. He displayed in the palm of his right hand what appeared to me to be an old morsel of salami.

"No, I do not deny it," Mr. K answered. "That is what I throw to the creatures in Central Park."

Rev. VanderCork jumped on his acknowledgment. "Then it IS you who feeds them this horrible poison?"

"Not poison," everlastingly patient Mr. K explained as though to a petulant child. "Is sausage. Kielbasa. Polish sausage. Is good meat."

"Oh, you are clever, Mr. Karbowski, very clever," the leader almost sneered. "But you won't get away with it. No one would feed good meat to the pigeons!"

Rev. VanderCork turned to his pickets and shouted, "He wants us to believe he feeds good meat to the birds! Do you believe that?"

His flock responded in unison, "No! No! No!"

"It is true! True!" Mr. K shouted back at them. He turned to Rev. VanderCork and said, very sadly, "Is very embarrassing. I am Polish, but I do not like kielbasa. I cannot eat it. See?" He went on, reaching into his pocket for what I had seen him remove from his refrigerator. "Here is more. I throw it to stray dogs and hungry cats and also to the birds. Here, taste. It is alright. Not poison. I no poison pigeons. I love birds!"

He lowered his voice and went on. "My wife, she thinks I like to eat kielbasa. She buys it all the time. I pretend to eat it in the Park so she does not become unhappy. But instead I feed God's creatures my Helena's kielbasa."

Obviously moved by Mr. K's comments, Rev. VanderCork quietly asked one of the more agitated pickets to come forward. "Is this the man you saw feeding meat to the pigeons?" he whispered. "Is this the man you followed home?"

"Yes, Joshua," she answered. "That is the man."

"Did you actually see any pigeons die after eating the meat?" VanderCork said.

The woman paused. "No, Joshua," she admitted. "But you know what a terrible pigeon mortality rate we have this year. This MUST be the cause."

She looked uncertain now and looked to her friends for support.

A scowl appeared on Rev. VanderCork's face then he jerkily pointed at Mr. K in an admonishing manner. From his lips, however, emerged a quiet apology. "Please forgive us. sir. We know not what we do."

He then turned to face the pickets and threw his arms in the air. making the victory V sign with both hands.

"Let us go, brothers and sisters," he called. "He promises to love all birds and to kill no more. Let us put away the signs and return to our homes."

As the crowd dispersed. Mr. K shook his head. "Franklin," he said, sighing with disbelief, "New York is a funny place. People don't seem to complain about taxes or noise or bad police. No, instead they worry about pigeons in the Park. Are you sure you want to be a superintendent in New York?"

Good question. At that point I wasn't even sure I wanted to BE in New York.

CHAPTER 2

The Country Boy Goes to New York

M y path to New York City had been far from straight. I was raised in several small towns and on two small farms in Pennsylvania's Pocono Mountains, about a hundred miles west of Manhattan. When I turned 17, two months after World War II ended, I persuaded my parents to let me enlist in the Army. Thus, while millions of Americans were being mustered out of the military, I was beginning my training as a medical laboratory technician at Fort Sam Houston in San Antonio, Texas.

To my great disappointment, during my three-year hitch I never persuaded my superiors to send me to an overseas post. Instead, I got stuck splitting my time between Fort Sam Houston and Fitzsimons General Hospital in Denver, Colorado, as a lowly technician fifth grade.

Shortly before being discharged in 1949, I found myself listening to a fast-talking Army Reserve recruiter. "Look, corporal," he argued, "think about two things. First, no matter what you do when you get out, you'll need money, right? Okay. As a member of the Reserves, you'll get it for damned little of your time. Second, what happens to you if war breaks out again? If you're in the Reserves, you know exactly what you'll be doing and you'll have rank. If you aren't in the Reserves, you'll have to start all over again."

Not wanting to have that happen, I signed up as a member of the U.S. Army Medical Department's Reserves.

I was about to begin my second year of college at a small school in

Ohio when the Korean "incident" erupted. I had hardly returned to school when orders arrived directing me to report to my Reserve unit to await further orders. "Maybe this time I'll get to see something more than blood samples," I told one of my instructors. "It got so I was the fastest syringe in the West. Heck, I could draw blood in the dark and never spill a drop."

Professor Metz grimaced. "Don't make light of it, Franklin," he warned. "There might come a time when you'd like nothing better than to be back drawing blood."

"You may be right," I admitted. "But at least a free trip abroad goes with whatever I wind up doing."

I dropped out of school as ordered, returned home to await further orders and waited ... and waited. One month, two months, three, four. Still no final orders. Frustrated, bored and more than a little angry at this point. I decided to go to New York City, get a job and try to continue my studies at night. I figured that once orders arrived it wouldn't take long to break an apartment lease and drop out of yet another school.

Why New York City? For a very simple reason. My fiancée Cindy was there, and the prospect of another long separation made the move both logical and biologically compelling.

I wasted no time moving and had only just settled into a tiny furnished apartment in upper Manhattan when the Pentagon dropped the other shoe.

The announcement I received, garbled in the usual gobbledy- gook of the military bureaucracy, boiled down to this: My Reserve unit and five others should never have been called up. Thousands of guys like me – and me! – had been left in official limbo for close to six months.

What to do?

It was too late to return to the Ohio school for the second semester. And besides, I quickly found that yet another separation of any kind from Cindy was out of the question.

After phone calls to City College of New York, Fordham, Columbia, and New York Universities, I determined that it was still possible to enroll in Columbia University's School of General Studies for night courses. I did so for three courses the very day I called.

Enrollment was easy since Columbia readily accepted students under the GI Bill. But as far as the Veterans Administration knew, I was still somewhere in Ohio, so survival until they untangled some of their red tape again wasn't going to be easy.

"Sir," I asked a bearded, obviously weary man in the Bursar's Office as I was completing the enrollment process, "can you tell me if Columbia has a job placement office? I figure I'm going to get very hungry before my monthly GI checks begin arriving again, and I'd like to get a job, any job, fast."

"Yeah, we have a good placement office," he said. "It's right around the corner. Ask for Matilda — Matilda Thayer. She always has jobs for hungry students." All this he said without ever looking up from the papers he was surveying.

I easily found the office and was surprised to find it open so late at night. It was then nearly nine o'clock.

The middle-aged, plump but attractive woman seated at the only desk behind the counter quickly stood up and asked, "Can I help you? My name is Thayer, Mrs. Matilda Thayer."

"How do you do," I smiled, reaching to shake her hand. "I'm pleased to meet you. I just enrolled for some night courses under the GI Bill, but I'm sure it will be two or three months before my support payments reach me. I need a job so I can eat and pay the rent."

She chuckled. "Welcome to my world! We specialize in keeping ex-GI's alive. What's your name?"

Army style, I spit out, "Noyes, Franklin, 321 558 246."

Mrs. Thayer looked at me very solemnly. "Franklin," she said, "the only number Columbia will ever request from you is your phone number. The time has come to put away your Army serial number."

Mrs. Thayer — or Mother Matilda as she had come to be known to a generation of Columbia students — quickly got down to the business at hand.

"What work experience do you have? What kind of a job would you like?"

"I was born in a small town," I told the kindly woman, "raised on a farm until I was 13, worked summers in resort hotels until I was 17, and have served three years in the Army. I'm used to menial and even degrading jobs. I'll try any job you give me. I'm sure I'll be able to handle most of them."

And handle them I did. I babysat for professors. I bartended for a dean, I analyzed feces in the medical lab at St. Luke's Hospital, I stocked groceries at a neighborhood store, and I was a bed-pan jockey at a convalescent home.

By the summer of 1951 I had made two decisions: The first was that I wanted to marry Cindy as soon as possible. The second was to resume my education full-time.

Cindy and I had met in high school in the Poconos and had become engaged via incessantly passionate correspondence while I was in the Army. She was two years younger than I. Immediately after graduation from high school, she had left the farm where she was born and raised to take nurses' training at a medical center in Brooklyn. And now, with both of us in New York, we assumed that we would be married after she had completed her training in August. This assumption quickly melted in the heat of our unaccustomed propinquity, however, and we secretly tied the knot in May. Secretly, because the nursing school she attended did not tolerate married students.

After a too-short, two-day honeymoon, Cindy returned to her training and I returned to my cubbyhole apartment — to which Cindy refused to accompany me for fear our secret would be discovered.

The combination of monetary need and unfulfilled biological urges made it mandatory that I find yet another job, one that would so supplement my GI Bill income that Cindy and I could afford a larger apartment so that we could be together.

CHAPTER 3

The New Super

Columbia didn't have summer sessions, so I spent my first married summer taking two courses at New York University's Washington Square Campus in lower Manhattan and working at whatever jobs I could locate on my own or through Mother Matilda. Summer jobs, however, were few and far between.

By August my GI Bill checks still weren't arriving and I was surviving by borrowing from an older sister. On a particularly hot day that month I was so broke and desperate for money that I decided to splurge the last of my pocket change on carfare to Columbia to personally see Mother Matilda and beg her for a job. I was prepared to impose on her to the point that she could even send me to jobs for which I was not qualified.

"Franklin!" she cried as soon as she spied me. "Where have you been? I've been trying to reach you all day! I think I have the job you've been looking for all summer. Here, read this!"

The notice she handed me read:

NEED AN APARTMENT AND A JOB?
Get both as a package.
I'm part-time Super of 20 apartments
and get my apartment rent-free in return.
Am finishing school about Labor Day
and need replacement soon.
Contact David Weiss
through the Placement Office.

Obviously David Weiss was aiming his notice directly at me since I did need an apartment and a job. To get them both at once would be the height of good fortune. Matilda gave me David Weiss' phone number and commanded me to use her phone. I dialed as fast as my anxious fingers could manage and got him on the first ring.

In less than a minute I established my interest in his notice, assured him that I didn't mind collecting garbage or cleaning dirty hallways and that, yes, I could be at 8 West 90th Street in exactly one hour to talk it over and perhaps see the landlord, who would make the final hiring decision.

I arrived at the five-story brownstone just off Central Park West with seven minutes to spare, and was soon being effusively greeted by David Weiss. He told me that he was completing his Master's degree in English and was leaving for Ohio and his first teaching post over Labor Day Weekend.

"David," I asked him, "what does a superintendent do? You mentioned some things on the phone. Could you elaborate a little?"

He grinned. "A Super's duties are basically what we called shit work in the Army. The most important thing is to collect the garbage every night and put the garbage cans out every morning. Once a week you also have to clean. Vacuum the halls, wipe the baseboards and railings, polish the mailboxes and front doorknobs, stuff like that. Other than that, it depends on what happens. You have to replace light bulbs in the halls, and you have to fix such things as leaky faucets and broken light switches."

I nodded. While I didn't have the slightest idea how to do either of those last two things, I wasn't about to admit it.

"Thanks for the description. Shit work is my forte," I assured him. "I'm sure I can handle the job."

"Good. Let me call Mr. K. I know he's anxious to meet you. Oh, yes. You should know Mr. K is a Polish emigrant and his English isn't very good. Listen carefully and watch his hands and eyes, and you should be able to follow the flow of the conversation."

David called the landlord and was urged to bring me over immediately. Mr. K lived in the adjoining building, 6 West.

My introduction to my prospective employer was brief and to the point.

"Mr. K," David said, "this is Franklin Noyes. He's a student at Columbia like me, he wants the job, and please send him back to my apartment when you're through." With that, David shot me a reassuring wink and left.

Mr. K, whose full name I soon learned was Zbigniew Karbowski, gave me the once-over and I looked back. Short and compact, his muscular arms, broad shoulders and flat stomach made him look like a stevedore. He had a graying crew cut and a large crescent-shaped scar under his right eye. He grunted a welcome and motioned me to sit.

In heavily accented English augmented with sign and body language that involved almost every digit and moveable anatomical part, I was haltingly but thoroughly interrogated to his satisfaction. It didn't take him long to determine that, newly married and desperately in want of an apartment for two, I was willing to do whatever had to be done … and probably more, much more.

The "arrangement," as Mr. K explained it, was fairly simple. If he hired me, I would be paid $100 a month for my labors. For the same amount he would rent me the apartment now occupied by David Weiss. At the end of each month he would give me his check and I in turn would give him mine. It was all very proper and legal. So, while the apartment wasn't exactly rent-free, it ended up that way.

My duties would be those David had already described, and I would also be expected to sweep the sidewalks as needed, respond to the "Ring for Super" bell, occasionally handle odd but necessary jobs and always try to be helpful to the tenants in 6 and 8 West.

Suddenly I realized he had stopped talking and I looked around to try and find out why he was staring at me.

"Sir?" I said. more as a question than anything. "Is something wrong?"

He frowned. "Wrong? No, nothing wrong. I wait for you to accept job."

"I didn't know you had formally offered … " My voice faded. "Oh! Yes SIR!" I nearly shouted, realizing he was offering me the job. "Thank you!"

I happily agreed to do whatever was required, plus whatever else might be necessary and was greeted with a firm handshake from my new boss. Starting Labor Day, 1951, I would be the superintendent – the "Super" – of 6 and 8 West 90th Street, New York City, New York.

CHAPTER 4

6 and 8 West Visited

I visited David again two days before he moved out so he could show me through the buildings and brief me on the tenants.

Six and eight West 90th Street were identical five-story brownstones built at the turn of the century for gracious urban living by the affluent, then largely untaxed middle class.

As a private home the typical brownstone was entered from the sidewalk on two levels. The help – cooks, scullery maids, and upstairs girls – stepped down three or four stairs into the kitchen and pantry level.

The family of the house stepped up eight or ten stairs and entered a spacious foyer. This in turn led to a sitting room, a living room and a spacious, usually chandeliered, dining room.

The third level was the domain of the parents. It housed their bedroom and bath, sometimes a nursery and usually a study or sewing room.

The fourth level was the domain of the children. It housed their bedrooms, a commodious bathroom and, depending on the number of children, a playroom.

The fifth level housed the live-in help. It contained their bedrooms and a bath and, depending on the number of help, a storeroom or two.

As renovated by Mr. K into ten small but functional apartments, the only charms retained of the original brownstones were in their facades.

Mr. K's renovation scheme had been simplicity itself. The stairwells were moved to the left wall and the remaining space was split down the middle on each floor. This produced ten apartments of about equal size in each building.

Each apartment had a bedroom, living room, kitchenette and bath. The apartments on the second floors had slightly more space than those on the first because of window bays, and the rear apartments on the fourth floors had small balconies. The first level rear apartments also had small gardens.

David and I began our physical tour in the basement of 8 West. This was identical to the basement in 6 West, I was told. In both basements were kept the tools Mr. K had purchased over the years for maintenance purposes. There were screwdrivers, pliers, well-used monkey wrenches, and plumber's helpers.

And, to remind me that the sidewalks would require occasional attention, there were also two ancient push brooms, a heavy-duty scraper, and a battered snow shovel. The basements contained three separate rooms. The stairs descending to the basement revealed the largest, which took up two thirds of the floor area of the building. This room contained the gas furnace, hot water heating system and the largest waste pipes I had ever seen.

"Keep your eyes on those pipes," David warned. "You'll see rats that have been here since the Indians sold Manhattan. The pipes are apparently part of one of their favorite trails."

To the rear of the large room were two smaller ones. One was the Super's workshop. I would come to use this one and Mr. K would generally use the one in 6 West. The other small room, tightly sealed with an assortment of locks on a solid oak door, contained odds and ends of tenants' furniture and personal belongings.

"This is your domain," David said as we examined the Super's workshop. "Almost everything you need is right here."

With that he emptied a large tin full of nuts, bolts, washers, screws and the like onto an old desk. "See? Three penny nails, five penny nails, hinges, knobs, the works. All here. Mr. K salvaged most of this during the renovation. You're allowed to go to the hardware store only if you can't make do with what's here."

"Did you ever need to go to the hardware store?" I teased.

"Only to find out how to use some of this stuff," he grinned. When I first came here, I couldn't tell the difference between a wrench and a hinge."

I exaggerated my gulp of helplessness. "I still don't!"

"Don't worry, Frank," David smiled. "When you have to, it's not hard to learn."

The desk held other goodies. A vise, more tools, rags and cleaning products of all kinds. I saw soaps, waxes, furniture polish, silver polish, brass polish and bottles of ammonia. I also saw assorted attachments for the Super's vacuum cleaner.

The walls of the workshop were covered with fuse boxes and electric meters for each apartment in the building.

"These buildings are still so new that there isn't much maintenance," David said. "Mostly you get broken light switches or an occasional blown fuse. The job really comes down to three things. There's daily collection of the trash, weekly cleaning of the halls, stairs and foyers, and, whenever a tenant moves out, a thorough cleaning of the apartment. Think you can handle it?"

Suddenly I didn't feel as overwhelmed as I had. "Sure, David," I said. "No problem. But what about the tenants? What can you tell me about them?"

"What do you want to know?"

"Are they friendly? Do they give you much trouble? Are they demanding?"

"To tell the truth, there's really little I can tell you," David admitted. "I had so little contact with them. You see, I'm a night person and an opera buff.

I frowned. What did that have to do with my question?

David continued. "I usually collected trash about two or three in the morning. Not many people up then."

I nodded but still wanted to know more.

"I really enjoy people," I persisted. "I feel I can learn more about history by letting people talk about their lives than reading a book. So I encourage people to talk about themselves. "Do you think the tenants will?"

"No reason why they shouldn't. But be prepared for Jon Hauser. He'll probably proposition you every Saturday morning. He's a persistent character."

Other than that, David could only say that the tenants were fairly quiet, not abnormally dirty and generally undemanding. They became testy only during periods when Mr. K, rigidly adhering to New York City laws, refused to turn on the heat on chilly spring mornings after April 15 or on cold autumn days before October 15.

Thus briefed by David, I was more or less prepared to move in and assume my new duties.

CHAPTER 5

Mr. K and the Lovely Helena

The prospect of having a live-in wife by Labor Day spurred my latent organizational talents into an efficient frenzy so the move into the Weiss apartment was easy.

My friend Dick Simpson made himself and his 1949 Studebaker available for the big event, and he appeared at my room at 8:00 a.m. the next Saturday. It took only ten minutes for the two of us to carry out my clothing and books and for me to return my key to the landlady.

The first stop David and I made was the nurses' quarters at The Brooklyn Hospital for Cindy and her few things. By nine o'clock Dick, my bride and I arrived at 8 West 90th Street and took possession of No. 8, fourth floor rear.

The lack of furniture never bothers a Super, I soon learned. Thanks to moves, planned or otherwise, marital disruptions, births, deaths, accidents and all the other unforeseen events that make waves in a tenant's life, a Super is never without furniture.

Cindy and I started our married life together at 8 West with the Weiss legacy: a tarnished brass bed with squeaking springs and a lumpy mattress; a hilariously seedy and rickety overstuffed chair which, eons ago, had been fully covered with leather; one card table with three good legs; two straight-back chairs whose only redeeming feature was sturdiness; and, important to me, a full-time student now, a very large, battered old desk.

Apparently, this was all the furniture David Weiss had felt he needed.

Shortly after we had hauled our meager belongings upstairs, Mr.

K appeared at the door. He surveyed the state of our furnishings and got Dick and me to follow him to the basement. There, in one of the locked rear rooms, he pointed to a chest of drawers and Windsor chair, both in excellent shape, and insisted that I take them. Dick helped me get them up to the fourth floor and suddenly the Noyes' apartment was as fully furnished as most rooms in college dorms.

Mr. K proved to be a consistently generous and thoughtful boss. Few holidays passed without a remembrance of some kind from him and his wife, and both of them were always available to help when occasional sickness made it impossible for me to fulfill my janitorial duties.

Over the two-year period Cindy and I lived and worked in 6 and 8 West, we were able to piece together the Karbowskis' story from numerous sessions with one or both of them and from occasional conversations with tenants who were friends or surrogate children of the K's.

While Mr. K's English was sometimes barely penetrable, Mrs. K's was quite good, and her gestures were less dramatic and more readily interpreted than her volcanic husband's.

Zbigniew and Helena Karbowski had been Polish aristocrats who fled Poland shortly before World War II. Unable to liquidate their extensive land holdings, they nevertheless escaped to England with a small fortune in jewelry, religious icons and portable art objects. By the time Hitler's forces had invaded Poland, the Karbowskis had decided to move on to Canada. In 1945 they emigrated to the United States and settled in Manhattan.

"We were not expert in selling our jewelry and art," Mrs. K explained to me one day, "so we had to get jobs or make an investment that would give us a regular income. I was not trained for any job I could find in New York. And Zbigniew was a gentleman trained to manage property that was run with peasant labor. No demand for him, either."

So they sold their jewelry and art and used the cash to buy 6 and 8 West 90th Street, two spacious turn-of-the- century brownstones, their charms long since sacrificed to the Depression. Mr. K had the buildings gutted and renovated into two apartment buildings containing ten apartments each. The Ks moved into their apartment on July 1, 1946, and by the end of that month, in apartment-shy New York City, both of the K's buildings were fully occupied.

When Cindy and I moved in some five years later, Mr. K must have been in his 60's and his Helena, lovely and voluptuous, fully two decades younger. Whatever Mr. K's age, he had the strength of an athlete and the energy of a 20-year-old.

He was a driven man with a great passion: the liberation of Poland!

On most occasions when I visited him, he was at his desk writing furiously or searching through masses of books, papers and documents that looked like they would form a devastating avalanche given the slightest jolt or quiver. I had been Super several months before I summoned the courage to ask what his research was all about.

"Pook," he smiled.

"Pook?" I couldn't imagine what he was telling me. Mr. K noticed my puzzlement and pointed to a dog-eared volume.

"Oh, book," I exclaimed, suddenly understanding.

Mrs. K picked up the conversation. "Poland has a tragic history," she said, her husband nodding in agreement. "But never more tragic than the last fifteen years. Zbigniew is writing what happened. How Poland was betrayed by friends and enemies. He is also looking ahead. How will Poland regain her freedom? By war? By revolution? The more he thinks about it, the more he feels there must be a revolt. And then war! And this is what he is urging in his book."

The Ks hosted an endless stream of visitors, many of whom, I later realized, must have been part of whatever plot Mr. K was concocting to overthrow the communist overlords of Poland. I was meeting with Mr. K one day when unexpected visitors arrived.

The two men were about Mr. K's age or a little younger and were quite distinguished looking in their fine clothes and straight bearing. They launched into an agitated discussion with Mr. K, in what I guessed was Polish, the second they entered the apartment.

Feeling I was intruding, I edged towards the door to leave.

"Please forgive us, Franklin," Helena said, "this is Admiral —- and General —-. They have some important news for my husband about the liberation."

I didn't catch their names and didn't want to. If anyone ever inquired about them, I preferred to be innocent of such information. I nodded a greeting and left. The visitors didn't leave until several hours later.

Helena had obviously trained herself to be a supportive wife and skilled and entertaining hostess.

She was statuesque, very blonde, slightly overweight and altogether lovely, the perfect model for a Rubens or Rembrandt painting. Her physical virtues were enhanced by her training in music and the domestic arts. She played the piano beautifully and she was an excellent cook.

While her Polish wardrobe was out of style in Manhattan, she enjoyed displaying her finery while entertaining friends and Zbigniew's co-conspirators.

Helena also had her own great passions.

One was to feed, clothe and spiritually nourish her sister's family in Krakow. I often saw her going to the post office to send them food, clothing and religious literature.

Her other passion was the Church. "To a Pole, nothing is more important than that," she told me. "We may fail as a people or a country, but we shall never, never fail as Christians. Nothing shakes our belief in Christ and the Church."

Her actions during all the time I knew her proved her belief time and time again.

In time I learned that to the tenants of both their apartment buildings the Karbowskis were perceived as slightly mysterious, more than slightly odd, or totally nuts. Their lease undoubtedly had a lot to do with this perception.

In the five years the Karbowskis had owned 6 and 8 West, they had been afflicted with a brood of eccentrically talented tenants.

One, a former munitions expert in the Army, had kept assorted shells and bombs throughout his apartment, ostensibly as part of the decor. Another, I had been told, had kept accidentally setting fires by forgetting food in the oven or on the stove until, somehow, it ignited.

Such eccentricities greatly troubled Mr. K, and he sought to exorcise them through "the law" – in his case, the lease that governed landlord-tenant relations.

The last page of a Karbowski lease was an incredible collection of forbidden activities, all gleaned from a mere 60 months as a landlord. One tenant, a man who had had some legal training, said the Ks' lease made "the Ten Commandments look like kid stuff." The Karbowski commandments numbered 34 when I arrived, or an average of seven a year for five years. What, I wondered, would they number when I left?

And what events, I also wondered, would lead to any increase, while *I* was the Super? I didn't know whether to feel curious or glum.

CHAPTER 6

The Super's Job

Our third Saturday night in residence Cindy was not working and we splurged on a bottle of red wine to accompany the spaghetti and meatballs Cindy was beginning to cook fairly well.

"Franny, how's the job going?" she asked. "You don't say much about it. Can you handle it? Are you having any trouble?"

"Trouble?" I asked. "No, I'm not really having any trouble. Somebody always seems to have a minor problem of some kind, but I'm coping. I took your father's advice. Before I fix a switch or change a washer, I study how the thing comes apart. I even draw diagrams. Then I try to put it back together the same way I took it apart. No catastrophes yet."

"But what about the trash?' And all the cleaning?

I smiled. "The trash is about as straightforward a proposition as you can get. I pick it up. I lug it to the cans in front of the building. I stomp on it till it fits in the cans, and I put the cans at the curb in the morning. Very uncomplicated. Except ..."

"Except what?" Cindy asked, looking slightly alarmed.

"Oh, nothing bad, really," I reassured her. "It's just that today I learned that we have a large trash pickup every three months. And I'm just hoping that no one throws out a couch. I'll have to move it myself."

"I'll help you."

"You? You're too tiny," I told my wife, loving her for her offer her help. "I don't think you're strong enough and I wouldn't want you to get hurt."

A rare flash of anger clouded Cindy's face. "You don't know how strong I am!" she snapped. "If you'd ever really watched a nurse at work, you'd know she often has to lift and turn sick people. Sometimes they're VERY ILL; and sometimes they're VERY heavy. That's just about dead weight! Besides, all I did was ask you about the cleaning!"

I felt embarrassed at having underestimated my wife. There was, I realized, still a lot I had to learn about her.

"I'm sorry, honey," I apologized. "I really am." And then I remembered she had mentioned the cleaning again.

"What about the cleaning?" I asked. "Does this building look dirty?" I was half-joking, half-serious.

Cindy looked slightly intimidated. "No, Franny, it's fine," she said. "Just fine."

We kissed briefly then stood with our arms around each other.

"I love you," I whispered, "and I'm sorry."

"I love you, too," Cindy whispered back, squeezing me tighter.

Once I learned the routine, my job as Super was fairly easy.

Even during a trying week it rarely required more than 15 hours of my time. My job was never dull, however, not even when it came to the most basic of my daily duties – the collection of trash.

David Weiss had somehow acquired a large canvas post office mail bag and this became my trademark. Each evening at ten I would shut my books, leave Cindy, if she wasn't working that evening, and hurry to the top floor of 8 West. There I began my descent, stuffing the bag with trash and discards left outside each door. I emptied the bag into trash cans at the sidewalk and then repeated the routine in 6 West. If there were no interruptions, I could complete the rounds of the 20 apartments in 22 minutes flat.

Interruptions, however, were initially the rule, not the exception.

"Evening, Franklin," some tenant or another would say. "We're just having a nightcap. Why not join us?"

Others insisted I worked too hard or too long and said I deserved a break. "Let's visit for a few moments!" was another common invitation.

Anxious to meet as many people as possible and make new friends, I accepted their invitations. On evenings when as many as four people asked me in for a drink, I barely managed to finish my rounds. Cindy soon let me know how she felt about such occasions.

"Franny, it's nice that you're friendly," she said, "but this is ridiculous. You'll become an alcoholic if you keep it up. And whether you know it or not, you're a lousy lover when you've been drinking."

I couldn't deny it. From then on I became highly selective in accepting drinks of any kind when collecting trash or doing other work in the two buildings.

And other work there was. There were often faucets which leaked or light switches which didn't work. I would learn about these on my trash rounds then attend to them during the day while the tenants were at work.

My other fixed duties took place on Saturday mornings. First I vacuumed the halls and stairs of both buildings, then I dropped to my knees for a good hour or so to dust or wet-clean the baseboards, step edges and stair spindles, and finally I polished the brass mail boxes and front door handles.

Cleaning baseboards was always an olfactory adventure. My nose within inches of rug and dust-covered wood, I soon began to distinguish between soot, soil, face powder, residue from cleansers and the vapors and patches left by spilled food and drink, and animal and even human urine. Any time I detected a new smell, it became an adventure to identify it, and I told Cindy that the human history of a building could surely be reconstructed from an analysis of the residues left on its pathways. She never disagreed.

The polishing of the mail boxes and front door handles was exciting. The odor of the brass polish was not only sharply different from other cleaning potions, but its use resulted in a highly satisfying transformation in both the color and brightness of the brass. The brass polishing was thus always my last and most rewarding cleaning act of the week.

Brass polish aside, I was intrigued to learn that there was a cyclical rhythm to all the smells of 6 and 8 West 90th Street.

In summer, when windows were open and fans running in most rooms, the air was incredibly heavy with heat and soot, especially on the upper two floors. In this atmosphere, cooking created micro-environments of shockingly sharp odors. Fish and cabbage bothered me most during my trash rounds, but garlic, sausage and curry ran close seconds.

The lower floors of the building smelled musty and moist, yet stayed cool and welcome even during heat waves.

But in winter, when all windows were closed tight and the gas-fired hot air heaters running constantly, the air was light and dry and delicately scented with pleasant cooking smells.

When Christmas approached, the air near most apartments was redolent with the sweet smells of holiday cookies and pastries. The scents of Mrs. K's babka baking and the deliciously intoxicating odors of tenants' fruitcakes and pies are forever engraved on my mind.

What of the other two seasons? Apartment buildings don't have smells for spring and autumn. Those are new grass or burning leaves, and neither exists within four walls.

Besides smells, other cycles existed in 6 and 8 West. The flow of mail to the tenants was one of them. Most checks arrived the first day or two of the month, and most magazines arrived on Friday or Saturday. The two weeks preceding Christmas saw me summoned by mailmen or deliverymen to receive packages as often as three times every day, including Sundays.

Another cycle involved not tenants but visitors. There were times when the Super's most challenging duty was to cope with the mixed bag of humanity who punched or thumbed or leaned on the "Ring for Superintendent" bell. Fuller brush salesmen, magazine or book salesmen of all types, Jehovah's Witnesses, apartment seekers, street peddlers, fruit and vegetable vendors, and solicitors for every cause known to mankind all had their seasons. This large and exotic assortment of solicitors never failed to fascinate Cindy.

"Who rang the bell today?" she'd ask when she got home from work. "Anyone new?"

"Oh, nobody special. A few peddlers. Some guy trying to check the credit of one of the tenants. And I'm not sure, but I think that last woman may have been a whore."

"Franklin, darling," Cindy hissed, "just what do you mean 'may have been a whore'? Was she or wasn't she? What did she look like? What did she say?"

"Well, she wore sort of a uniform," I teased. "Slinky, tight-fitting dress. Very revealing. Asked if I had any work for her."

"And what did you say?"

"What could I say? I said, 'No, ma'am, we're too poor to afford extra help.'"

"Extra help! You call a whore extra help?" Cindy yelped.

"Cindy," I laughed, "I never took a course in talking to whores. What should I have said?"

My wife said nothing – for over an hour.

Through it all I collected trash. I collected leaky bags stuffed to overflowing, dog-eared magazines, broken household items and old shoes. I removed discarded toys, piles of newspapers and empty bottles. And occasionally I carted down broken furniture and worn-out rugs. In return I got to keep the occasional penny I found while wiping baseboards, and hundreds of cookies and many, many bottles of liquor at Christmas. Oh, yes. I also gained the benefit of many valuable lessons in the nature of the human species.

CHAPTER 7
Jack Be Nimble, Jack Be Quick

Excluding Mr. K, the very first tenant I met was Uncle Louie. He greeted me at the door of apartment No.8 in 6 West as I bent over to swoop a bag of trash into my converted mail bag. He licked my left cheek, made a soft noise in his throat and grasped my shirt sleeve in his mouth, gently, as if trying to tug me into the apartment.

Uncle Louie was a delightful little dog of dubious origin who stood about a foot high and stretched no more than three feet from his blackberry nose to the far end of his long tail. His dominant traits were obviously collie since his coloring and physiognomy were all but AKC certifiable. I would learn he belonged to Jack and Donna Ripon.

The Ripon's front door, invariably ajar, made it possible for Uncle Louie and me to become good friends long before I ever encountered his master and mistress. I finally met them late that first summer when their apartment door was wide open and they were in the midst of a subdued but evidently warm celebration.

In the time it took me to pick up the trash — measurable in seconds — two voices had proposed toasts to "...Jack, on his good fortune."

At the start of the second toast and as I was about to straighten up to continue my rounds, ebullient Uncle Louie again locked gently onto me and tugged me into the apartment.

Showing little surprise at my presence, a pretty woman greeted me, shooed Uncle Louie away and informed me that her husband, an actor, had just landed a role in a Broadway play.

"Please join us in celebrating our good fortune," she invited. "I'm Donna Ripon. What a wonderful way to meet you!"

Before I could answer she placed a bottle of beer into my empty right hand.

The Ripons, several years older than Cindy and me, soon become our very close friends. Jack, who described himself as either "obese" or "portly", was six feet tall, had long, wavy brownish-red hair and a waistline of Falstaffian proportions. During the time we knew the Ripons, he was in a succession of plays and television shows. But his life, Jack said, was divided into three parts: making love to Donna, walking Uncle Louie, and waiting for his agent to call with news, any news. There were periods – one lasting nearly three months – when Jack had no work, and the Ripons were flat broke. Then they lived on small loans from Donna's father. Jack, however, was so committed to what he called his "one- week-chicken, the next-week-feathers" existence that he never became depressed. The mere mention of a part was enough to jolt his latent charisma into instant readiness.

The early 1950's were years in which the Broadway theater began to decline and television began a period of explosive growth. Because most TV shows were televised live, filming being expensive and taping not yet invented, Jack soon gained recognition as a TV director's dream. He had the unique talent of being able to successfully contend with any on-stage catastrophe, and on-stage catastrophes apparently were the price paid by many ambitious TV productions that were televised live after short rehearsal periods.

Donna's father had given her a TV set, and it became Donna's custom to invite Cindy and me over to watch whenever Jack was performing. I can remember three such evenings that persuaded me that Jack Ripon was the most poised, most composed and fastest-thinking actor on the American stage.

The scene: Versailles during the reign of Louis XV. Jack is playing one of His Imperial Highness's ministers and enters Louis's chamber to discuss an upcoming conference. Madame de Pompadour is sedately seated in the background.

Louis summons a servant to bring wine, and the meeting begins. The discussions start as the servant enters with the wine carafe and glasses on a tray. He approaches Louis, stumbles on an unseen TV cable, and launches the carafe and glasses on a perfect trajectory towards Louis' face and ruffled front.

"Ah, shit!" exploded the unrehearsed line from an unkingly king.

Jack to the rescue. "Of course, Excellency," he purrs. "Ashidt will be the perfect setting for the conference. It is such a charming village. I shall make the arrangements immediately!" Exit Jack, the camera following. Dissolve. Commercial. Commercial.

When next seen, Versailles is composed.

Even funnier and more memorable was the time Jack played one of the Founding Fathers from Massachusetts. The stage was divided into three sets: a Philadelphia street scene, the meeting room in Independence Hall where the Founding Fathers would be deadlocked in their discussions on declaring independence, and the Massachusetts living room of the forefather Jack was portraying.

Scene: A bitterly cold winter night in Massachusetts. A hard knock at the front door; the wife crosses the stage and opens the door to be greeted by her husband (Jack) dressed in a warm, heavy coat. They embrace, they disengage, and Jack closes the door and starts to take off his coat, all the while anxious to embrace his wife again. His coat pocket catches the door knob, Jack vigorously turns to sling the coat aside, and the wall of the set collapses on Jack and the woman. The transfixed camera records the whole scene, especially Jack's instant commentary.

"My god, wife," he admonished but with no sternness in his voice, "why didn't you tell me the house was in such terrible shape? I would have returned from Philadelphia long before this to attend to repairs. Is freedom worth such sacrifices? Think how noble you have been, wife, to make such a contribution to the freedom of these Colonies!"

Dissolve eventually, then back to Independence Hall. Jack saved the day — and the play.

Our third memorable evening with the Ripon's TV set was when we joined Donna in watching Jack perform in his first commercial, a live one.

The early 50's was the period in which movie stars and somewhat lesser luminaries of the stage were debating whether or not they should appear in television commercials. Would such appearances be demeaning? Would their souls forever be possessed by General Motors or General Electric or Colgate if they appeared in one of their commercials?

Jack had no such problems. He was neither star nor lesser luminary. He was just a hungry actor who was delighted to get work.

The setting: A circular table with several bottles of a little-known carbonated beverage and two glasses with ice. To the right of the table was Jack seated in a comfortable chair; to the left, a gorgeous woman, Jack's stage wife, who was about to speak her first words on any stage anywhere. The 60-second spot called for Jack to open the first bottle of soda, extol its virtues then pour the contents into his wife's glass and his. She would sip the soda and join Jack in praising the product. Jack was then to open the second bottle, a different flavor, and accompany his wife in urging the viewers to sample the maker's complete line of ten different flavors.

Lights, camera, action.

Jack: "Ladies and gentlemen, if you haven't tasted THESE beverages, you don't know what you're missing! This (lifting bottle) is the finest root beer you can buy! At our house, on a warm day like this, our family drinks six or eight bottles (applying opener to glass bottle) since it not only quenches your thirst but provides you with much-needed energy."

At this point, the bottle top flew off and the contents exploded into the woman's face and down, as dictated by gravity, into her décolletage. Jack calmly swung his chair away from the table and the camera followed him.

"Yes, indeed, ladies and gentlemen," he ad-libbed, "this is the liveliest, tastiest, most refreshing drink in town. If your taste runs to orange, there's also a superb orange soda made from the finest natural ingredients." (He edged back to the table and picked up the orange soda. The camera remained on him.)

"This is my wife's favorite…either over ice or as a mixer for a variety of interesting drinks and desserts. Honey, let me have your glass." (At which point this new bottle also opened explosively and gushed into his "wife's" hair.) "There you are, honey," he smiled and reached his arm toward her with a glass half-full of the residue of the orange pop.

"See, folks," he continued, not missing a beat, "she's so crazy about this luscious drink she's speechless. Remember, folks, THESE beverages are THE BEST. Be SURE to pick some up at your grocery store first thing in the morning."

Dissolve. Back to main production.

The repercussions of that commercial could have been the basis for a television show! The model's agent threatened Jack's agent with suit, alleging that Jack deliberately impeded his client's professional progress by not permitting her to speak during the commercial. The beverage people were so pleased with the improvised spot that they asked Jack to be their exclusive spokesman. But he declined; he was planning to move to the West Coast. Jack's agent then shrewdly recommended the woman and they agreed to try her, and they used her exclusively until she became pregnant and abandoned her career. The father? The cameraman who had toweled her so vigorously after the root beer explosion that they both nearly ran off together on the spot.

Jack and Donna remained our good friends during all the time I was their Super. Eventually, though, they left for Hollywood, and Jack made a respectable name for himself as a film actor. Long after I was graduated from college, Cindy and I continued to hear from them. The letters they always signed "love" always contained the postscript "Uncle Louie says 'Me, too!'"

CHAPTER 8
Baldy the Boat Builder

While in the Army, my best friend had been James Christian Baldwin. His more cynical — that is, envious — associates called him J.C., but his friends called him Baldy.

The only child of a very late marriage, Baldy had always been something of a prodigy. His mother, a public school teacher in a small Georgia town, had instilled her love of music in him to the point where, at age ten, he could identify most classical music by composer, period and even movement. At 15 he was graduated from high school as valedictorian of his class, and at 18 he was graduated from the University of Georgia summa cum laude in physics.

Baldy, a year older than I, entered the Army two days after his college graduation. I first met him at Fort Sam Houston when we were assigned to the same platoon for basic training. For reasons neither of us understood, we were drawn to each other during that first hectic 13-week period in which the Army trains men how to survive and kill in combat.

Our paths temporarily parted at the end of basic training when Baldy went into Officers Candidate School and I moved on to the mundane task of learning how to examine human urine, feces and blood as a medical laboratory technician. After OCS, Baldy was assigned to San Francisco and Naples, lucky fellow, while I applied my analytical training at Army hospitals in Texas and Colorado.

While neither he nor I were very faithful correspondents, we did keep in touch, usually through Christmas cards and a brief letter or two during the year. During my first year as Super I received no letters from Baldy but I did receive a Christmas note. He was in

Naples but expected to return to the states for discharge in April.

One May afternoon I was studying for an exam when the phone rang and Baldy's familiar southern accent greeted me. "Franklin, ol' buddy, I'm here in your New York City! When are you going to shower me with your vaunted northern hospitality by buying me a drink?"

"'Vaunted,' Baldy?"

"Means you boast about it."

"Oh."

Cindy and I had Baldy over that night.

He told us that he had "moved North forever," was working as a technical writer for a nearby publishing firm, and had acquired several passions during his years as an officer and a gentleman. He no longer drank Scotch. His taste now ran to martinis, extraordinarily dry.

"Jes' gin on the rocks and vermouth forgotten," he drawled exaggeratedly.

He had discovered and now extolled the appeal of older women. "You know, those between 32 and 40," he winked. "They give so much, demand so little and are so-o-o-o grateful."

And he had a new avocation: The preparation and appreciation of food. He had studied cooking both in San Francisco and Naples and could now, with no effort whatsoever, prepare dishes from virtually any culture. This I soon learned that first time he visited Cindy and me in New York when he threw together an unforgettably delicious pasta dish for a late supper from ingredients Cindy would never have thought of combining. In common with any true gourmet, he could taste any recipe he read, and could discern all the ingredients of any dish he tasted.

Baldy was renting a room from a college classmate but hoped to move into an apartment of his own in the near future. After we discussed the prices of the apartments in 6 and 8 West, he urged me to let him know the next time one become available.

The first floor front apartment in 6 West, No.1, was vacated unexpectedly in mid-July, and I immediately asked Mr. K to let Baldy have it. He insisted on interviewing Baldy before agreeing to do so.

Baldy could just barely decipher what Mr. K was saying, and Mr. K never did penetrate Baldy's deep-South accent. Baldy won Mr. K over, however, by very strongly answering in his best military manner, "Yes, sir!" "No, sir!" or "You are absolutely right, sir!" whenever one of those responses seemed to fit Mr. K's expression.

He also won over Mrs. K by not only recognizing the Chopin piece she was playing when he entered the apartment but also by commenting on the history of the piece. Helena was overwhelmed that any American, and especially one so young, would know so much about the great Polish composer.

The interview was a smashing success.

Baldy's move into No.1, 6 West, in late July was easily accomplished. His only possessions were two large boxes of records, several hundred books, a record player, his Army clothing, a sleeping bag and a carton full of cooking utensils.

I saw almost nothing of him the next few months. And when we did finally have a chance to sit and talk, he explained that our paths were not crossing because he had been given the opportunity to design and build exhibits which his firm would use at trade shows. He enjoyed such creative challenges and threw himself into the work with his customary gusto for 12 and 14 hours a day. Baldy met the challenge so brilliantly that he was assigned to his company's public relations and promotion department. This was staffed, he told me, by three very talented and very beautiful women, all in their mid-to-late 30's, and I couldn't help smiling when he reminded me of his passion for "older women." The job lasted all of four months.

"Baldy," I asked him one day, "what happened? Why did you change jobs so quickly?"

He smiled. "Franklin," he said, "I should be able to give you a very sophisticated answer to that question. Like a quote from Shakespeare or Tennessee Williams. But I can't. What happened was that I got very friendly with one of my beautiful colleagues and then I was forced to work with another on a crash program to promote a book. Next thing I knew I was the center of a cat fight. Being a southern gentleman, it would have been unethical of me to keep them both miserable, so I made a strategic retreat."

Almost as an afterthought he mentioned that in his new job he would be working with a totally male staff.

Baldy had a passion for sailing. He subscribed to sailing magazines, read books on the Americas Cup races, devoured the New York Public Library's archives on naval architecture and, to my great surprise, began sketching plans for a sailboat which, in his mind, was to be named "Baldy's Dream."

Cindy and I had just finished dinner one February evening when Baldy visited us to make an announcement. "I'm going to start building myself a boat!" he declared. "A sailboat. My own boat! My plans are finished and I'm going to get the materials I need on Saturday."

"That's great, Baldy! Where are you going to build it?"

"In my apartment, of course."

"In a gnat's eye, Baldy! Mr. K will have a stroke and you'll get kicked out on your ass. Besides, how would you ever get it out?"

"How d'you think? In sections! I intend to build it in sections!"

After two stiff martinis, which I needed to build up my courage, I agreed to ask Mr. K for permission for Baldy to build his sailboat – not in his apartment, but in the basement.

We met with Mr. and Mrs. K the next night. I introduced the subject by pointing out what a genius Baldy was in building things and how important it was that such talent be encouraged. Baldy followed by explaining what it was he wanted to do, and produced sketches of the proposed boat and pictures of sailboats similar to the one he would build.

To my astonishment, Mr. K's skepticism was soon overcome by

Helena! Her unrestrained enthusiasm for the project stemmed from girlhood memories of summers in Poland spent sailing with her father.

"I was but 14," she said with nostalgia in her eyes, "but even so I had my own boat, and I won all the races."

How could Mr. K reject Baldy's request when his wife, whom he adored, would like nothing better than to see a sailboat actually being built? To show his assent, Mr. K opened a bottle of wine and we all drank a toast to the project's success.

Baldy and I cleaned the basement late into the night, and I had a key made for him the next day. Within a week he had assembled most of the construction materials he needed.

Once again I saw little of Baldy as winter mellowed into spring. The few times I heard activity in the basement and had time to stop in to check my friend's progress, Helena was there every time, sanding or caulking or stitching. The project had obviously fostered a warm relationship between them but just how warm I neither wished nor dared to ask.

Late in April Baldy proudly stopped me to say that the boat was done, except for the final assembly, and he invited Cindy and me to attend the launching from a friend's dock in Rowayton, Connecticut, the following Saturday. I accepted with enthusiasm.

While we were extracting the boat from the basement – which was surprisingly easy to do – I was puzzled that Helena was not present for this part of the ceremony.

"Baldy, where's Mrs. K?" I asked. "I'm surprised she's not in charge of these festivities after all the work she did."

"Oh she had to go to White Plains with Mr. K. I think it had something to do with his revolution," my friend answered vaguely.

Something told me he wouldn't answer any more questions about her, so I dropped the subject.

Once we got to Rowayton, the sailboat was as easy to assemble and launch as it had been to extract from the basement. But Baldy insisted on taking his creation out for her maiden voyage alone. My job, Baldy explained, was very simple but important nonetheless. Just keep pushing the button on the camera so the maiden voyage could be recorded for posterity. I did so with increasing interest as the main sail became engorged with wind and revealed the name painted on the boat. It appeared to be Greek letters.

"What do they mean?" Cindy and I both asked Baldy when he finally came ashore, delighted with his boat's performance.

"Want to take a quick sail?" he answered.

"Baldy, what's the name of your sailboat? What do the letters mean ?"

Realizing we wouldn't shut up until he told us, he said, "Why, what do you think they mean? Baldy's Dream, of course. Now get on board, or it'll be dark by the time we get back."

Several weeks later I was looking at the photographs of the launching, which I paid to have processed as sort of a christening gift for Baldy and which I had just brought back from the drug store, when Sam Morris, another tenant, stopped by to ask me to unplug a drain. I showed him the pictures of Baldy's Dream and boasted about its origin and how well it sailed.

Sam looked at me, puzzled, and asked, "Frank, what did you say the name of that boat is?"

"Those Greek letters translate into 'Baldy's Dream.'"

"I know they're Greek letters," Sam acknowledged, "but they sure don't mean Baldy's Dream or anybody's dream. Those letters spell out 'The Master's Helena.' What do you suppose that means? Sounds ambiguous as hell."

"Does, doesn't it?" I answered, flustered. "I don't know what it all means, either."

After Sam left, I thought about the non-name some more. I thought, could it be an act of gratitude? I was grateful I didn't know.

CHAPTER 9

The Major and the Inspector

I became familiar with Roderick St. John (pronounced sin-JUN) a glimpse at a time. I would see him, in a posture I would learn was typical of him, slightly stooped and peering around his door at apartment No. 1 of 8 West at the ascending figures of female tenants. Or I would see him tangled in leashes as he walked Vicky, Eddy and Georgy, his three miniature Schnauzers named after English monarchs. But it was a full year before I was properly introduced to him.

The St. Johns were both "to the manor born," I was told, a good decade before the turn of the century, in Victorian England. Roderick had chosen a military career, and he and Mrs. St. John had spent nearly 30 years of that career in India. Shortly before World War II, Mrs. St. John returned to England but remained only briefly before emigrating to the United States. The reason for her emigration wasn't clear to me, though various residents of 8 West who had met the couple speculated that the St. Johns had lost most of both family fortunes through bad investments and simply couldn't afford to live in England in the style in which their aristocratic traditions demanded. Roderick St. John followed Felicia as soon as his retirement papers were processed after the war ended in 1945.

Roderick was a small man, barely 5' 1", whom I doubted ever weighed more than 125 pounds. His thin, dark hair was always neatly slicked back, and his large, black-rimmed glasses gave him something of an owlish look.

He was a dapper bundle of energy.

Once I had met Roderick, I learned that he spent much of each day doing double time on his typewriter.

Since his separation from the British Army, Roderick had written 15 detective mysteries. An avid fan of that kind of tale all his life, he decided to try his hand at writing detective stories while he was in India. It was during this time that his fertile imagination gave birth to Detective Donald Brisbane, the character who would become the central focus in all his books. I had read over a dozen of them.

Brisbane was an appealing character, a Scot. Tall, handsome and bewhiskered, he could run the mile in four minutes flat and stop a fleeing desperado in his tracks a hundred yards away with a boomerang. Brisbane smoked a hand-carved mahogany pipe and had a following of young women. Indeed, every Brisbane mystery ended with the Inspector nuzzling or bedding the grateful victim, invariably a gorgeous young blonde. The day I did shake Roderick St. John's hand for the first time is one I won't ever forget, for it was then that I got my first suspicion that Roderick attempted to play-act Detective Brisbane's escapades before they were put down on paper. How preposterous, I thought, that such a funny little man could envision himself in all those exciting adventures and lusty interludes.

It was at the Karbowskis' apartment on a day it had been necessary to hire a plumber to try and track down periodic and perplexing eruptions of soap suds in the sinks and tubs of apartments in 8 West.

"Franklin!" Mr. K had demanded, "meet Mister Saint John. He is a book writer."

"Er," (cough) "that's Sin-Jun, my dear Mr. K," Roderick interjected. "Delighted, young man. You work for our friend here?"

"Part-time, Mr. ... er ... sir. The rest of the time I'm a student at Columbia."

"Well, hail Columbia — that's a little joke — and good for you. And don't worry about pronouncing my name properly," he picked up. "I put the accent on 'sin' because I don't live up to the 'saint'."

He obviously had said this many times before because no sooner had he heard himself than he broke into a loud chortle. I shared his joke and laughed too.

"I write books about a man who would speak like that," he offered. "So I must keep in practice."

Not daring to guess whether he was referring only to dialogue or to antics as well, I shook his hand once more and went on my way.

For a long time afterwards, each time I saw Roderick St. John, he would give me a sly wink as if we were partners to some mysterious secret. What that secret was I wasn't sure, but I did begin to wonder if it had something to do with his constant peerings.

It seemed more and more that he was spying on something or someone, but I decided that I was imagining it only because I now knew who and what he was. You're more aware of a familiar face, I thought to myself. That's why you've become more aware of his habit of stooping and peering. It's really nothing to worry about.

Still, I couldn't entirely dispel my growing suspicion that Roderick was a voyeur. But, wanting to give him the benefit of the doubt, I made myself remember that Roderick was also the creator of Inspector Brisbane. No doubt he was researching facts and checking situations for his adventures.

I wanted to believe the latter since Roderick's latest novel had featured situations and personalities which were distinctly familiar to me. Indeed, there was no doubt in my mind that the woman Inspector Brisbane had rescued from a fate worse than death in his most recent effort was Elise Saxon, an upstairs tenant, and that the shimmeringly seductive temptress he had saved from being impressed into a prostitute's career was Dottie Rodgers, who lived next door to Elise.

I was being forced to believe the former by the sheer weight of evidence.

More than once I had passed Claudine Plouvier, a fourth-floor tenant, muttering something in French as she went up the stairs with one or both of her sons.

This meant nothing to me, however, until the day I met Dottie Rodgers and her roommate Helen Jason coming in the front door. Roderick and his dogs had just left the building. Helen and Dottie were laughing and chatting animatedly.

"Did you see what I saw?" Dottie was asking. "That little guy had mirrors on the tips of his shoes! Wait till the weather gets warmer! I'll give him a show!"

Helen laughed. "What do you think he'd do if we invited him up to the apartment? God, he seems full of energy. With all those years he spent in India, he might know something we don't."

"Shhh," Dottie tittered, now seeing me.

They were still laughing as they disappeared up the stairs.

The final confirmation came from Cindy. As I kissed her when she came home from work one Sunday afternoon, she pulled back a bit and started to laugh.

"What's so funny?" I asked, suddenly peeved. "You act like the way I kiss you is stupid!"

She could hardly talk for laughing. "Frank, it's not you! It's your Mr. 'Sin' John! I couldn't believe my eyes. I was just coming up the stairs when his door opened and he began staring up at me through binoculars! That poor man has a problem!"

Perhaps he did. But as long as the female residents of 8 West could take it so lightly, it would remain his problem and not mine.

While cleaning the hallway one Saturday morning I was surprised to see the St. Johns' door propped open with a large book. I had hardly approached the area in front of the door with the vacuum cleaner when Vicky, Georgy and Eddie surrounded me, yipping with all the fury they could muster. This quickly brought the Major, who shushed them and got them inside. No sooner had I started vacuuming than the Major reappeared.

"Franklin, please turn that thing off," he said. "Come in, come in. Have some tea with me."

The invitation was a surprise, and the tea was surprisingly good.

"I get my tea directly from Malaya," he informed me. "They blend it to my specifications. I'm very fussy about my tea."

"I can see you are, Major," I said, and I meant it. "The taste is wonderful. When did you become a tea expert? When you were in India?"

"That's right. I was a transportation officer in the British Army so I traveled much of the time throughout the Indian sub-continent and Southeast Asia. I always enjoyed visiting the great tea plantations in the Malaysian Peninsula."

"Did you have interests besides the Army and tea?"

"Indeed I did. Felicia, whom I sometimes accuse of looking like Buddha, became involved with religions and exotic things like the I Ching and the Tarot and ESP. Not I. I enjoyed shooting and British sports and the marvelous foods of that part of the world. I did share one thing with Felicia, though. She's a psychologist, you know. A good one, I'm told. I studied some things along with her. Psychology of sex. Abnormal psychology. Things like that."

Somehow not surprised to hear this, I asked more questions.

"Why did you come to New York? Why didn't you retire to England?"

The Major's face reflected a small, sad smile. "You haven't been to England, have you," he asked. "It has changed – and it is still changing rapidly. The life Felicia and I knew as children is no longer possible. Only the very rich can afford servants now. And the bloody Socialists have fixed things so that inheritances are a thing of the past. We wanted to leave the things we have to museums, not the government, so we came here. But that's not the main reason we're here. New York is a vital city, an exciting place to live. We love it. I have a publisher, and Felicia has everything she wants. God knows, she seems to be studying everything at once these days – life, death, ESP, psychokinesis, theosophy. Makes we wonder at times what world she's living in."

"Major, where did you acquire all these magnificent things?" I was referring to the awe-inspiring collections of art that surrounded me and were everywhere I looked in the St. Johns' apartment.

"We acquired most of these things in India and Asia," the Major said. "The jade and ivory items are from India mostly. These prayer wheels are from Tibet, and the large silk screens and porcelain vases are from China. The rosewood prayer table is also from China. The incense burners – God, how I hate the smell of incense – are from India for the most part. The jewelry, the emeralds and rubies especially, are Indian. We're quite proud of our collections. Some of it's quite sexual, too. Many of the items are sex symbols. Damned if we'll leave them to the bloody government!"

Enjoying his rare expansiveness, I asked, "Are you working on a new book?"

"Franklin," he pronounced, "as long as I can breathe, I shall write. I love to write. The writing, and the research one must do before writing, keeps one young. You must try it sometime, young man. Why, if I can write a book – and I was 51 when I wrote my first one – anyone can. I now write two and three a year. Great discipline! Really keeps the old brain alive! And it's such fun! Oh, I have had such fun with the one I am now writing!"

I soon learned that one man's fun can be another man's terror.

A few weeks after my very pleasant visit with the Major I was summoned to the Karbowskis'.

"Franklin, what is going on in 8 West?" Mrs. K asked sternly.

My perplexed look and mute presence led her to blurt out, "Who is shooting in the house?"

My perplexed state continued. I managed to mutter, "Shooting? I don't understand."

"Franklin, someone is shooting a gun in 8 West," Mrs. K repeated. "Anastasia de Maupeou, one of the tenants in that building, hears it every morning. She is terrified. She has already called the police but they do not listen to her. Please, stop the shooting in 8 West."

"Mrs. K, if anyone is shooting in 8 West, I certainly want to know about it," I answered. "I live here, too. Please, what more can you tell me? Does it happen every day? Just once in a while? At a certain time of day?"

"Anastasia said it is mornings, usually about ten o'clock. She says she can hear the shots very clearly. They must be close to her."

This exchange occurred just before the Easter break at Columbia. Obviously I would have to spend some of my vacation researching the shootings rather than my studies.

Every day during the Easter break I walked the halls of 8 West between ten and eleven each morning, listening for gun shots. I also left my door open other times so that I could catch sounds from throughout the building. My researches were rewarded the last day of the school break.

I had hardly started out the apartment door when I heard what I thought was a shot down below. I cautiously worked my way down to the first level when I heard a second shot — which had to have come from the basement. The basement door was open and the light from below was so great that it nearly blinded me. It also scared the daylights out of me.

Standing in the basement doorway I shouted, "Who's shooting down there? What's going on?" With that, I jumped back to listen in safety.

"Franklin, is that you?" It was the Major's voice. Franklin, why are you shouting? What on earth is wrong with you?"

Relieved that it was the Major, I presented myself in the stairway. "What are you doing?" I challenged. "What are you shooting? You have terrified some of the tenants!"

The Major looked not the slightest bit nonplussed. "Doing? I'm researching a situation for my latest book. The Inspector has been hurt. His right arm and leg are broken and he's a little woozy. I am trying to see what happens when he shoots unnaturally with his left hand. Come down and take a look at my target. I have it beautifully illuminated."

I didn't move. "Major, how did you get down here? Where did you get the key?"

"Key? Why, Mr. Karbowski gave it to me. I explained what I wanted to do and he seemed very pleased. Gave me the key immediately."

Excuses aside, I still had some nervous tenants to settle. "Are you about done with your research? I'm afraid your next-door neighbor is about to die from fright."

"I'm done, yes. I have just worked out what I needed to know. Here," he said as he ascended the stairs. "Give the key back to Mr. K."

"The Major said you gave him permission," I explained to the K's as I returned the key. "He said he told you what he wanted to do and you gave him the key."

I could see Mr. K was in thought. "Oh, oh, he must have said players, players in his book. I thought he said prayers. I thought he wanted to get away from his wife to pray to God. I always encourage prayer."

When I returned to 8 West I remembered the Major's invitation to look at his target. I let myself in the basement, turned on the main light and cautiously descended the stairs. There in front of me was the target, a cardboard creation about three feet square backed with sand bags. Pasted to the cardboard was a picture of a naked woman of Buddha-like proportions with pistol shots through her eyes, her heart and her navel. Without the shots, I would have guessed the target to be the Major's beloved Felicia, whom I had heard was quite fat. With the shots, the target could have been an illustration out of a medical text.

I could hardly wait for the Major's new book to be published!

CHAPTER 10

Felicia to the Rescue

It was a Sunday morning and I was comfortably settled with a pot of coffee and The New York Times when the phone rang.

"Franklin, I am sorry to bother you on a Sunday." It was Mrs. K. "Zbigniew would like to talk to you. Can you come over?" I could and I did.

Mr. K apologized for bothering me on the Sabbath, but he had a project on his mind, he said. His nature would not permit him to delay talking about it.

"The roofs need fixing," he said. "And the chimneys need pointing. At least that's what I thought he said. Now that I could more easily penetrate his accent, he seemed easier to understand. He went on. "I will do the work, but I need help in getting the materials and tools to the roof. Can you help me?"

"Certainly," I consented. "What has to be taken to the roof? And when do you want to do it?"

"You will take the heavier things, please," he explained. "A bag of cement. Some sand. Some large cans of roof coating. I will take the tools and the rope."

"Rope?"

"Yes," he went on. "I always tie myself to the chimney when I work on the roof. If I slip on the edge I will be safe. I learned this when climbing mountains."

"Oh, well, let me know when you want me to take the cement and stuff up. I'll be glad to do it," I said, all the time mentally groaning at the thought of lugging cement and tar up the ladder which linked the fifth floor with the roof.

Returning to my apartment, I met the Saint Johns about to enter the building with their yapping mutts. They were both carrying bags of groceries.

"Ah, Franklin," the Major greeted me. "We've been stocking our pantry. Have you met my, ah, better half? This is Felicia."

If opposites do attract, Mrs. St. John was indeed the perfect mate for the Major. She was a good head taller than he and she outweighed him by at least 75 pounds. Her salt and pepper hair was undoubtedly combed from time to time, but right now it looked wild and wispy. Her eyes, however, reflected an extraordinary serenity.

"How d'you do, Mr. Noyes," she smiled. "I *am* pleased to meet you!"

"I'm also pleased to meet you, Mrs. St. John," I answered, shaking her hand. "I've seen you a few times at a distance and I apologize that it has taken me so long to say hello."

"I've heard much about you, Mr. Noyes."

"You have? Good things I hope?"

"Veddy good indeed," she said. "In fact, you are eggs-ACT-ly the sort of person I'm looking for."

My puzzlement must have showed all over my face, and Felicia St. John hastened to explain her statement.

"I am the head of the local Theosophical Society, and we're always looking for qualified members. I believe you would qualify."

"Theosophical Society?"

"Yes, indeed," she nodded. "It was founded by Madame Helena Petrovna Blavatsky in 1854 after she had spent seven years in Tibet being initiated into the mysteries of the occult. Do you wish to know more?"

Taking my lack of response as an affirmative answer, she went on.

"Mrs. Blavatsky remains in touch with her occult teachers, myself included, through a form of telepathy, and we use the information we exchange in telepathic transmissions as the basis for many of her continuing works, most notably 'The Secret Doctrine.'"

I was fascinated. To hear Mrs. St. John tell it, not only was a long-dead woman creating books, but there was also a publisher producing them. What great pearls of wisdom could this disheveled woman's group be uncovering?

As if reading my mind (maybe she <u>was</u> reading my mind!), Mrs. St. John invited me to attend the next meeting of her Theosophical Society. On a whim I accepted.

Thus I sat in on a few Friday night sessions which were held at the St. Johns'. Felicia (as she insisted on being called) explained that the first and most fundamental idea of occultism is that everything in the universe is one. As a Christian, albeit not a regular practitioner, this idea made sense to me.

As we progressed into more advanced ideas — that all matter exists in different states; that life evolves within the form; that the laws of periodicity, of ebb and flow, flux and reflux are universal — I was unable to relate these ideas to my own life or limited experience and so I lost interest.

I returned to more sessions of the Theosophical Society, however, not so much to learn more about theosophy as to learn more about Felicia herself.

I learned that she had begun her studies in psychology as the precocious daughter of an eminent English surgeon. Through her father she met Sigmund Freud and William James and later became a disciple and faithful correspondent of Carl Gustav Jung.

When the Major's career took him to India, with occasional holiday journeys to Tibet and China, Felicia took advantage of every opportunity to learn more about the occult arts which flourished in those countries.

She became an expert in symbology, astrology, numerology, phrenology, the Tarot and I Ching; and she was cataloging stories of persons who had had ESP, psychokinetic and life-after-death experiences. At one point the Major told me that Felicia had had several experiences with ESP herself.

It didn't take Felicia long to realize that I had no real interest in displacing my Christian beliefs with Madame Blavatsky's occult wisdom. However, I was so obviously interested in learning more about the I Ching that she enrolled me in her four-week course. The sessions were held in the St. Johns' room at three o'clock on four successive Saturday afternoons.

The second session was about half over when Felicia stopped talking, sat up rigidly in her chair and appeared to stare into space. The students – three others besides me – looked at each other in wonderment. Was she all right? Should we do something? Should we call the Major?

My thoughts were shattered by a scream from Felicia.

"Franklin, quickly, quickly! Go to the roof! Every second counts!"

I looked at her in bewilderment and didn't move.

"Franklin," she repeated, "Don't stare dumbly! Get to the roof of this house immediately! Move!"

And move I did, though I didn't know why.

I shot up the stairs to the fifth floor and then up the ladder to the roof. I scanned the roof, and quickly saw Mr. K. flat on the roof, his face almost in the cement mixture he was using to point the chimney. When I got to him I saw that he was unconscious and tangled in the rope that he said he tied around his waist and the chimney whenever he worked on the roof. Now said rope was tautly engaged around his right leg in his crotch. How had this happened?

Felicia and my fellow classmates reminded me of a puppet show as one head would appear at the top of the ladder to the roof only to be quickly replaced by another. When Felicia's head appeared I shouted to her to call for help. The screeching sirens let me know that she had already done that.

The fire emergency people revived Mr. K, fit him with an oxygen mask and quickly removed him to an ambulance. At my request they took him to St. Luke's with Cindy and Mrs. K following in a cab. I stayed behind to clean up the mess on the roof, all the time wondering how Mr. K could have possibly slipped or spun or kicked to move the rope around his waist to his right leg. And why? Did he have a stroke or a fit of some kind that triggered a bizarre sequence of events? From questions I asked him later, I pieced together that Mr. K had been attacked by what he called a "wild cat". Swinging his arms like a whirling Dervish to protect himself, be became entangled in the rope, fell and was knocked out. I assumed the "wild cat" was one of the many feral cats prowling Manhattan.

Mr. K. was home within three days as vigorous as ever. Helena told Cindy that Mr. K. did blackout occasionally but was not concerned. Why? A fellow conspirator from Poland, not a physician, assured Mr. K. that he was "as fit as a thirty-year old." Cindy knew better. She read his chart and saw that several physicians urgently recommended a complete cardiac work-up. She tried to discuss the matter with Helena who just shook her head and said, "Not to worry, my Zbig is fine."

When I told Mr. K. how I had come to help him, he had no doubt that God had worked His life-saving wonders through Felicia. He was in such awe of her, and so willing to do anything she asked, that the Karbowski-Noyes ESP incident achieved a certain amount of notoriety in psychical circles. Felicia turned the incident into such an interesting article for the Journal of the American Psychical Society that Mr. K. and I were asked by visiting scholars of psychical phenomena to reenact the incident three different times.

He and Felicia did. In the safety of Felicia's living room.

CHAPTER 11

Of God and Polish Freedom

I was vacuuming the halls one Saturday morning when Mr. K intercepted me and asked me to stop by that afternoon. He had important matters to discuss, he said.

It was about three o'clock when I stepped up to knock on the Karbowskis' apartment door. I stopped momentarily because I heard Mrs. K playing the piano. I didn't know what she was playing but I was enthralled. She played magnificently.

At the first break in the music I knocked quickly. Helena answered.

"Ah, Franklin, come in. We have been expecting you."

"Thank you. I was standing in the hallway listening to you play. You're great!"

"Do you know what I was playing?"

"No. I can't sing or read music. Mostly I'm musically illiterate. But I loved what you were playing."

"It was the music of an old family friend," Helena said. "Ignace Jan Paderewski. Zbigniew and he worked on many matters together. "

I whistled softly. "I *am* impressed," I said.

Mr. K came forward to greet me and steered me to a couch.

"We have many things to talk about," he said. "The exterminators will come here Wednesday. You must let them in. And the roof next door. I need..." The phone rang and he jumped to answer it.

Because my day of considerable physical activity had tired me, I leaned back in the plush couch and was semi-somnolent when Mrs. K sat next to me. Mr. K's animated voice rose and fell in the background.

"Franklin, are you and Cindy happy in New York City?" Helena asked.

"We sure are," I told her. "Everything is still so new and exciting. We love the theater and have already seen several plays. And we have made many fine friends. What about you, Mrs. K? Are you and your husband happy here?"

"We are happy," she answered, "And sad. Happy to be free and to be near so many Polish friends. And sad not to be in Poland with our families and in our own homes."

"I've heard your husband talking about overthrowing the communists and making Poland free once again," I continued. "Does he really think this is possible?"

"What do you know about Polish history?" Helena asked.

"Very little. Why?"

"Zbigniew is a nationalist. As a very young man, he fought against the Russians. When the Germans took over in 1916, he fought against them. In 1919 and 1920, he fought against the Russians once again to restore Poland's old borders. And he served in the republican government during the 1920's before returning to his family's lands. Yes, he thinks it is possible to beat the Russians, if the Americans will help. We fled to help organize Polish forces worldwide."

We both turned to look at Mr. K.

Judging from the tone and volume of his telephone conversation, the revolution he planned to lead wasn't going well.

"He's talking to a judge," Helena whispered. "He's an old friend. Zbigniew gets very excited when the judge insists that the revolution must not violate Polish law. Have you ever heard of a legal revolution?"

I admitted I hadn't and told her it sounded like a contradiction of terms. I asked, "How do you feel about all this? Do you think you will live to see a free Poland?"

Helena draw a hand across her forehead. "Do you know my husband has never asked me that question?" she said quietly. "He assumes that I support him in all that he does. And I do. But I do not believe in his revolution."

She shook her head sadly and it didn't appear she would say anything more.

"Tell me what you believe," I urged.

"Franklin, I believe in God," Helena said with conviction. "And only God can make Poland truly free."

I didn't know what to say at this point. All of my political studies, and my meager Methodist upbringing, failed to prepare me for this type of discussion. So I fell silent.

"Poland is probably the most Christian nation in the world," Helena continued in a moment. "Nowhere is the Church stronger. Does not that sound strange to you? A strong church in a communist country?"

I nodded but said nothing.

Helena continued. "It is no accident. We have lost our political freedom many times. But we have never lost our belief in God and His church. It is the Holy Spirit at work in us and our captors which will make Poland free. I don't think I will see it in my lifetime, though. But you may in yours."

Again we both turned to look at Mr. K. He was now walking around with the phone, shouting at it like a father deeply aggrieved by a son's behavior. When he stopped I could hear what sounded like two other voices shouting back. I looked quizzically at Mrs. K.

"I think you must go," she whispered. "The Polish general staff in-exile is obviously not in agreement on something. That means only one thing. They will soon be here. I must be sure I have enough coffee and bread and kielbasa and ham. My Zbigniew's general staff works well only with a full stomach." I waved to Mr. K as I stood to leave.

"Tell him I'll let the exterminators in on Wednesday," I said over my shoulder to Helena. "And I'm available to talk any evening."

"Do you have a record player?" Helena asked suddenly.

"Yes, but why?"

"Wait just a moment." She walked over to the piano and picked up two records.

"Take these," she said. "Think of us when you play them. This one is by Chopin, a great Pole who left his country at age 21 and never returned. And this one is by the other great Pole I mentioned, Paderewski. He was a great patriot. Twice he led his country. Two great musicians whose stories tell much about Poland. But for Christmas I shall give you something much more important. A Polish house prayer. God shall be Poland's savior. Not my Zbigniew's general staff."

I smiled my thanks and gave her a light kiss on the cheek. She nodded and I let myself quietly out.

I was playing the Paderewski record when Cindy got home from work.

"That's beautiful," she commented, listening. "Where'd you get it?"

"Mrs. K gave it to me. I was there this afternoon. I'll tell you about it during dinner. We had a great visit."

And during the next two hours my wife and I talked about how lucky we were to have such good and generous friends as the Karbowskis.

And meanwhile I, still befuddled by Helena's absolute belief that God would save Poland, tried to figure out how.

CHAPTER 12

The Transients

The first tenants I met in 6 West's apartment No. 2 were the screaming Donatuccis, Phil and Ellen. Their screaming matches started their second night in residence and continued until they departed, separately, about a month later. They usually began their shouting at dinnertime. "You sonofabitch," Ellen would start, loud enough to be heard on the third floor. "Drinking already? Did you pick up the meat like I told you? What the hell do you expect me to cook? Ever tried fried shit?"

"Everything you cook tastes like fried shit," would come the equally loud reply. "Who the hell d'you think you're talking to, anyway? Your fat-ass mother?"

From that point the decibels of the scatological comments escalated either until I was summoned by neighboring tenants or until the police had been informed that the domestic tranquility of No.2, 6 West, had again been shattered.

I had had no experience in quelling domestic uprisings and was a most timid and reluctant mediator the few times I entered the Donatuccis' apartment.

"Please!" I would beg. "Please keep your voices down! The neighbors are complaining and Mr. K is threatening to evict you."

"Evict us? Ha! That's a laugh!" Ellen would screech. "Who's that dumb fart think he's dealing with anyway? A coupla dumb dagos? We'll sue the shit out of him if he tries to evict us!"

Despite such exchanges, my visits usually restored quiet for a day or so.

About three weeks after they moved in, the Donatuccis' apartment became strangely quiet. And their nightly deposit of trash no longer contained garbage, only liquor bottles. I made it my business to find out why.

Ellen had moved out and had left Phil to devote his waking hours to inducing drunken stupors. Within a week, he too moved out. He left a note saying he could no longer afford the apartment and was moving to California.

He bequeathed to Cindy and me what remained of their furnishings: a stuffed chair, a bathroom scale and a near-new floor lamp.

The screaming Donatuccis were replaced by the shattering Bronsons.

Johnson and Carole, both medical lab technicians at St. Luke's Hospital, were in their late 20's and recently married. What they lacked in furniture they appeared to make up for in loving attention to each other. For almost a week.

Soon, Mrs. K began calling me to report strange noises coming from No. 2. Would I please investigate? I did but heard nothing.

Then other reports of noises emanating from No. 2 started coming from neighboring tenants. It sounded like breaking glass, they said. Still I heard nothing when I went to check.

On a Saturday morning about five weeks after the Bronsons' arrival, I was plugging in the vacuum cleaner outside their apartment when I heard the sound of glass smashing against the door. Voices rose and were soon followed by a blast of music, the volume of which was enough to shatter eardrums.

I then heard Johnson scream, "Stop it, Carole! Stop it! Are you mad? Don't throw that flask!"

Johnson's plea was followed by more glass-breaking sounds and, shortly, the eruption through the apartment door of Johnson, dripping purple fluid from his head.

Johnson left that same day and Carole followed two days later, at the insistence of Mr. K.

But not before I learned from Carole that she and her husband had been using various beakers and flasks from their lab as household dishes. As their young marriage began to deteriorate, these had become handy weapons for their matrimonial war. The ultimate weapon proved to be a flask of gentian violet which Johnson Bronson had been using to treat a persistent case of athlete's foot.

As I scrubbed and scoured and tried to remove purple stains from the walls and floor, I began to wonder if this apartment, No.2, was jinxed. It certainly looked that way.

CHAPTER 13

The Citron Certainty

Cindy and I were so busy adjusting to our new home and responsibilities that it was months before I yielded to my sister's importunings to "stop next door for a minute and introduce yourself to the Blacks." They were practically family, I was told.

Indeed they were, for despite the fact that neither Cindy nor I had ever met them, we knew a lot about them. Ken and Frances Black, in No. 6 in 6 West, were related to my sister's neighbors in the Poconos.

The family Frances had worked for was the Clarence Blacks of Nyack, New York. While only a housemaid, Frances was an integral and indispensable part of their family even before she and Kenneth Black fell in love. Since Ken was the heir apparent to the considerable Black fortune, Ken's father hoped for a "proper" marriage for his son and openly discouraged the tender feelings Ken and Frances occasionally let show in public. So they were married secretly, and for over a year they were able to occupy a conjugal bed only occasionally.

That was 1929, the year of the stock market crash.

In a matter of months, father Black joined that maudlin legion of financiers and industrialists who saw their fortunes dwindle and disappear. He and his wife sold their home and furniture and lived in a small cottage which their daughter occupied near Morristown, New Jersey.

The parents were both so traumatized by the Crash and ensuing depression that neither of them lived more than two years beyond Black Friday.

Ken and Frances had revealed their marriage and moved into New York City shortly after the Crash. They survived for several years largely on odd jobs which Frances found among those of the Black's' friends who were still solvent. Sometimes Frances did housecleaning, sometimes washing and ironing, but most often she did cooking for special occasions. She was a miracle worker with food and a superb pastry chef whose exquisite confections were frequently mentioned in newspaper social columns. Each such mention would bring her two or three more engagements. And so, with flour and eggs, she was able to hold body and soul together during the harsh depression years.

Ken, who had studied psychology at New York University, had wanted a career in personnel management. His father, however, had insisted instead that Ken join him in his enterprise of arranging financing for small businesses. Part of the father's insistence was for a very special reason: Ken had suffered from rheumatic fever as a child and had a severely damaged heart. The father wanted to make sure that his son's physical and mental stresses were minimal.

Ken had never been very strong since his illness. As a "special" child who could not engage in physical activities of any kind, he used to spend physical education periods at prep school in the library stacks instead. On one of his visits there he discovered astrology. He grew to be such an avid student of the subject that he became convinced it was his destiny to become an astrologer. When he and Frances moved to New York, he was pleasantly surprised to find some of his father's old friends and colleagues begging him for horoscopes. They asked him to cast charts and to advise them, astrologically, whether their attempts to find a successful niche in the diminished world of American business would be fruitful.

As the result of this interest and his still-serious physical limitations, Ken decided to make his living as a professional astrologer. It took only four years for his practice to produce enough for the Blacks to live on. By the time I knocked on the Blacks' door that summer morning, Ken had a thriving practice, and his wife had been able to reduce her commercial baking to the annual preparation of fruitcakes – only enough to be mailed to an elite list of 500 people throughout the country.

Ken and Frances immediately chided me for not stopping by before this, and both insisted that I fetch Cindy so that the four of us could "meet properly" over coffee and cake. From that morning on, the Blacks remained our devoted "adopted" parents. Indeed, there were times, usually when I was preparing for tests or writing class papers, that Cindy spent many of her non-working hours with them.

Ken's impish manner fit his looks perfectly. His azure eyes were large, wide set and slightly bulging. They seemed to sparkle in harmony with his perfect teeth which were fully revealed every time he smiled, and this he did frequently and broadly. To his doctor's dismay, Ken smoked, deferring only slightly to his doctor's admonitions to quit by using a very long cigarette holder. There were times when I watched him that, with his wide grin and cigarette holder clenched in his teeth, he looked very much like a *New Yorker* cartoon version of Franklin Roosevelt.

Frances was a good partner for Ken. Very attractive, plump from enjoying her own cooking and baking, she was his equal in impishness and playfulness. She loved nothing better than to tell jokes that clearly revealed her earthy upbringing.

When I first met the Blacks, Ken told me that through interpreting his dreams and visions he had reconstructed his life through three reincarnations. In his earliest life, in medieval England, he said he had been a court astrologer; during the time of Henry VIII, he had been a tax collector; and during the early years of Victoria's reign, he had been a royal physician, he said.

It was Ken's interest and strong belief in reincarnation that led him to Felicia St. John, living next door, and her theosophy sessions. The two of them soon become interested in research to prove life after death.

Their research was challenging, Ken told me. Whenever they learned of someone who had been brought back from the dead — usually persons saved from death by drowning through artificial respiration — Felicia would interview the person using a questionnaire devised by Ken.

Their research, slow due to the dearth of subjects, was producing a definite and fairly consistent picture of life after death, I learned. Most of the subjects described a strikingly similar sequence of events: travel down a long, dark tunnel at great speed until they saw a light and exited, at which point an out-of-body experience began; floating above the body and watching revival efforts with largely dispassionate interest; hearing voices of dead relatives and friends but not being able to respond; and the appearance of a bright, warm, all-encompassing light which communicated telepathically. Ken saw this research as the first step in a series of projects which could ultimately prove the reality of reincarnation and demonstrate that in the life-death cycle it was not unusual for human souls to return — sometimes even in the form of animals.

Whenever Ken launched into this particular discussion, Frances would observe somewhat sarcastically, but not unkindly, that Ken's theory stemmed from the fact that he looked like a sheep.

"And you, my dear, look like a pelican," he would always reply, nonplussed. "Your eyes can hold more than your belly can."

As dedicated as Ken was to his research, it took a piece of fruitcake to produce what Ken insisted was proof positive of life after death — at least as far as he was concerned.

It was a gray, dreary January afternoon. I was at school. Cindy was working nights and using any spare time she could find during her waking hours to transform a Christmas gift of Pendleton wool fabric into a winter outfit for herself. Whenever she encountered a sewing problem, she found Frances a willing and able teacher.

This afternoon she had sought Frances' advice about 4:30, and

Frances suggested the problem should be handled over coffee and homemade fruitcake. Ken decided to join them.

Frances and Cindy were deep in a discussion about how to make bound buttonholes when they simultaneously realized that something was wrong with Ken. His face was tomato red, his eyes were moving rapidly from side to side, and his hand was grasping at his throat. Cindy immediately realized he was asphyxiating from something lodged in his windpipe.

"What's in your throat?" she shouted. "Francis, call the operator. Get an ambulance! Quick!"

Ken pointed to a small piece of fruitcake on his plate, and Cindy realized in horror that a piece of candied fruit was probably what was choking him.

Frances had not made any move to call for help. Instead, she lurched toward Ken, first in wonder then in shock. As Cindy moved to slap Ken's back, Frances moved in to hug her husband, babbling.

Cindy slapped her, roughly pushed her aside, and sternly ordered her to make the call. Sobered, Frances moved to the telephone.

By the time the ambulance arrived only three or four minutes later, Ken's badly diseased heart had stopped functioning. The quick-witted ambulance doctor knew exactly what to do first. He made an incision and luckily found the offending foreign object – a large chunk of citron – immediately.

Then he started to administer oxygen through a device cleverly inserted in Ken's windpipe.

"And I've found a heartbeat again!" the young man in white cried jubilantly.

Ken began breathing again and soon he was being carried out the door on a stretcher and taken to St. Luke's Hospital.

Cindy was waiting to leave when I arrived home. She quickly told me what had happened and said we would be having dinner at the hospital cafeteria tonight. On the bus to the hospital, she recounted to me the details of the traumatic incident.

"Is he going to die?" I asked anxiously.

"No, I don't think so. The ambulance people arrived in time to save him."

Only slightly relieved, I couldn't wait to see Ken and decide for myself what his chances were.

After dinner, we were allowed to see him for a few moments. I was pleased to see that he was apparently breathing normally. Frances, however, was still in shock. Cindy took her in tow and in fact stayed with her in the Blacks' apartment through the several days it took Frances to recover from the near-tragedy.

Ken's recuperation was rapid. On the third day of his stay in the hospital, he said he was ready to go home, but his physician insisted he remain a week.

It was the fifth day after the choking incident, and I went to visit Ken on my way home from school.

"I'm so glad to see you!" he greeted me. "This certainly has been an extraordinary week for me."

"You can say that again," I declared, stressing every word.

"No, not for the reason you think," he said. "I'm talking about something I've decided to call 'The Citron Certainty.' See?"

He pushed some papers across his hospital tray-table toward me.

"I've been writing furiously and can't get it down on paper fast enough," he went on. "Do you know what I'm writing? I'm writing PROOF of immortality!"

Mentally I had been prepared to verbally stroke a near-dead patient with platitudes and pleasantries. Ken's philosophical sledge hammer was therefore almost more than I could take in, and Ken sensed it immediately.

"Franklin, I'm not dead, and I'm no longer near death either," he explained jubilantly. "And do you know something? I'm almost sorry that I'm not in either state."

Seeing what must have been a very strange expression on my face, he said, "Sounds crazy, doesn't it? But it's not."

"Oh?" I mustered, waiting.

"It's like this," he went on. "When I stopped breathing five days ago, I started experiencing the same sequence of events which Felicia and I had been identifying in our research. I was zooming down this black tunnel until a light appeared and I left the tunnel. Then I saw myself leave my body and I floated over it, all the time watching Cindy and Frances and the doctor trying to save me. My parents' voices, and the voices of dead friends greeted me, but I couldn't answer. Then I felt like I was on a Florida beach with warm, bright light all around me and I was being asked 'Are you ready to die?' And scenes of my life were passing before me. But something, I don't know what, kept saying 'You have to go back.' And suddenly I was. Franklin, I think I have proven immortality, possibly even reincarnation. It's something for which I shall always to grateful to Frances."

"Frances?" I questioned, surprised. What Cindy had told me about Frances freezing from fright flashed across my memory. "What did Frances have to do with it?"

"The citron!" Ken declared. "The citron I nearly choked to death on! It came from a fruitcake which she had made with her own loving hands. If she hadn't made that cake, I wouldn't have had the life-death experience. So I want her to be recognized for the opportunity she gave me."

"Well?"

"Well, I couldn't think of a suitable phrase using Frances' name. You know, like the Pythagorean theorem or the Aristotelian mean. So I'm doing the next best thing. I'm calling my discovery 'The Citron Certainty'! And I shall attribute it to three people: Felicia St. John, Frances Black, and myself. Yes, in one fell swoop I shall immortalize Frances and her fruitcake!"

Wow! I left the hospital smiling. No greater love hath any man than one who immortalizes his wife for almost choking him to death. I felt honored to have been the first one to hear the words 'Citron Certainty' spoken out loud.

CHAPTER 14

Of Astrology and Fruitcakes

As interested as I was in Ken's metaphysical research, nothing fascinated me more than his astrology practice. And the way his interest in astrology touched almost everything he did was interesting to observe indeed.

Since his sheltered childhood days, he had been a dedicated ham radio operator and electrical wizard. When his father, whose very fortune depended on the telephone, began losing his hearing, Ken created what he called "Black's Bell Blaster."

He rigged the apartment phone with a microphone and speaker which greatly magnified the voice of any caller. When the Blaster was switched on, which Ken occasionally did for my edification, Ken's own conversations with his clients could be heard throughout the Black apartment.

Caller: "Ken? Sam here. We got the long-term contract with Penney and another with Montgomery Ward. It means we have to expand production. I intend to subcontract for a while, but I want to build a new plant. Where should I build it?"

Ken: "Most of the shirt business is here in Manhattan or down South. That's where the workers will be."

Sam: "I know, I know. I want you to look at my horoscope and tell me where to build the plant. I don't care where you say it is, I'll get the workers. Just be sure the location is right, astrologically."

Ken: "Okay, Sam. Let me check your 'scope and I'll get back to you later today."

My incredulous look made Ken laugh.

"What's the matter?" he chuckled. "Isn't that the way your professors taught you plant location occurs? Want to know something? Sam is one of the most successful shirt manufacturers in the country, and he doesn't bid on a contract or make any major decision without checking with me."

"Do you really believe astrology should be used to make business decisions?" I asked.

"I don't dare think otherwise. This is my bread and butter."

"Did you ever try to use astrology to advise your father?"

"Just once...I tried," he answered a bit sheepishly. "I can still hear him laughing."

Most of Ken's clients were business people and stage performers, few of whom would make a decision without consulting him. To each Ken attempted to give a full and accurate answer, as much as his star castings would permit, and it was not unusual for him to be contacted any hour of the day or night.

Many of Ken's clients were also Frances' customers – for her fruit-cakes, which she baked in two- and three-pound sizes.

In September a steady procession of purveyors would begin their deliveries to the Blacks. Fifty and hundred-pound bags of citron, glazed oranges, raisins, currants and assorted nutmeats arrived, followed by sacks of flour and sugar, packages of spices, and bottles of rum and brandy.

From October to late November, all of 6 West exuded tantalizing odors of fruitcakes, and from early December through the middle of the month Frances' trips to the post office were more frequent and heavier than those of the mailman who served 6 and 8 West both.

Our last Christmas season in New York, I was so concerned about Frances' frantic pace that I made it a point to visit her at least once a day so I could help her carry the heavy cakes to the post office.

On one of these visits I was in the kitchen helping her load up her two-wheeled shopping cart when she stuck her face next to mine, held her finger up to her lips and whispered, "Shhh. Listen for a minute."

What I heard was a conversation between Ken and a client. Thanks to the Blaster, both sides of the conversation could be heard in the kitchen.

"I agree," Ken was saying. "Any time in the next year is a good time for you or your son to start a new business."

"Great! Great!" boomed a reply. "But what kind of business? I want something my son can build slowly and yet make a little money. I don't want him to go into the finance business. Look, my father was in the garment business. He wouldn't let me go in it. Said it was for whores. I feel the same way about the finance business. What does Bill's horoscope say? What should he do?"

"It says he should go in business," Ken answered. "A quiet business. A select business. One with dignity."

"Great!" the voice boomed again. "But what the hell kind of business are you talking about?"

"What's Billy like to do?" Ken asked. "What are his hobbies? What interests him?"

I heard a sigh come through the Blaster.

"He's a gentleman, Ken," said the father. "A gentleman. He likes the theater, the movies…the ballet. And, well, he likes to cook. Drives his mother crazy. He's always trying to cook or bake something."

Ken asked if his baking was any good.

"Damned good," came the enthusiastic reply. "His bread and cakes are a treat."

There was silence for a long few seconds as if Ken was trying to sort out the words for his reply.

"Bill?"

"Yeah, Ken, I'm here…waiting."

"I have an idea for a business for Billy which will fit him like a glove.

Frances, who had been eavesdropping all along as I had, raised her eyebrows as she glanced at me. I shrugged but said nothing, afraid I'd miss something Ken said.

Ken went on.

"Here's my idea, Bill. I suggest you buy my wife's secret fruitcake recipe and client list and put Billy in the fruitcake business."

Frances look astonished — and relieved — to hear her husband's words. She opened her mouth to say something but decided against it, hearing Ken start a sales pitch.

"With damned little effort," he was saying, "he should be able to expand her list into the thousands. And I'm sure she'll throw in the testimonial letters at no charge. She has hundreds of them."

"Terrific!" father Bill shouted. "When can we wrap up the details?"

At this point I could no longer keep quiet.

"Did you know he was going to do that?" I whispered.

Frances shook her head. "No, I didn't. But I'm delighted. I wonder what my business is worth? Do you suppose we'll get enough for Ken and me to finally have a honeymoon?"

It took only a few weeks to find out. Ken and Frances decided that $10,000 was a good price for her recipe and customer list. However, they also insisted that thirty of their family members and friends — including Cindy and me — were each to receive three-pound fruitcakes in the Blacks' name each Christmas for the next fifteen years.

That made me very happy. I had never tasted anything as good as Frances' fruitcakes.

Certain of my favorite fruitcake until I was nearly 40, I remember our last pre-Christmas session with the Blacks with special fondness.

Frances was serving her fruitcake, of course, and she matched it with equally delicious coffee, thick as caramel syrup. The combination of her coffee and cake and Ken's astrological musings for the year to come produced memories that neither Cindy nor I ever forgot.

"Next year will be a good one for both of you," Ken told us. "Franklin, I've checked your horoscope, and you'll get that graduate school fellowship you're after."

I was impressed! I had never even mentioned the subject to Ken.

Ken went on, pleased. "And Cindy and you will be very happy in Philadelphia."

Philadelphia? This time both Cindy and I jumped. But Ken would not elaborate.

"Well, will Cindy get pregnant?" I asked, winking at my wife.

"Not according to this horoscope, yet," Ken smiled. "And assuming you keep the diaphragm patched," he added.

Frances jumped on that comment.

"Kenneth Brown, all you think of is sex, sex, sex. Can't you keep this conversation in tune with the season?"

"It is, m'dear," Ken answered, unruffled. "Isn't this the time of the year when we celebrate birth?"

Cindy piped in. "Ken, please, enough. Be serious. What great events do you see in 1953?"

"I'm not a great prognosticator like my associates in the newspaper columns," Ken said in mock seriousness, "so I don't try to predict what kings will die or what famous actress will sleep with what unknown actor. These two things I can predict, though. The war in Korea will end. I can see that in the movement of Mars. And Frances will get fatter. I can see that by looking across the table."

"Kenneth Black!" Frances exploded. "How dare you? Just for that, do you know what I'm going to get you for Christmas?"

"Yep, sure do. A pair of blinders so that I only see the better parts of you at any one time."

Cindy and I weren't sure what protocol or the horoscopes dictated at that point. However, when verbal love play becomes that intense, we did the one thing common sense dictates. We quickly wished them a happy holiday season, thanked them for the coffee and cake, and left, chuckling.

And sure enough, no matter where we were, each Christmas for the next 15 years a three-pound fruitcake caught up with us, reminding both of us of our good friends Ken and Frances Black.

CHAPTER 15

Country Girl/City Girl

The first year of our married life, Cindy had two urgent missions: To get the new Noyes' nest in order as quickly as possible and to adjust to the roaring, frantic chaos of Manhattan.

I suppose I wasn't surprised to learn that nest-building was Cindy's forte.

We had only just moved in when she decided the apartment needed painting which, indeed, it did, badly. Since we had no spare money for paint, unknown to me she visited Mr. K and persuaded him to supply the paint and some plaster to get our walls and ceilings into shape. Receiving the promise from Cindy that we would do all the work ourselves, Mr. K was pleased to be the benefactor.

Furniture? With the items David Weiss had left behind and what Mr. K had given us, we didn't need much more. With a $40 furniture budget, the Salvation Army store filled any gaps. We bought a fairly stable stool; two lamps; a faded, chintz-covered bedroom chair; two unmatched end tables; and three collapsible wooden chairs. Added to this was a new, two-seater sofa purchased with wedding-gift money from my parents.

So we painted and plastered the apartment and installed our "new" furniture, then Cindy began sewing like a demon.

The bedroom window, until now covered only with a shade, got curtains. The new sofa received a protective cover, tablecloths were made for our card table and my desk, and the living room windows got drapes.

Cindy kept on and she made aprons, placemats, throw rugs, pillow cases, kitchen towels, toss cushions, lampshade covers and more. On and on she sewed, and never before had her sewing machine, bought with high school graduation money, been pushed so hard. Remarkably, by the end of our first summer most of our needs had been met.

For Cindy to adjust to New York City was a different matter and much more difficult than turning our sow's ear of an apartment into a silk purse of a home on very little money.

Cindy had grown up on a small farm in the Poconos which had severely limited her contacts with the "outside" world. The farm had had no electricity, no telephone service and no indoor plumbing. It did have a rigid farm routine – the care and feeding of the livestock every single day, starting at 5:00 a.m., and the continual planting and harvesting of crops, starting in May and ending in October. Life, while busy, was never hurried and never disorderly.

Nurses' training in Brooklyn was hurried and occasionally disorderly, but it was similar in many ways to the farm. Cindy worked with a limited number of people in a highly structured society which had little contact with the outside world. She often compared it to living in a convent, an analogy that was apt in more ways than not.

So, for Cindy, marriage and the move to 8 West 90th Street represented a very difficult change. Under the best of circumstances, Manhattan is hurried, disorderly, dirty and unpredictable. Under the worst of circumstances, it is chaos.

To Cindy, Manhattan was pure chaos.

Commuting to St. Luke's Hospital became a necessary evil that Cindy grew to dread. In buses and subways, she detested being crammed against strangers, especially those who pinched and rubbed and felt with every lurch and veer of the vehicle. And she was desolated when one of those strangers, a skilled pickpocket, stole her wallet and a cameo necklace which had been in her family for generations.

Moreover, Manhattan was the place which ended Cindy's sheltered world in which until now there had been absolutely no confusion about which sex was which. The people visiting and living in Jon

Hauser's apartment upstairs contributed to Cindy's feeling of confusion and concern. There, sex roles apparently had no clearly definable niches, she was to discover, and it did not seem to detract from the sexual delights of a creative foursome who gathered in that apartment. But more about that later.

I'm sure I too contributed to Cindy's general fretting. During our first few months at 6 and 8 West, four times I had literally staggered back to the apartment after my trash collection rounds near drunk from get-acquainted cocktails from various tenants. Was her Prince Charming a lush?

It took two young Danes to persuade Cindy that Manhattan was exciting fun, not chaos, and that her husband was just a normally convivial Dane, not a lush.

An ad in the Columbia University paper had read: "Danish student seeks American student to share expenses on trip to West Coast."

I telephoned the number given, explained that my father was a Dane and that while I wasn't interested in traveling west, I would like to learn Danish. Would he be willing to give me lessons?

Møgens Sørenson arrived after dinner the next evening. We never got to the first lesson. Instead, we spent five hours developing a firm and lasting friendship.

Møgens ("Mrs. Noyes, my name is MO-enz, please, not Mr. Sørenson"), age 21, was from the Danish coastal town of Esbjerg. He had come to the United States "to study American business methods," fresh from the Gymnasium, the Danish secondary education unit, on a two-year scholarship from the American Scandinavian Foundation. He was now working on Fifth Avenue at Georg Jensen's, a seller of fine glass, china, and silverware, but he planned to take two summers off to see America. He was anxious to visit Florida, Texas and California where he had names of Danish emigrants to visit.

To hear Møgens, Manhattan was heaven, the ultimate in culture and fun.

"I love the crowds," he would declare, "and the noises, the dirt, and the so many diverse peoples. Also I love the richness of New York's cultural institutions, the tastes of America's beers, and the texture and taste of white bread." Cindy loved his way with English words.

For Møgens, every day in Manhattan was an adventure to be enjoyed to the fullest.

I never had classes on Sunday but almost always needed Sunday afternoons and evenings to work on papers or prepare for classes. Cindy, on the other hand, did have some Sundays off entirely and, on others, had the afternoon free since her working day sometimes began at 11:00 p.m.

So, when both of them were free, Møgens invited Cindy to "play tourist." And play tourist they did – from the Metropolitan Museum and the Fulton Fish Market to walking tours of Greenwich Village and community craft shows and fairs . Cindy's world began to take on dimensions she thought were possible only in her mind.

"Franklin," she'd challenge me, "do you know where to find nests for birds' nest soup? I do!" Or. "Do you know there's a place less than a mile from here which still makes collar stays from real whalebones?" Or, once, "Franklin, we did a survey. Did you know that New York prostitutes are taller than most women?"

Coming from Cindy, these were interesting revelations indeed.

About six months after we had met Møgens, Carl Johan Petersen joined us. He was a childhood friend of Møgens, and his family had moved to Copenhagen when he and Møgens were 12. Like Møgens, Carl had a grant from a foundation and was just beginning to study American business methods, also at Georg Jensen's.

Where Møgens was high-strung and energetic, always ready to tackle new challenges, Carl had a very low-keyed personality and doted on twin vices: whisky and women. Both Møgens and Carl had ready laughs and a keen sense of humor, though, and we admired both of them.

Carl was appalled that Cindy and I had yet to have our first dinner party. Moreover, I was told that, as a proper Dane, it was time I got some beer and schnapps in the house. So, with very careful budgeting, and considerable trepidation on Cindy's part, we set a date for a party. It would be a seafood-spaghetti affair, and the guests would be the Blacks, Møgens, Carl, and my friend Dick Simpson. With care, that many people could be seated around the card table and the desk.

At seven o'clock the morning of the party Carl, Møgens and I were at Fulton Fish Market to buy the seafood. Carl, taking charge and thinking out loud, said, "Let's see, seven people. We must purchase six dozen of clams. Four dozen shall be steamed and two dozen shall be for Cindy's spaghetti sauce. What else?"

"Hey, hold it, Carl," I begged. "We're not millionaires."

"It is not necessary to fret, Franklin," Carl assured me. "We shall eat like royalty but pay like paupers. You shall see. Let us mix some scallops and smoked oysters in the salad. Squid? No, that shall be another party."

Carl was so confident about his selections that I, an expert on nothing but peanut butter on white and baloney on rye, was pleased not to be consulted.

By 9:00 a.m. the clams and beer and schnapps were on ice in the bathtub and the spaghetti sauce was beginning to bubble on the stove. At midday, the apartment was redolent with the tantalizing odor of spaghetti sauce, and Carl and Møgens opened their first schnapps.

By 5:30, when the guests began arriving, everything was ready. Carl made it his responsibility to see that everyone had and continued to have something to drink, and he officially started the festivities with a toast to Cindy and me. Then, again and again, whenever the spirit or schnapps moved them, Carl and Møgens would shout "Skol!" – an irresistible demand that glasses be raised and schnapps tasted. By the end of the spaghetti course, everyone was happily offering skols and following the sips of schnapps with swallows of beer. Next came the salad.

Dick Simpson came back for third helpings. The Blacks were enchanted with everything.

"Your culinary talents are exceeded only by your contagious hospitality," waxed Ken to no one in particular.

"Is there dessert?" asked Frances, mentally stroking her sweet tooth.

"What would be such a feast without a magnificent dessert?" crooned Carl. "Not even the Danish gods have dined so well."

The dessert was, indeed, fit for the gods. It was a Møgens special – a hot plum soup which, in Denmark, would have been served as a first course. Dark, thick and piquant, it soon disappeared. So deliciously rich it was, Carl decided it would be the object and subject of a special toast.

Rising to carry out his pleasant chore, he forgot how tight our dining arrangements were and quickly discovered how tight he had become. He lost his balance, fought to regain it and fell against the card table, knocking it over and tipping dishes, coffee and beer and schnapps over everyone and everything.

"Oh dear, oh dear, oh dear," was all he could say. Four soup bowls, three cups and several glasses were broken, and everyone received a thorough splattering.

The mess was quickly cleared up, but poor Cindy. Though she hid it well, I knew she was distraught over the loss of the dishes and glasses. Nonetheless, the party, which lasted until midnight, was a huge success.

In bed later that night we talked about our first dinner party.

"The smoked oysters in the salad were a good idea, weren't they?" I said.

"Beats hard-boiled eggs hands down," chuckled Cindy. "They liked my spaghetti sauce, didn't they?"

"I know they did," I answered. "It was the best part of all."

I knew Cindy well enough to know that she was asking me in her own quiet way whether I thought Carl and Møgens had really been responsible for the success of the food.

"Your spaghetti was the best part of all," I repeated, then kissed her goodnight.

She turned over and, just as I was about to fall asleep, I heard her say, "Sure was a shame about those dishes, though."

"Hmmmm."

Three days later, Carl and Møgens stopped around for a post- dinner visit.

"Do you mind if we bring in something with us?" called Carl from the foyer. "Cindy! Clear off Franklin's desk!"

Knowing better than to question a determined Dane, Cindy rushed to comply, and soon in came Carl and Møgens sharing the carrying of a carton that obviously contained something very delicate.

"Be careful, Møgens, be careful," Carl kept saying.

"You're the one who should be careful," Møgens huffed as both of them angled their way across the floor to the desk.

"Don't peek until we have taken our coats off, both of you," Møgens said. He was smiling and very pleased about something.

"Now we are ready, Madame Noyes," said Carl. "You will please start removing the contents."

Again Cindy, smiling and sharing their enthusiasm, did as she was told.

After armsful of crumpled newspaper balls had been removed, the real contents of the box started to appear and Cindy gasped.

"Oh, you two, you shouldn't have!"

"Yes, we should. You deserve it."

Out came a magnificent Flora Danica cup, the best china Denmark had to offer.

"It has a scratch on the bottom," Carl explained. "That does not affect its use but Georg Jensen's cannot sell it that way, so now it is yours."

Each succeeding piece had some slight and sometimes barely detectable flaw which the Danes rushed to point out, but you never would have known by Cindy. She was near tears with delight and crowing with pleasure.

The cup was followed by four Royal Copenhagen soup dishes, also from Georg Jensen's storerooms and basements.

"That was designed for Danish royalty," Møgens explained.

"I know, I know, Møgens," answered Cindy, "and they truly are magnificent." She sounded breathless.

Møgens showed her the tiny chips in the dishes which had been the cause of their removal from the sales floor. She nodded, instantly making herself blind to the defects forever, and moved on with the unpacking.

Next came two bud vases, crystal and apparently unscathed; eight crystal water glasses, not nicked or scratched but ours now because they weren't perfectly symmetrical; and two very, very large drinking glasses, each of which would hold a quart of beer or iced tea.

"These are not from the cellar," Møgens said, putting his hands around Cindy's. "They are the real thing and our gift to you for being so good to us."

"You and Franklin shall please use them when we are not here," Carl chimed in, "but we hope you will let Møgens and me drink from them each time we visit. Please?"

Carl's intensity made Cindy laugh.

"You sillies!" she said. "You know you are always welcome here. The broken dishes at the dinner party didn't change anything. You are our friends!"

Carl in particular looked very relieved.

Cindy was overwhelmed with her new treasures and thanked the two over and over again. Standing up and moving towards the kitchen stove to put on water for tea, she could only summon up one more comment for the Danes.

"Where but in Manhattan – or Copenhagen – could this happen?"

To Cindy, Manhattan was no longer chaos. It was home.

CHAPTER 16

The Plouviers

One of the more memorable ménages was our neighbors, the Plouviers, who occupied Apartment No. 7 in 8 West.

The Plouvier family consisted of father Jean, mother Claudine, and sons Jacques and Philippe. They were native French and all spoke to each other animatedly with vigorous gestures, parries, thrusts and shouts. The word that always reminds me of the Plouviers is noise.

According to the Karbowskis, Jean Plouvier, in his early 30's, was a brilliant chemist who was employed in the highly competitive and profitable cosmetics business. In 1951, I was told, Jean had been persuaded to come to New York to work for Helena Rubinstein, and he did so with an arrangement that made his wife his principal assistant.

Claudine Plouvier was a capable chemist in her own right. A strikingly attractive brunette with dark, sparkling eyes, at 30 she looked no more than 20, despite having given Jean two lively sons: Jacques, now age 7, and Philippe, age 4.

Jean had been in New York only three months when he was enticed to leave Helena Rubinstein for another cosmetics firm. The arrangement this time did not include Claudine, who chose not to stay at Helena Rubinstein without her husband. Instead, she chose to devote all her time to her boys and her home.

The door to the Plouvier apartment was open, if only a crack, most of the time.

While Jacques was at school, Philippe would flit in and out. The hallway had evolved into his playroom, and by the time the older brother returned home each day, many of Philippe's toys and cloth books would be scattered about the halls.

The dangers inherent in toys scattered in dimly lit halls were well known to me. I was the first to step on one of Philippe's wooden blocks, and my twisted ankle ached for days. In my pained condition, I pleaded with Claudine to keep her younger son's toys inside their apartment.

Shortly after I twisted my ankle, one of the tenants who lived one floor down from the Plouviers, Elise Saxon, called on me.

"What's going on around here?" she demanded. "Are we deliberately booby-trapping the hallways?"

I asked her what she meant.

"A friend of my uncle's stepped on a wooden block last night," she said by way of explanation, "and he nearly fell backwards down the stairs. Franklin, whatever's going on has to stop before someone gets seriously hurt."

I vehemently agreed – but I wasn't certain I could get Claudine to confine Philippe to the apartment.

The next time I saw her, I pointed out to Claudine that I had hurt my ankle and I told her that other tenants or friends had been hurt or could have been. Her only reaction was to shrug her shoulders, roll her eyes and shoosh Philippe behind her as she eased back to close the door and thus the conversation.

Tenants' complaints about Philippe's playing habits became so severe and frequent that I seemed to be in constant negotiation with Claudine or Jean or both.

Tenant bitterness also erupted into a new form of dark humor which Jon Hauser called "Philippephobia." Suggested cures for Philippephobia, especially those embellished by Jon, made medieval tortures sound like child's play.

Ironically, it was not Philippe's toys but his toilet habits which caused a near-tragedy among the residents of 8 West.

One day about noon, Philippe started down the stairs to retrieve a block which had fallen to the second floor hallway. On the way down, nature overwhelmed his young bowels and feces cascaded in sausage-like links from his short pants. By the time he reached his destination, his fecal matter reposed on nearly a dozen steps. Only a few moments later, Helen Jason, one of two tenants in the third floor front unit, left her apartment. Always brisk and precise, she started rapidly down the stairs. She was half-way down the flight when her right foot connected with a link. She skidded, lost her balance and was launched into a bumpy ride down to the landing on her backside. Cindy and Claudine, both hearing the clatter, rushed to help – and both also slipped on Philippe's deposits and shared a similarly uncomfortable ride down to the landing.

When their hysteria subsided enough for them to concentrate on disentangling – carefully, for the evidence was now smeared all around – the three queried each other about breaks or bruises.

"You okay, Helen?" Cindy asked. "It's bad enough to fall without having me land on top of you."

"I think so," Helen said, slightly dazed. "My right hip hurts but I'm sure it's just a bruise." Suddenly she wrinkled her nose. "But shit!" she exploded. "I reek of shit! I have it on my shoes, my legs, my uniform, my arms that little bas…"

Suddenly remembering that Philippe's mother was there with them, Helen amended what she had been going to say. She said, "… that little boy sure knew how to, er, spread it around."

Cindy, thoroughly mortified by what had happened, didn't know where to put herself. "You think you reek!" she said. "Look at me! I think I even have some on my face!"

Suddenly feeling helpless, she leaned back on one elbow and made no effort to move. "Helen," she said, "when was the last time you were so … fecally saturated?"

Helen snorted a chuckle. "God, but you're delicate," she declared. "The last time I had shit allover me was in nurse's training. I was cleaning some old man's backside and he exploded all over me."

"Same here," Cindy mused. "In the Emergency Room. Poor devil. He was a young man. So badly banged up he didn't know where he was. We were cleaning him up when the gusher hit. It was awful. I was sprayed from head to toe."

Suddenly Helen saw the humor in their "accident" and began to laugh wildly. Cindy soon joined in. They determined they were okay and, as they helped each other up, continued their shrieks of laughter as they considered what must be every nurse's occupational hazard.

Claudine, who had been quiet through the laughter, was totally chagrined. She could think of nothing more to do than shoo her two laughing companions back to their apartments. Then she undertook the odious task of cleaning up her son's mess. It took two long hours.

The next day, as an apology, Claudine left a package at our doorstep and an identical one at No. 5 for Helen. They were beautifully wrapped boxes of French cosmetic items – lipstick, cologne and perfume.

She didn't stop there.

Shortly after the dignity-damaging incident, Philippe was placed in a nursery school and Claudine returned to work.

In this incident, as in several others, Jon Hauser had the last word.

"I told you that kid would have to mend his ways or the shit would fly," he teased. "But I never expected flying shit to lead to peace and quiet. Do you have an explanation for that?"

No explanation, I told him. No matter, though. What made me happy was that our tenants, the Plouviers, were, for the time being, causing no more complaints.

CHAPTER 17

Of Cats and Rats
and Leaking Toilets

I'll never forget the first time my limited skills as a plumber were put to the test.

It was a Saturday morning, and as I was vacuuming my way down the halls and stairs of 6 West, Sally Dixon stuck her head out of No. 5 and asked if I would look at her toilet. I switched off the vacuum cleaner and went into her apartment. Almost immediately I noticed a trail of wet towels.

Jim and Sally Dixon had been awake only four or five minutes. They discovered that a very small leak near where the water pipe entered the toilet tank had become much larger during the night. The dripping could no longer be controlled by a towel on the bathroom floor.

I turned off the valve which fed the toilet and, in my most authoritative voice, suggested they fill the bathtub so they could use buckets to flush until I could fix the leak. Jim asked me to hurry since he was expecting students at noon and dinner guests at six.

As I hurried down to the basement to gather some tools and washers, I thought about the first time I met the Dixons.

One night early in my superintendency, I was bending over to pick up the Dixon's trash a few seconds after Sally had placed it outside their door. She was going back into the apartment when she saw me.

"Oh, hello. Are you the new Super? I'm Sally Dixon."

"Hi. Yes, I am. How're you?"

"Fine ... and your name is ... ?"

Why did introductions always fluster me?

"Oh I, er, forgot," I spluttered. "I mean, I didn't forget my name. I forgot to tell you what it is."

"Yes?"

"Yes?"

"Your name?"

Blushing furiously, I was sure, and furious at myself for having it happen, I tried again.

"I'm Franklin Noyes, when I can remember to tell people my name."

Sally chuckled. "Well, come in for a drink, Franklin Noyes," she urged, "now that I know who you are. I'd like you to meet my husband Jim. And Archie. And this is Smudge."

Smudge was a magnificent white Persian cat that Sally was wearing around her neck like a fur collar. Being carried in such a manner seemed not to bother the cat in the least.

I was introduced to Jim and learned he was a musician who had graduated from Julliard School of Music three years earlier. Now he was the voice coach for some of Broadway's finest young singers.

And Archie was not a person, as I had imagined, but a second cat — a blue-point Siamese which also draped itself around Sally's neck or occupied her lap when Smudge was being the fur piece.

Well, despite such an awkward start, the Dixons and I got along very well. I did accept Sally's offer of a drink, and Jim was friendly. We small-talked for almost an hour and I left feeling good. But after that, whenever I bent at the Dixon's door to pick up their trash, I experienced a fleeting sensation of acute embarrassment.

And now, seeking the tools to repair their toilet pipe, I was not anxious to embarrass myself again because of my lack of plumbing know-how. I took the cake tin full of washers, two wrenches, several screwdrivers and a pair of pliers and started back upstairs.

Back in the Dixon's apartment, I was dismayed to discover that the building contractors had not left enough room in the bathroom for an inept, inexperienced, ill-equipped person like me to make repairs, if ever they were needed.

The Dixon's toilet, in common with all the toilets in both buildings, was located immediately inside the bathroom door. The left edge of the toilet tank was separated from the wall by barely half an inch. The water pipe entered the tank from the left and allowed only about eight inches of working space between the base of the commode and the wall. Worse, there was practically no working space between the pipe and the wall.

No matter. What I lacked in skill and space I would make up for in zeal. After an hour and a half, during which I skinned my knuckles and scarred the wall in four places, I had loosened the connection and removed the faulty washer. Now all I had to do was find a replacement washer and put everything back together.

I emptied the contents of the cake tin onto the bathroom floor. While I was searching for a washer, Smudge strolled in to join me. With an effortless leap, he landed on the toilet seat. And while I watched in wonder, he straddled and relieved himself just like a GI using an open pit. With another leap he was gone.

The cat's performance so astonished me that I could not have found the proper washer had the tin been full of them.

I shuffled out of the apartment muttering, "I'll be back," and headed back to the basement in search of washers. Actually, I was stalling for time to regain my composure.

When I pulled the chain to switch on the light above the workbench, I was terrified to find myself eye to eye with the largest rat New York had ever bred. It was an enormous brown thing that must have been a foot long and weighed five pounds or more. The creature had apparently entered the basement on a waste pipe and traveled the tops of the basement walls into the workroom.

Where were Archie and Smudge when I needed them? And what do you say when your nose in only six inches away (it felt like only six inches) from a hideously large rat? I didn't stop to find out. I just ran like hell, slamming shut behind me as many doors as I could find.

Since Cindy was sleeping, I decided to recover from the cat and rat shocks by taking a very slow walk to the hardware store.

When I returned to the Dixon's about an hour later, Jim was running two voice students through basic drills. I quietly entered the bathroom, wriggled alongside the commode and inserted the new washer. Because the space between the pipe and the wall was so limited, I couldn't use the wrenches. Instead, I struggled with the ancient pliers, trying to tighten the fitting to the tank. It didn't work. Nothing would tighten. I couldn't get a good grip and the pliers kept flying off the mounting. Try as I might, the toilet resisted me.

A long time later, Sally handed me a bottle of beer, and I very gratefully accepted it.

At two o'clock Archie joined me at the toilet. He walked disdainfully over my legs, leaped to the toilet seat and repeated Smudge's performance. Lightheaded from beer and the constricted working quarters, I accepted Archie's performance as perfectly natural. *Weren't all cats toilet trained?* I asked myself. As I sloshed a half-bucket of water into the toilet to flush away the cat's deposit, I was sure they were.

At 2:30, with every knuckle skinned or bruised, I was becoming desperate. It was obvious I would never get the fitting on properly with the existing tools. My options were very narrow. Either I had to find a slim tool that would work in a small space or admit defeat and ask Mr. K to call a plumber.

I sighed, hitched up my pants and told the Dixons there was something else I needed. This time I went down to the basement workshop with a flashlight in hand. I saw no rat, but when I pulled on the overhead light I saw what appeared to be the head of a very large snake withdrawing into the darkened area where the floor beams met the foundation walls. Snake? How could a snake survive in the bowels of New York City? No, I decided, it was no snake. It was just me hallucinating from an exasperating day in which I would soon have to humiliate myself before Mr. K because of my mechanical ineptness.

There were no more or better tools, of course, so I sought out Mr. K, explained the situation and asked him to call a plumber. He said no! He refused to do anything until he tried to right what I had done wrong. Back we went to the Dixons'.

Once he got his big, square body crammed into the tiny working space, Mr. K's efforts to secure the fitting were not without their amusing moments. When he jammed a knuckle, he deliberately shook all four of his limbs to hasten the passage of shock through his body. Despite my misery, I had to force myself not to laugh. It was just that it reminded me very much of the puppets in a Punch and Judy show.

When Mr. K got a flake of rust in his eye, he uttered something apparently profane in Polish and flooded both his eye and the bathroom floor in his efforts to remove the foreign object.

I stifled another laugh.

Vision restored, Mr. K jammed his frame back between the wall and commode, applied the pliers to the fitting and came to a dead halt. Archie had ascended the commode to repeat his morning performance. Mr. K viewed these feline maneuvers with a look suggesting Black Magic, squirmed free, handed me the pliers and said, "I call plumber."

Naturally, the plumber didn't arrive until the Dixons were in the middle of their dinner party. Mercifully, the plumber had the right tool – and the expertise – for the job. In only a matter of minutes he had sealed up the leaking tank.

I collected all my tools, cleaned up the mess I had left earlier, petted Smudge as he entered the bathroom, and quietly ducked out of the Dixon's apartment.

I reflected on my day and sighed again. Cats, rats, knuckles, pliers and humiliation. Snakes, washers, wrenches and feline toilet habits. This definitely had been a day I dearly wanted to forget.

CHAPTER 18

The Kleptolagniac

I had stopped in the University bookstore for some typing paper and remained to browse. I drifted over to the small section devoted to fiction and was surprised to be confronted by a display touting the latest Inspector Brisbane novel. The title was intriguing: *The Mixoscopic Murderer.*

The book's front cover featured an artist's rendering of supersleuth Brisbane collaring what appeared to be a Peeping Tom. The back cover was a recent picture of the Major walking his three dogs.

I bought a copy of the book and started reading it on the way home and quickly discovered that mixoscopia is a condition in which one experiences sexual pleasure by secretly watching sexual acts. In short, voyeurism. Recalling several questionable incidents in which the Major had been at least partially involved, I suddenly realized how he had mastered his subject.

I was so fascinated with the book that I decided to ask the Major to autograph my copy of it that very afternoon.

Felicia responded to my buzz.

"Good afternoon, Franklin," she chirped. "So good to see you! What can I do for you?"

I showed her the copy of her husband's book. "I just bought this," I answered. "Do you suppose the Major would autograph it for me?"

"He's not in just at the moment," she said, "but I expect him any time. Do let me get you some tea."

Over her strong brew I asked her how her husband researched his books.

"He says he is doing research all the time," Felicia answered, pouring a little more cream into her teacup. "I believe him. Look."

She stood up, went over to a dresser and returned with her hands full. "These are the tools of the voyeur," she said, handing me opera glasses, small mirrors and assorted lenses. "Roderick has been doing his research right here. I can never be sure until his latest book is published. Have you read many of them?"

"Yes, most of them."

She hesitated slightly. "Have you noticed anything unusual about them?"

"Unusual?" I searched her face for a clue. "They're always good mysteries," I volunteered, "but they do deal with sex more than Agatha Christie or some of the other popular mystery writers."

"Not just sex," Felicia went on. "Out-of-the-ordinary sex. Do you remember *Inspector Brisbane Smells a Murderer*? That book dealt with osphresiolognia, or sexual pleasure aroused by body odors. And do you remember *Burn, Inspector, Burn*? That one was about pyrolagnia — sexual pleasures aroused by fires. What Roderick does is mix sex and murder quite unlike anyone else ever has."

"Now that you mention it, you're right," I agreed. "In most mysteries, sex is usually a passing thing. In the Major's books sex is always the prime motive behind the murders. And the sex is usually bizarre."

"Don't be misled by that," Felicia warned. "The Major and I have always had a quite normal sex life."

I was totally unprepared for that remark. I think I muttered "Oh, how nice," or something equally innocuous to cover the awkwardness I always experienced when talking to an older person about sex. To change the subject I got up and walked over to the St. John's exquisite collection of jade carvings.

Felicia followed me. "Why are you shy about talking about sex?" I didn't answer. "It's a fundamental of life, possibly the essence of immortality," she explained. She took my right hand and started stroking it. "Besides, it's fun. Don't you agree?"

The sound of the Major arriving masked the knocking of my knees.

"Hello, my dear," Felicia said to her husband, stepping rapidly away from me. "Franklin just stopped by to get your autograph on your latest masterpiece. Naturally, while we were waiting, we talked about sex."

The Major never even so much as raised an eyebrow. "Of course," he answered, "of course." He held out his hand for my book. "I'll be pleased to inscribe it." Once he did I thanked him and quickly made my goodbyes.

When I got back to our apartment my head was spinning. This was a Felicia most unlike the one I knew at theosophy meetings and symbology sessions. I had always considered her pedantic and somewhat other-worldly, a brilliant professional totally absorbed in thought and work. Very stuffy. Very British. But today's Felicia was human and down to earth. Had she been making a pass at me? What did the Major think of her comment that we were talking about sex? And where in this world did the Major do his research on his earlier books?

I had calmed down by the time Cindy came in from work. I said nothing about my encounter with the St. Johns since I didn't understand it well enough myself to explain it.

Early the next morning Felicia telephoned.

"Please stop by!" she almost shouted. "I think we have been robbed! "

She hung up before I could ask any questions, and my adrenaline was pumping hard by the time I knocked on the St. John's door. It must have showed.

"Goodness, you look like a wild man," Felicia said. "Calm down."

"Yes, I will, I will," I answered hurriedly, "but tell me, what has been stolen?"

Many of the jade things you were admiring yesterday. Look, most of them are gone. I just started preparing a list of the missing items. Curious, though. They were all sexual symbols."

Uh-oh, I though, she's trying to pick up where she left off yesterday.

"Where's the Major," I asked her. "Does he know these items are missing? Have you called the police?"

"Whoa, Franklin! One question at a time! The Major is walking the dogs. He knows the items are missing. He does not wish to call the police. But I thought you should know. You might want to change the locks or something."

"First I had better tell Mr. K," I said. "This will be very disturbing to him. He may want to change all the locks in the building."

"No, no, you must not do that! Roderick said only you are to know. You are not to tell Mr. K."

Not tell the police? Not tell Mr. K? It began to look very much like the Major was working on another book. I calmed down quickly.

Felicia started to talk again.

"The disturbing thing is that my favorite phallus is missing," she said, sadness in her eyes. "The quite explicit jade one. I bought it in Delhi many years ago as a present for the Major. It never failed to excite me. For years we had it in our bedroom."

Ignoring her personal comments, I asked her to finish her list and put it in my mailbox. "I'll see about the locks," I promised, "but now I must get to school. Excuse me."

I was sure the Major was researching a new book. But I wasn't the least bit sure what Mrs. St. John was about. And I didn't intend to stay around to find out.

In the next month I was summoned to the St. John apartment three more times. The first two were to report additional thefts, again from Mrs. St. John's mini-museum; the third was to report that everything had been mysteriously returned. With one exception. Her favorite phallus was still missing.

On the last occasion I noted that the Major was present but totally preoccupied with his typewriter. Obviously a new Inspector Brisbane mystery was in gestation.

I was on my way to school a few days later when I encountered the Major and his three yipping schnauzers. We swapped greetings and small-talked for a few moments, then I asked him if he would mind if I asked him a question or two.

"Shoot!" came his immediate reply.

"Are you working on your next Brisbane mystery?"

"Yes. And it's going very well. Very well indeed."

"Great. Tell me, is the murderer this time a man who gets sexual pleasure out of stealing?"

"Yes, indeed he is," the Major nodded, surprised. "The murderer is a kleptolagniac. I see you saw through my little thefts."

I shrugged. "It was just a guess. Can I ask you one more question? Dare I ask about the still-missing phallus? Why didn't you return the jade one? Your wife is very fond of it."

"Yes, she is, isn't she?" he said, almost in a whisper. "It was a fine addition to our marriage. I shall have to ask the Inspector to find it." With that, he jogged off behind schnauzers Vicky, Eddy and Georgy.

Ask the Inspector to find it? Is that phallus to be featured in a future Brisbane mystery, I asked myself. Or have the Major and the Inspector become interchangeable personalities? I didn't know the answers to the questions. But I was fairly sure I had not seen the last of the missing phallus.

CHAPTER 19

Sammy the Surprise

It was Sunday morning. Cindy had left for work at 6:30 and I had arisen an hour and a half later to confront the day. As usual, my first Sunday act, even before making coffee, had been to walk to Amsterdam Avenue for the Sunday paper. For me, Sundays didn't officially begin until *The Times*, the coffee pot and I were united in the living room.

Coming back into 8 West, I noticed an envelope folded into the slot of our mailbox. I pulled it out, stuffed it into my shirt pocket and bounded up the stairs to our apartment.

When the coffee was ready, my languid brain began to stir as I stirred my first cup. Suddenly I remembered the envelope. I ripped it open and found inside a note penciled on a page of green paper. Curious, I read:

Mr. Noyes,

My husband and I moved out last night. We are going to another city far from Manhattan.

I'm sorry we have been so secretive all these months, but we didn't think Mr. Karbowski would have understood our love for reptiles and fish.

We made the hole in the living room floor to hold our aquarium for our tropical fish collection. The stains on the floor around the edge of the living room and bedroom are from moisture from tanks which held our snakes and plants. We promise to send Mr. Karbowski a check large enough to pay for the repairs.

The reason for this note, however, is to tell you about our beloved Sammy. He disappeared several nights ago. When you find him, please give him to the zoo.

Sincerely,

Margot Stengler

P.S. Sammy is a boa constrictor. He is nine feet long but very docile. Maybe he is wrapped around a heating duct.

Dear God! A boa constrictor loose in the next-door building? It suddenly flashed to me that I thought I had recently seen a snake in my building's basement as I was getting things to repair the Dixons' toilet.

What was I to do now? Call the police? Tell Mr. K? Alert the tenants and maybe cause a building-wide panic?

I forced myself to try and be calm. Docile. How docile can anything nine feet long be? And what do snakes eat? Would this Sammy be likely to fancy Smudge and Archie, the Dixon's cats, or Uncle Louie, the Ripons' dog, for breakfast?

My knowledge of boas – indeed, of all snakes – was limited to what I had seen as a kid at Saturday afternoon movies. They squeezed people to death then feasted on whole chickens and pigs.

I had even less knowledge of the Stenglers. In fact, until I read the note, I never knew that Mrs. Stengler's first name was Margot. Of the 20 apartments I tended, the one she and her husband had just vacated, no. 7 on the fourth floor of 6 West, was the only one I had never been inside. And now they were gone … leaving their snake behind.

Where was it likely to be? Would it follow the heating ducts throughout 6 West? Could it have gotten into 8 West? Might it actually be lurking behind the hot air vent in the Karbowskis' apartment even now?

My panic-prompted adrenals rapidly pushed me to the brink of terror, but by re-reading Mrs. Stengler's letter I managed to lurch back. Suddenly a hopeful thought occurred to me. Why should that damned boa attack me or any of the other tenants if it apparently had never touched the Stenglers? That sounded reasonable enough.

Pulling myself together but still breathing heavily, I took the master key and went outside and next door, upstairs to No.7. I could actually see my heart moving my shirt with its pounding as I slowly eased open the door. After I carefully looked behind it, I stepped inside. No Sammy. I checked the kitchen, then the bath, my skin crawling. Still no Sammy.

Reaching the living room, I was dismayed to see a large hole cut into the floor, the one Mrs. Stengler had written about. What had she said about it? An aquarium? Mr. K would pop a vein when he saw it.

Skirting the hole – I still wasn't convinced that a nine-foot snake couldn't spring out from under the lip of the hole and kill me instantly – I tiptoed to the bedroom. And there, curled into a comfortable coil and warming himself in the Sunday morning sunshine, I found Sammy on the windowsill.

As I stared, too frightened to move, I found myself both traumatized and fascinated. Sammy was a beautiful creature, ruddy brown in color with a brick-red tail. A row of large tan and cream saddle-shaped patterns lined his back.

He appeared to be sleeping and I certainly wasn't about to disturb his rest. Afraid he'd detect my presence and wake up, I backed out, carefully closed and locked the apartment door and fled back to my apartment.

Safely home, I tried to think what to do next. I decided to try my father's prescription for almost everything -— a good stiff shot of whiskey in a cup of coffee. As the whiskey took hold, my panic subsided and I re-read Mrs. Stengler's startling message a third time. Suddenly something she had written clicked into place. The zoo! Hell, yes, who would know more about snakes than a zoo? Call the zoo!

I rapidly learned that spring Sundays are busy times for zoological gardens. For nearly half an hour I desperately tried to reach the Manhattan and Bronx zoos. Never had telephone busy signals created such agitation. Finally I managed to get an operator at the New York Zoological Gardens to answer.

"I'd like to talk to someone who knows about snakes," I begged, positive the woman would be able to detect the alarm in my voice.

"That line is busy, sir."

"It's an emergency! I've got a wild Boa Constrictor here!"

"That line is still..." Her patronizing voice infuriated me.

"Dammit, woman, I know it's still busy. Cut it! Matter of life and death!"

She clicked off the line without answering. Soon I was talking to someone else, the first of several false starts, but finally I was connected to the Chief Veterinarian. He seemed amused at my predicament.

"There's no one here today capable of handling large snakes," he said, "but don't worry. Boas are quite docile. Most of them like people."

"What if this is an exception?" I asked, not reassured.

"You already told me the creature was asleep, didn't you?" he said. "He's content to be in the sunshine. It's not unusual for them to wrap themselves around their keepers for warmth. So don't panic. I'll send someone over to pick him up tomorrow."

The tone of his voice hinted that I shouldn't press him further.

"Look, sir," I said, "at this point I'm controlling my panic with whiskey. So can I ask you one more question? What do boas eat?"

"Nothing fancy. Mostly rodents – mice, rats, whatever is common to their environment. They also like chickens."

"What about dogs and cats? Will they eat those?"

"I guess so," he chuckled. "But only if they were very hungry."

He promised again that someone from the zoo would come tomorrow to collect Sammy. "Until then," he suggested, "keep the apartment as warm as possible. Boas are used to very warm surroundings."

I hung up, not very happy. After a third cup of coffee generously laced with whiskey, I wondered what to do next. Should I tell Mr. K? I decided he had to know. If anything happened, if Sammy decided to leave No. 7 and visit another apartment or feast on a pet, it was Mr. K's insurance policies or lawyers which would have to rectify the damages, actual or emotional.

I combed my hair and splashed cold water on my face. Wouldn't do to let the Karbowskis see me looking like a mad man.

They were pleased to see me, but they soon discovered I had been drinking.

"Franklin," Mrs. K admonished gently, "why have you been drinking on the Sabbath? And at such an early hour? What is wrong?"

"There's a gigantic snake loose somewhere in 6 West," I said, too wrung out to select less blunt words. "And the zoo can't come to get him till tomorrow."

As I hurriedly related the events of the morning and showed them Mrs. Stengler's letter, they both turned sickly pale. Highly agitated, Mrs. K explained why.

"More than anything we are deathly afraid of snakes of any kind, both my husband and I. Even little ones." She started to cry.

I realized that neither of them could offer me any help. They were too petrified to do anything at this point, or even offer a suggestion. So I withdrew. Never had I felt so alone.

When Cindy came in from work that afternoon, I was in an alcoholic fog. I told her why.

"Well," she declared in her most authoritative nurse's voice, "there's nothing more we can do about it today, is there? So I suggest we go for a walk. Maybe it'll get your mind off Sammy."

Relieved to have someone help me decide that it was all right not to worry, I agreed. Soon we were strolling in Central Park and I started to unwind.

Next morning at ten my bell rang, and I opened the front door to admit the zoo's herpetologist and his assistant carrying a black case five feet long and about a foot deep.

"Is that to carry the snake back in?" I asked, hoping my question was a guarantee that the snake would indeed be removed.

"You think it's my lunch inside?" the assistant sneered.

"Now, now, Johnson," his superior said, "let's not be rude. Our work is cut out for us and this gentleman obviously needs our help. And where is the snake you called about?" he asked, turning to me then looking up the stairwell.

"Oh, it's not in this building," I said. "It's somewhere next door. I'll show you."

He nodded and I led the way.

When we reached the Stenglers' apartment, the herpetologist, just like I had done, opened the door slowly and looked behind it.

"He's in the bedroom," I volunteered.

But Sammy was not in the bedroom. Nor was he in the bathroom or the living room or the kitchen. Yesterday's panic slammed back into the pit of my stomach. The snake must have gone off to find warmer quarters along the heating ducts. But how could we reach them?

"Let's start in the basement," I told them. "Then, if necessary, we'll remove the heating vents in every apartment until we find him."

"Look, mister, the assistant said, sighing at the prospect of a long,

long hunt, "all we expected was a simple pick-up. We got more work we gotta do back at the zoo."

The herpetologist became angry at his helper's impatience and rudeness. "Watch your tongue," he snapped. "While we have no intention of spending our entire day here, this man still needs our help. And so, no doubt, does the snake."

Agreeing, I nodded, grateful for his words. "The basement's down this way."

Our search was thankfully short.

Just as we were about to enter the basement, the door in front of us burst open and Mr. K, deathly pale and his eyes bulging in distress, exploded past. Not for a moment did I doubt he had seen Sammy.

"Please get it away from here," he groaned. "Please remove it!"

The zoo people collected Sammy from a duct just above the furnace where he had wrapped himself for the heat.

"Thank you *both* for your help," I called after them as they maneuvered their long case into their car. "I'm really grateful."

The assistant looked back. "Yeah, sure," he said, very grudgingly. "Sure."

"Did you touch it?" Cindy asked later, out of the blue.

"Touch what?"

"The snake. Sammy. Did you touch it?"

"Are you kidding?" I laughed. "Course not. The only pets I touch have four legs."

"Guess that lets me out, huh?" she challenged, playing. "I only have two."

I pulled her toward me and held her close the way I knew she wanted me to do. "But yours are twice as long."

"You're nuts," she chuckled into my shoulder.

"And I'm a squirrel. That's why I love you so much."

"Want to prove it?"

I didn't need a second invitation and, for a while at least, Sammy was temporarily forgotten.

Later, though, the Sammy incident became one I would never forget. Nor, I am certain, would future tenants of 6 and 8 West. Thanks to one very docile boa constrictor and one very large hole in a living room floor, the number of clauses in Mr. K's litany of leasing horrors took a giant leap upward. Again.

CHAPTER 20

Anastasia

I remember meeting Anastasia de Maupeou.

She telephoned our apartment to ask if the Super could repair the switch to her ceiling light in her living room. She told Cindy she relied on this light for much of the illumination in her apartment, the rear unit of the first floor of 6 West.

The next day I went to answer her call.

I knocked and she opened the door. "I've come to switch your broken light repair," I babbled.

She was that stunning. But she didn't know who I was or what I meant and I tried again, making it worse.

"I mean, I've come to light your broken repair switch."

Awesome Anastasia stood in front of me trying to decipher my senseless words. A hauntingly beautiful woman in her forties, she had violet eyes, unbelievably long eyelashes and jet black hair pulled straight back and braided. The combination of my awe of her presence and her confusion practically paralyzed me with intimidation.

Then the reason for my visit came to her and her expression fell into one of bemusement. "Ah, the rescue force," she said, "come to chase away my darkness." And she beckoned me in.

Once inside, I took a deep breath, picked a point on the wall beyond her right shoulder on which to concentrate my eyes and tried again. Sure enough, the third try was my lucky one.

"Miss de Maupeou," I started slowly, "I am Franklin Noyes, the superintendent, and I'm here to repair your broken light switch."

What a lady! She made no mention of my first two futile efforts but instead told me how pleased she was I had responded so promptly to her call and asked if I'd like to have a cup of tea while I worked.

Gratefully I accepted and off she went, soon to return with a tray set with dainty china and a plate of tiny golden cookies.

"I still call them 'biscuits'," she said then drew me into such an interesting, comfortable conversation that I forgot my earlier abashment forever. What we talked about I no longer remember, but I do know that on that afternoon I made a new friend.

Back home, I described Anastasia to Cindy as intense. Yet it wasn't much later that I was to describe her as tragic.

Mrs. K. told me that Anastasia's parents had been very close friends of the Karbowskis and that Mr. K treated Anastasia as family, as a niece. She was the only child of Polish aristocrats and had been educated in Catholic schools in Poland. In 1922, when she was 16, she had been sent to the Sorbonne to pursue her interest in languages. She could already speak and write Polish, French, Czech, Russian, German, Spanish and English fluently, and by the end of her first year at the Sorbonne had translated the works of several Polish poets into French.

By the end of her second year at the Sorbonne she had met and married Pascal de Maupeou, a brilliant linguist and student of Latin American government who was about to leave for his first diplomatic assignment in Uruguay.

The de Maupeous thrived on the diplomatic environment. Pascal proved to be a very perceptive student of life in whatever Latin American country he was assigned to and an able spokesman and negotiator for French interests.

Anastasia, an imaginative hostess and gifted conversationalist who loved to give parties, was the perfect mate for the ambitious young diplomat.

Then, in 1936, tragedy entered Anastasia's life twice within a month.

Her parents were killed in a train crash near Paris and, less than a month later, Anastasia, recently returned to Mexico City from Warsaw, fractured a lumbar vertebra when she was thrown from a horse. She was hospitalized for many months, her body almost covered in plaster and bandages. When she finally did return home, she was in constant pain which was exacerbated day after day by the exercises she forced herself to do to return tone and responsiveness to her flaccid muscles.

By the time she was able to function as a wife and diplomatic hostess once again, her marriage had collapsed.

Pascal had met and fallen in love with a young Mexican beauty whose parents were very rich. The girl's parents so approved of the match that they drafted an agreement which proposed Anastasia as the sole beneficiary during her lifetime of the income from a sizeable trust fund, provided she agreed to terminate her marriage to Pascal in a manner acceptable to the Church so that their daughter could marry him.

Apparently because of her constant pain and feeling that her life would never be the same again, Anastasia signed the marriage termination agreement and in August, 1937, returned to Paris to build a career as an interpreter. By mid-1938 she emigrated to New York City, so sure was she that Europe would soon be in flames.

It was many months before she was able to find a job. She became the assistant manager of a small bookshop which specialized in foreign books, however, and was soon not only happily employed but also in a position to meet a wide range of writers and scholars, many of whom later used her considerable talents as an interpreter.

When the Karbowskis sought her out in 1947, she was working as an interpreter for Columbia University Press. When 6 and 8 West were renovated, at the insistence of Mr. K she was one of the first tenants to move into 6 West.

Anastasia was never completely free of pain, even when she took pain-killing drugs. At times the pain was so intense, Mrs. K told me,

Anastasia could be heard sobbing or emitting suppressed screams or moans.

But the day I went to her apartment, during a visit much later to fix a noisy toilet, she was calm and seemed to want to talk. She informed me that she would soon be entering Columbia-Presbyterian Hospital for a spinal fusion.

"May I call you Franklin?" she inquired. Without waiting for my answer, she continued. "Well, Franklin, some years ago I fell from a horse and injured my back. It was never fully healed. The doctors think I will get relief if they fuse some of my backbones. It means I will be in a full body cast for about nine months and I will have to stay in bed."

Sympathetic but not knowing what to say, I pursed my lips and slowly shook my head.

Anastasia seemed determined to finish speaking words which by now I knew she had rehearsed to herself before I arrived. "It also means I will need help," she continued. "Nursing help. Housecleaning help. I know your wife is a nurse. Do you think she would consider working for me an hour or so a day?"

Knowing it hadn't been easy for her to ask, I made my reply as short and direct as I could. "I'm sure she would, Miss de Maupeou."

And Cindy accepted. The modest pay offered would be a welcome addition to our income.

It was a raw November day when the ambulance returned Anastasia to 6 West from the hospital. I was picking up our mail when she arrived.

Wanting to help, I held the doors open then used my passkey to open Anastasia's apartment door. As the attendants wheeled her in, I was surprised to notice that she was accompanied by an elderly man who could have been the double of the always dapper, very distinguished actor Adolph Menjou. Even the mustache approached the perfection of Menjou's.

As groggy as she was, once she was settled in her bed and the attendants had left, Anastasia introduced me to her companion.

"This is Professor Mischa Toplitsky," she said, smiling fondly. "He is my mentor and I am his interpreter. We are both displaced eastern Europeans. I try to forget that fact, but he writes about it. He writes poetry, too. Bad poetry. He is an incurable romantic and sentimentalist."

Prof. Toplitsky beamed delightedly at her then reached and shook my hand. His grasp was firm and enthusiastic.

"I am pleased to meet you," he told me. "And pay no attention to this child. She is a fine student of languages and a very sensitive interpreter. But she knows nothing, nothing whatsoever, about poetry."

Anastasia smiled a weak and tired smile of the drugged.

"Hah!" she snorted gently, "and you, dear friend, know nothing about love. Even though that is all your poetry is about."

Prof. Toplitsky beamed at her again.

After promising to have Cindy look in on her later in the day, I took my leave.

From my occasional visits, and from Cindy's daily reports, there was no doubt that the Professor was Anastasia's inseparable companion. He cooked for her, cleaned up after her, bathed and massaged the exposed parts of her body and read to her constantly in languages that were a mystery to me.

Prof. Toplitsky did such a thorough job that Cindy's daily visits became shorter and shorter. After two months they stopped entirely. It appeared that Anastasia's recuperation was taking an uneventful course.

I was vacuuming the hall one Saturday morning about four months after Anastasia's return when the Professor tapped me on the shoulder. His haggard appearance gave me a start. He was unshaven and his moustache was positively shaggy. This, combined with his gray hair and sallow complexion, gave him the look of a corpse, a very old corpse.

"Franklin, can we talk?" he whispered anxiously. "Please, I must talk to someone."

In an instant I had unplugged the vacuum cleaner and coiled the cord safely away. "Yes, of course we can," I told him, thoroughly alarmed at his tone and appearance. "Let's go to my apartment for a cup of coffee. You look like you could use it."

He was almost done with his coffee when he looked up, took a deep, trembling breath and began to speak. His eyes were dull and unfocused.

"I'm worried about Anastasia," he droned. "Deeply worried. She has been in pain ever since the operation, and the doctor has been increasing her daily dose of narcotics. Every time he increases the dosage, her personality changes. One day she was a little girl again and thought I was her father. Another day she thought I was her husband. She screamed at me and threw a glass at me. Franklin, this morning she swore most vilely at me in six languages. I do not know what to do any more. I do not know."

I didn't know what to do either. But I thought talking might help.

"How long have you known Anastasia?" I prodded. "When did you first meet her?"

As distraught as he was, my question stirred a flicker of interest.

"I will answer your question," he said, "but first tell me, how old do you think I am?"

"I don't know. I would guess in your sixties, maybe 65."

"You're close. I'm 71. I met Anastasia when I was 41. And she was a beautiful, brilliant child of 16. I was teaching languages at the Sorbonne. When she appeared as a student I soon learned that she was gifted as a linguist. In her first year there she translated two novels from Polish to French and English. However, she came to me when she was asked to translate some poetry. She wasn't sure of the nuances, she told me, the subtleties that are so important to poetry. That's why she calls me her mentor."

"Are you married? Have you ever been?"

"No, Franklin, I have never married. I was considering marriage in 1915 when I got caught up in the war. And I nearly married in 1939 but my fiancée was imprisoned in Auschwitz and perished. I fled from Europe that same year."

I winced but kept up the questions.

"What have you been doing in this country. Did you resume teaching?"

"Yes. I had a job at Columbia the day I arrived. I retired last year."

"And after all those years, where did you meet Anastasia again? Had you kept in touch with her through it all?"

"No, we had not kept in touch. I met her again at Columbia. She was doing some translation work for Columbia University Press, and the Press was publishing some of my poetry. We accidentally met in an editor's office one day. We re-established our friendship immediately."

"And have you spoken to the doctor about Miss de Maupeou's personality changes?" I asked. "Does the doctor know what's happening?"

The Professor sighed again. "Yes, but he does not seem concerned. He said all fusion patients have a psychologically difficult recuperation."

I was stymied. "Let me talk to Cindy about it," I offered. "Perhaps she has some suggestions."

"Who can tell?" the poor Professor ventured. "I hope so."

I walked him back over to Anastasia's apartment and had hardly resumed my vacuuming when back came the Professor, screaming as if he had seen a ghost.

"Franklin, Franklin, come quickly! Please! I think Anastasia is dead!"

This time I did not take the time to put the vacuum cleaner safely aside. I merely dropped it and ran after my distraught friend.

There was no doubt as to what had happened. Pill containers, mostly empty, were strewn on the bed and floor. Without checking Anastasia, I grabbed the telephone and hurriedly asked the operator to call an ambulance. I also telephoned Anastasia's doctor and reported what had happened.

"Is she alive?" he demanded.

"I don't know! I think so. What should I check? Pulse? Breathing?"

"Quit talking, you fool," he roared at me, "and check her!"

She was alive. Her pulse was feeble and she was breathing, albeit very slowly. I reported this to the waiting doctor. And I also asked if I should try to make her vomit.

"No!" he ordered. "With the drugs I think she has taken, and that body cast, God only knows what would happen. Call me back as soon as you know what hospital they take her to."

By this time I could hear sirens, indicating the approaching ambulance.

Prof. Toplitsky had collapsed in a chair and appeared to be alternately sobbing and praying. I moved by him and propped open the apartment door and then the front doors to the building.

When the ambulance arrived moments later, the attendants scrambled from their seats, ripped open the rear doors of their vehicle and slid down a stretcher bed in the wink of an eye. Almost as fast they found Anastasia and removed her to St. Luke's Hospital, a fact I rushed to report to her doctor.

The Professor was still slumped in the chair when I went to close the apartment door.

"Try not to worry," I said, trying to sound confident. "The intern on the ambulance said he thinks she'll be all right. Are *you* all right?"

He ignored my question.

"I love her so much. So much that I shall kill myself if she dies."

I opened my mouth to say something, anything, but he motioned me not to speak.

"We've never made love," he said, not to me in particular, "and we have never even kissed. I have never even told her I love her. I am so old and she is so young. I was afraid she would laugh at me. But I know now that I cannot live without her. If she dies, I too will die."

This was more than I could handle. I patted the Professor on the back and withdrew to leave him with his grief. Once back with the protective noise of the vacuum cleaner, I managed to compose myself. Soon I switched off the machine again and went to break the news to the Karbowskis. They were almost as distraught as the Professor. They invited him up to their apartment, and I felt better that he wasn't going to be alone for the next hour or so.

Time, and a new doctor, did wonders for Anastasia. She was home again in barely four weeks and was mentally sharper than she had been in months. One morning several weeks after her return, she telephoned me and asked me to come over. I went immediately.

"Hello!" she said brightly, and then she paused and seemed to carefully reach for words. "I want to thank you for saving my life. Mischa told me what you did. I'm glad you saved me. I really want to live."

"Miss de Maupeou, please don't..."

"Call me Anastasia..."

"Anastasia, then. Please don't thank me. Thank the Professor. Thank Mischa. He's the one who saved you. If he hadn't come back to your apartment when he did, well... In case you haven't noticed, your life is his life. He literally can't live without you. Don't you know that? He loves you!"

Anastasia looked startled. "What makes you say Mischa loves me?"

"He told me. He told me he couldn't live without you. And if you had seen him here when ... well, that day, you would *know* he adores you. Besides, how could one lavish the care on you that he did and not love you?"

She didn't answer. She turned her head and then I heard her start to sob. I left quietly.

Anastasia's recuperation was uneventful after that. The cast was removed at the end of nine months, and the slow, painful effort to restore tone to her atrophied muscles began.

As before, Professor Toplitsky was ever at her side, and he helped her in her walking exercises and ministered to her reborn muscles and tendons.

As soon as she could, Anastasia returned to work for Columbia University Press. I saw less and less of the Professor who, Anastasia told me, was deeply immersed in finishing an epic love poem, his greatest work yet.

It was a lovely spring day when Anastasia telephoned me and insisted that Cindy and I come to her apartment. There was something she wanted to show us.

It was a wedding cake. She and her Mischa had been married that morning, and they wanted us and the Karbowkis to join them in a modest celebration before they left for Bermuda on their honeymoon.

The Professor was ecstatic, literally glowing with love and joy.

"A toast," he beamed. "To my beloved bride — and her family. You four are her family, you know. I hope you will welcome this old, broken-down academic into it."

He was hugged by everyone with delight.

"With pleasure" and "with pride" came the flattered responses.

"Professor," I asked, "what shall I call you? What manner of relatives are we to be?"

"Hereafter I shall call you son," he announced. "What do you say to that?"

"What else but amen?" I shot back, and from the look of pure pride on my new "father's" face, I knew I had said the right thing.

As Cindy and I were taking leave of "father" Mischa and the other celebrants, Anastasia took me aside and whispered in my ear. "You should know," she said softly, "that I proposed to him. He was too shy to do it. He thought he was too old for me. Thank you, my dear, dear friend, for telling me."

"For love you give thanks? For love, you should always give thanks!"

CHAPTER 21

When's A Burglar
Not A Burglar?

There was a memorable occasion when the Plouviers added irony to my life. Did I say memorable? It was unforgettable! They almost cost me my job.

The Plouviers, the noisiest household in the building, generally disappeared on Sundays until late at night, for which we, the tenants of 8 West, were grateful. On that one day the building was quiet. No one knew where the Plouviers went, or cared, until one fateful Sunday.

On that day Cindy was working and I was deeply immersed in studying for a quiz. Around two o'clock the door buzzer rang and I got up to answer it. Peering down the stairwell to find out who the visitor was, I soon saw a very formally dressed gentleman of about 50 with a strikingly shaped goatee. He was bounding up the stairs two at a time. Passing right by me, he continued to the Plouviers' apartment and began hammering on their door very agitatedly.

"They're out for the day," I called to the man. "They always go out on Sundays."

He looked positively heartbroken and volunteered the reason for his dismay. In heavily accented but perfect English he told me it was urgent he see Jean.

"I work wiz him," he said, "and Jean 'az some papers I need to finish a chemical process we are working on. It is urgent zat I finish zis work today because someone is coming tomorrow to consider purchasing zis process."

I expressed my regret that the Plouviers were not in and told him there was no way I could help.

"Zen may I see ze owner of zis building?" he pleaded.

"M. Karbowski n'est pas ici, aussi," I replied in fractured French, trying hard to ease his consternation.

He made a clucking noise then left, muttering under his breath.

I had hardly settled back into my studies when the buzzer rang again. It was the Frenchman once more. "Are zay back yet?"

"No, monsieur, not yet."

"Alors, je m'excuse," came the exasperated response. "I shall return again later."

And he did, three more times in the same hour. Each time his question and my reply were repeated.

When the buzzer rang about 4 o'clock, I answered it from inside the apartment since I was expecting Cindy. Again, however, it was the Plouviers' friend demanding entrance to their apartment.

For reasons I will never understand, this time I permitted the man to enter their apartment – something I had never been permitted to do – and to remain there alone for about an hour.

When the Plouviers returned at nine that night, all hell broke loose. Hardly had they set foot in their place when they were pounding on my door. Things in their apartment had been disturbed! They were sure they had been robbed! Had I heard anything?

"Why, yes," I managed to squeeze in, "your associate with the goatee was here. He waited in your apartment for an hour or more. He…"

Jean exploded with rage. He spun around, strode back to his apartment and called the police!

Interrogations, accusations and reprimands lasted well into the night. One detective referred to me as a robber's best friend; another insisted I had a Robin Hood complex. Mr. K, called in soon after the authorities arrived, was baffled by my lack of judgment. And Jean stayed livid with anger. I heard him mumble "cretin" several times under his breath, and with each passing minute my spirits sank lower and lower, easily keeping pace with his sinking opinion of me.

Finally the story, the reason for Jean's rage, emerged. He had been developing a new and very powerful shampoo and the man with the goatee was his assistant, Pierre Boulanger. With Claudine no longer working with him, Jean had become increasingly suspicious of all assistants. A growing paranoia kept him feeling that they were all trying to steal his secrets.

I was ready for the worst. Images of Mme. Defarges and the Looking Glass Queen of Hearts shouting "chop off Franklin's head" flashed through my mind. But, thank God, I was to be spared. As far as Jean could see, once a measure of his reason returned, nothing had been stolen. And when he was totally calmed down, he became generous enough to tell me that he had had none of the shampoo papers in the apartment anyway.

I crept home to lick my wounded pride.

The nightmare ended the following evening when Jean returned home, arm in arm with none other than the goateed non-burglar!

His assistant was a genius, Jean now told me! After not finding the papers he needed in the Plouviers' apartment, Pierre had gone to the lab, found Jean's briefcase in a locker, located the papers he needed and completed the work on the shampoo process without Jean.

It was very fortunate that he had, I learned, since the prospective buyer had appeared at the lab first thing this morning, and by early afternoon he was so impressed with the new process that he purchased it on the spot for a very handsome fee.

Jean's opinion of my judgment had done an about-face and now he couldn't be more pleased with me.

Me? I was happy that Mr. K hadn't fired me. I remained ashamed of myself for several weeks. Why had I waived my judgment that day?

Why had I violated some of the most fundamental guarantees of our Constitution? To this day I cannot understand why I acted as I did that fateful day in violation of the Plouviers' right to privacy. And to this day I feel a rush of shame whenever I recall the incident.

CHAPTER 22

Suds, Suds, Suds

It was a bright, warm spring day.

I had fallen asleep while trying to review the last several chapters of a dull text on international economics. The phone rang and made me jump; I was in a sleepy fog when I answered.

"Can you come to our apartment for a few moments?" a voice was asking. "We need to talk about the awful suds."

"Of course," I answered, realizing Mrs. Karbowski had been talking to me. "I'll be right over."

Had she said suds? I must have heard her wrong.

"Has no one in 8 West spoken to you about the suds?" Helena called down the stairs as I made my way up to the Karbowskis' apartment. There. I heard her say suds again.

"No ... no one has," I answered, going inside. "Tell me what you're talking about. What suds?"

Mr. K, coming into the living room from somewhere else in the apartment, was very agitated. He was making strange gestures and expelling air from his mouth as though blowing the foam off a beer. But Mrs. K picked up the story.

"The St. Johns and Anastasia have been experiencing soap suds attacks for the past week. Suds have foamed up in their sinks and bathtubs. Toilets, too. What is causing this? What can be done about it? What..."

I threw up my hands, not knowing where to try and start answering. Mrs. K paused to wait for me to reply. Immediately Mr. K took up where his wife had left off but in Polish. He exploded, his face alternately turning red and purple as he spoke.

I was so startled that Mrs. K took my hand and started stroking it as if to allay my fears.

"My husband says the Communists are probably doing it to stop the revolution," she interpreted. "If not the Communists, it must be the stupid officials of this city, trying to justify more taxes."

By now fully awake, but still thoroughly confused, I assured the Karbowskis I would look into the matter instantly. I left as fast as my hand could turn their door knob.

I decided that a quick survey of all the apartments in 8 West was in order. That way, I'd be able to determine if the sudsy affliction was confined just to the first floor or rife throughout. I quickly found that the tenants on the first three floors had all suffered from suds eruptions in varying degrees, that no one had on the fourth floor, and that Joe Halstead on the fifth thought he and his roommate, Sam Browning, had on two occasions.

The more I thought about it, the more confused I became. Why suds?

It seemed logical to deduce that where there were suds there had to be soap of some kind. But where were the suds coming from? It could be from inside the building, where someone was pouring soap into the waste pipes, or it could be coming from outside with something sloshing in from New York's antiquated sewage system.

The Karbowskis had not been victimized by suds, neither had other residents of 6 West. I also checked with the owner of 10 West, and he looked at me as though I had lost my senses. The suds were apparently confined to my building.

What to do?

At my urging, Mr. K hired a plumber to investigate. He spoke to the St. Johns and Anastasia, spent some time in the cellar tracing the waste pipes, banged the waste pipes with his wrench at several junctions, and then rendered his $15 decision. "Buy salt," he declared. "Lots of salt. It breaks down suds. Don't fight it. It's bigger than all of us. Tell your tenants to salt the suds – just like you do a good beer. The salt will cure the problem."

While I was not very pleased with his suggestion, it did offer an interim solution.

But the sudsy affliction became worse, finally reaching even the Noyes' apartment. My repeated admonitions to "salt the suds" were now drawing some salty comments in response.

However, there were also moments of humor, albeit somewhat black.

There was the night, for example, when Helen Jason, wearing only a bath towel, pounded on our door. "I'm being attacked!" she screamed. "They're taking over my apartment! Please come quickly!"

Terrified that a street gang had somehow barged its way into her apartment, I hurried after her. The 'they' turned out, of course, to be soap suds. And Helen hadn't been kidding when she said they were taking over her apartment. Her tiny bathroom was full of suds from floor to ceiling, and suds were flowing into her kitchen and living area.

I rushed to turn off the water. It worked. The suds stopped gushing out almost immediately.

But Helen's story came to be typical.

Anastasia told me a similar thing soon thereafter. "I was taking a shower when I realized that suds were enveloping my ankles and even my knees," she reported. "I was in the middle of washing my hair, so I rushed and rinsed as quickly as I could. By then suds were up past my waist. I fled the bathroom in fear of suffocating. My husband was out. Never had I felt so alone."

And another night, Sam Browning came to tell me he was dying from some mysterious disease. Or hallucinating. "I had staggered home – as I often do," he said, "and I was desperate to pee. I had just started when I realized that foam was appearing seemingly out of nowhere. I thought it was coming from me! Hell, I was too drunk to figure it out, so I finished peeing and flushed. Suddenly, the whole hopper exploded with sudsy foam. I put the seat down and walked away. I'm still not sure if I imagined it all."

The source of the suds and also the reason I had never been invited into the Plouviers' apartment became obvious soon after they moved out. They moved thanks to the sale of their shampoo- making process, which made it possible for them to afford a much larger and fancier apartment on Central Park West.

When the movers removed the last item from No.7, I entered for the first time.

It was filthy, which surprised me because I had seen what a thorough cleaning job Claudine had done on her son's stairwell accident sometime back. But what surprised me more was what I found in the bedroom and bathroom. The bedroom walls were ablaze with lipstick scrawlings, the floor was thick with the overflow from lipstick molds, and damaged lipstick cases were scattered everywhere. The bathroom, however, showed me the solution to the mystery of the surging seas of suds. Next to the toilet and sink were dozens of bottles partially full of a thick liquid which a sniff told me was shampoo.

Obviously the Plouviers had either been manufacturing or testing their new shampoo at home and had been using the bathroom facilities to dispose of samples. The ebb and flow of suds throughout 8 West undoubtedly corresponded to the Plouviers' test schedule.

Even now when the toilet was flushed, suds formed and rose and overflowed into the bathroom for a full four minutes. Case closed ... and as I mopped and salted, I mentally retired my deerstalker hat and magnifying glass.

With the suds gone, I figured we'd all soon forget the Plouviers. But I figured wrong. Jean's moonlight manufacture and testing of lipstick and shampoo were directly responsible for yet another clause in Mr. K's leasing litany of horrors.

"There shall be absolutely no manufacture of cosmetic preparations within these walls," it read.

And to this day, whenever I flush a toilet, I half expect to see suds.

CHAPTER 23

Of Gays and Gals

While I was discovering how to be a building superintendent, I also discovered that there was a lot more to sex than anything I had ever heard or learned before coming to New York City.

Much of what I unwittingly discovered was thanks to Jonathan Hauser, one of two tenants above Cindy and me in No. 10. Jon was an easy-smiling blonde with unusual turquoise eyes, and he had no abashment whatsoever about revealing his enjoyment of sex.

In his late 30's, Jon's hedonistic philosophy boiled down to these phrases: "Life is short, short, short! Make every moment count! Live! Live!" And by live Jon meant that one should indulge oneself in all of life's pleasures.

I seldom saw Jon on my nightly trash rounds, and I seldom missed seeing him Saturday mornings when I took the vacuum cleaner and began my weekly cleaning chores, starting at the top floor of 8 West.

The lines varied but the setting rarely changed. Picture the Super, working the upright cleaner back and forth in front of him, working his way along the hallway towards the front apartment. The door to the rear apartment opens and reveals Jon Hauser, in most of his glory. He is dressed only in tights or jeans, and his hairless chest is never covered. He is over six feet tall, is lean and light, has a flawless physique.

The lines. "Good morning, Franklin. Coming in for a cup of coffee? Come now, I won't bite you – at least not very hard."

More lines. "Franklin, have you disposed of that stuffy bride of yours yet? I have lots and lots of room up here for you when you do."

I was used to his not-unfriendly teasing and always told him that I preferred a woman, my wife, to satisfy me.

Once he asked me to come to a party. "...Just you, of course," he challenged, "then I'll show you."

"Go to hell," I tossed over my shoulder.

"Gladly," came back the easy reply, "if you'll come with me."

Jon's constant importunings to me to join him in bed didn't endear him to Cindy. What troubled her even more, however, was the fact that he could sew better than she could.

Jon was a professional dancer. When, years back, he realized that he would never make it to the top of his profession, he shrewdly saw that many affluent city dwellers who sent their children to private schools would pay handsomely to endow their dear little ones with the poise and grace which dancing was supposed to provide.

Thus, Jon was the sole and growingly prosperous proprietor of a dancing school in mid-Manhattan. He worked with professional dancers-to-be each morning and with youngsters in the afternoon.

His most awesome responsibility in the course of a school year was his annual show for the parents for which practices were held Saturday afternoons.

Seldom could Jon purchase the precisely appropriate costumes for this show and, perfectionist that he was, he would never trust a parent to produce a costume which only he could visualize. So he made most of the costumes himself.

For a good month before the show, Jon's social life stopped dead. His every minute was spent over his sewing machine producing the frilly, lacy garments which would be just right for the big event.

Cindy had the misfortune to confront Jon in the hallway on two occasions when Jon was in his sewing season.

The first time he was reasonably calm.

"Are you still trying to sew, dear?" he smirked. Having seen the fruit of Cindy's sewing accomplishments all through our apartment, he oozed sarcasm.

"Trying?" Cindy retorted. "I sew perfectly adequately, thank you."

"What a shame," Jon again smirked. "Maybe it will get better."

The second time I was with Cindy, and I was wearing a clever, bias-cut shirt she had made for me. It caught Jon's eye.

"What a lovely shirt!" Jon gushed, closely examining the seams. "Shame the seams don't match exactly."

Cindy was in no mood for banter.

"What does a grown man like you know about sewing anyway?" she hissed. "Why don't you behave like the man you're supposed to be!"

That did it. Jon flounced off, and no sooner were we back in our apartment than he was at our door, his arms loaded with costumes.

"What do I know about sewing, dear?" he challenged. "Here, can you make this? Have you ever seen anything as intricate as this Colonial gown? Or this?"

On and on he went, as he peeled off and displayed one exotic piece after another. Cindy, thoroughly intimidated and somewhat afraid, looked to me for support.

"All right, Jon," I said. "You've made your point. Let's drop it."

He turned, picked up his work and, without another word, left. I could tell by his bearing that he felt he had won that round. I was left to calm down Cindy. Throughout our tenure at 8 West, she remained totally perplexed about the nature of a man who could sew so beautifully.

My Army experience had left me with no doubts about Jon's nature. He was a homosexual.

My thoughts were confirmed during my first year as Super. His numerous parties and occasional spats that could be heard from the streets were invariably attended by people, mostly men, who behaved much like Jon.

Twice I was called upon by tenants to quiet down Jon's parties, which were almost always noisy affairs.

"Franklin, we'll stop this noise just for you," Jon told me both times. "Just say the word."

Telling him to knock it off, I'd stay around only long enough for my presence to put a damper on the noise.

While Jon Hauser's apartment was frequently noisy, Helen Jason's third-floor apartment, No. 5, was always quiet.

An attractive, slender brunette, Helen was in her thirties and appeared to me to be totally dedicated to her career as an operating room nurse. On the occasions I had been asked to come to her apartment to repair something, I had been amazed, even awed, at the neatness and cleanliness of the place. I watched in wonder as she went about her housework. Never a wasted motion, never a hair out of place.

While Jon had a series of apartment mates, Helen had only one — Dorothy Rodgers. Dottie, a bubbly, petite gamine also in her late thirties, had been Helen's friend since school days. She was a legal secretary.

Helen and Dottie were so quiet that I was never aware if friends, male or female, visited them. Never, that is, until Jon Hauser entered their lives.

One very hot and humid Saturday morning in July as I was working my way down to the third floor with the vacuum cleaner and dust cloth, Jon came striding by. He seemed very light hearted and stopped to offer his usual indecent proposal. I, also as usual, declined his offer, and he continued on his way.

Soon afterwards, Helen came out.

"Who was that good looking man?"

"Jon Hauser. He lives upstairs in No. 10 with Bill Brochetti."

"Uh, will, you introduce him to me?"

I alluded to his homosexuality.

"That's none of my business," she answered politely. "Introduce me anyway, all right?"

So I did, 15 minutes later. By then I was cleaning the second floor. Jon came back up the stairs two at a time.

"Changed your mind yet?"

"No," I called after him, "but I have something to tell you. There's someone here who wants to meet you."

He turned and came back and I told him about Helen's request.

Allowing that "there's no time like the present," he accompanied me up one floor.

Thus did Jon Hauser become a new and vital part of not only the life of Helen Jason but of Dottie Rodgers', too.

And Bill Brochetti, Jon's current roommate, also became involved. Bill was a lecturer in physics at Columbia. A smallish man, he had dark brown hair, a nearly black mustache and eyes so deep brown the pupils could not be seen. His speech was precise, his diction perfect, and his manner curt. When he made a point, he expected no riposte – except from Jon, whom he adored.

When I made my trash rounds that night, I was surprised to find Jon's door open and Jon and Helen and Dottie and Bill obviously having a good time. They waved at me. My hands full of trash, I merely nodded back, but I felt pleased that I had enabled four people to make new friends.

From then on, my Saturday morning confrontations with Jon were less frequent and their nature changed rather dramatically. I was now confronted by a fully clad Jon who invited me to join the ménage à quatre for brunch. Helen, Bill and Dottie were all chattering animatedly and all were busy working on some portion of the meal.

I assumed that the four, while very proper in public, were getting into all kinds of matters sexual in private.

But another Saturday morning invitation made me rethink everything.

I was polishing the mailboxes in 8 West when Bill bounded in with a box of pastries from Lengacher's Swiss Pastry Shop down the street.

"Morning, Bill. Is that your brunch?"

"Sure is. Come up and join us. We hardly see you anymore."

I didn't want to interrupt anything, I felt I would be an intruder, so I started to beg off. Bill asked me why.

"Well," I said, "it seems to me that four's company but five's a crowd."

"That's stupid " Bill answered. "Why, we're just four people like any other four people. We all have friends and we like to have them around us. We consider you a friend."

I wasn't sure how to respond, so I blurted out exactly how I felt about the ménage I had imagined.

"I consider all of you my friends, too," I said. "But I can't cope with sexual, well, orgies. Homosexuality doesn't bother me because I was exposed to so much of it in the Army. Heterosexual is what Cindy and I and most people are. But bisexual? And anything-goes sex? It's new to me, Bill. It offends me. Maybe when I'm a little older, a little more worldly, I'll be able to handle it. But right now I can't."

Bill was stunned. He started to speak several times but only stammered. I couldn't understand why and felt extremely uncomfortable.

Bill actually blushed.

"You don't really know what it means to be a homosexual in our society, do you?" he asked quietly. "Sex orgies? Franklin, they're as offensive to me and Jon and the girls as they are to you."

I felt terrible and could think of nothing to say to relieve myself of the embarrassment.

Slowly Bill continued, searching for the right words.

"We aren't sybarites, you know. We don't have orgies. Jon and I are simply trying to survive in a hostile society together. We're fiercely monogamous – to each other. Don't you see?"

I tried, I really did. But then how did Helen and Dottie fit into their lives? My unspoken question was apparently easy for Bill to pick up because he took the words right out of my mouth. "What about Helen and Dottie? How do they fit in?"

I nodded.

"Don't you realize they're Lesbians?" he nearly whispered. I shook my head dumbly. Lesbians? "Well, they are," he said. "And in a way they're just like Jon and me. They're fiercely in love with each other. And monogamous. They, like us, have to live in a closet, so to speak, because society won't tolerate our kind."

"But the four of you are always so, well, intimate," I ventured.

"That's because we're so happy ... now," Bill replied, enthusiasm growing in his voice.

"It was Helen who found this way out for all of us. That's why she asked you to introduce her to Jon. Somehow, she had figured Jon and me out. She suggested we try to appear as two heterosexual couples, and it's working. Why, for three years I've been a lowly lecturer at Columbia with no apparent hope for promotion. But in the last few months I've taken Dottie to several faculty parties. And just yesterday I was informed that I was being appointed an associate professor of physics. Coincidence? Hardly. It's just normal prejudice toward homosexuality."

Stunned, amazed, I shook my head. And never had I felt more foolish or inadequate.

"Forgive me," I said with as much earnestness as I could muster, "but I honestly didn't understand, Bill. And today, well, if you don't mind, could I take a rain check on the brunch?"

Understanding that I needed time to digest all this new information, Bill kindly let me off and left to deliver the pastries.

Several weeks later I made it a point to be outside Jon's apartment with the vacuum cleaner at 11 o'clock, the ménage's usual brunch hour. The moment I switched on the vacuum, the partly opened door swung wide open and Jon bounded out.

"Come on, Franklin, join us," he urged. "We all understand. Besides, Bill has gotten some of the richest stuff from Lengacher's Bakery and we heed help."

Feeling a little abashed, I accepted his invitation. Our conversation was stilted at first, but it grew more comfortable and animated as it became apparent to the four of them and to me that I could indeed accept them as friends and not as freaks.

When Cindy and I left 6 and 8 West in 1953, Jon and Bill and Helen and Dottie were still quietly and delightedly enjoying life behind their façade. Mercifully, Mr. K never became aware that sexual "abnormalities" were loose in his small fiefdom. Had he known, his litany of leasing horrors would have made "Fannie Hill" seem as tame as "Little Women."

CHAPTER 24

David Haunts Goliath

"**Y**ou never had a real honeymoon?"

Mrs. K had stopped by to return a yardstick, and Cindy had invited her to stay for a cup of coffee.

"Well, no, not really," my wife answered. "We couldn't afford it."

"Could you now?"

Helena Karbowski, always the complete romantic, thought every young married pair should have fond memories of an unforgettable honeymoon.

Cindy's face brightened visibly at the thought of it.

"Oh, Franklin, do you think we could?"

Cindy and I had started our marriage with a hideaway weekend straight out of the Yokel's Tour Guide: two nights at the Dixie Hotel, convenient but seedy, broken by an afternoon at Radio City Music Hall.

Suddenly the thought of a week or so alone with Cindy in any place other than New York City became overpoweringly attractive. But could we afford it, now that we both had been working for a year? Together we had accumulated almost $300 in a savings account. Should we spend a chunk of it on a real honeymoon?

On an aggressively hot Sunday afternoon not long afterwards, Cindy made the decision. A poignant story in the travel section of the paper about Bailey's Island, a tiny place off the coast of Portland, Maine, did it. She wrote to a small inn on the island and asked for reservations for the second week in September, which was just before my Fall semester at Columbia would begin.

I was delighted with her decision, but it also put me in a quandary.

Who would handle my Super's duties while we were gone? Cindy was ready with the answer.

"Your bachelor friend Dick Simpson, of course. He hates that little room he lives in. He'd jump at the chance. He's a slob but I don't think he could do much damage in a week."

Dick was the answer. He was a second-year student at Columbia Law School, which opened two weeks earlier than the rest of the University, so he could accept my suggestion.

He was delighted to have the relative luxuries of our apartment for a week in exchange for collecting the trash and handling my other menial chores.

I cleared the arrangement with Mr. K, who gave his permission only because his wife prodded him to. Then I helped Cindy with the final preparations for our honeymoon vacation.

We flew to Portland then took a motor launch to Bailey's Island. Our inn was charming and comfortable and, being the only guests there, we were spoiled silly. Our unforgettable week of swimming and loving and feasting on lobster for fully half our meals passed all too rapidly. When, thoroughly rested and refreshed, Cindy and I returned to New York and 6 and 8 West, we were ready to face anything.

What faced us was Dick completely packed and ready to leave the instant we arrived. He thanked us for letting him enjoy our apartment, apologized to Cindy for leaving it in such a mess, assured me that all was well on the tenant and landlord fronts, and quickly departed.

Only moments after Dick closed the door, someone was banging on it. It was Mr. K, his face beet red, his eyes bulging and his breathing labored and loud.

Striding into the apartment in a most ungentlemanly manner, very out of character for my boss, he glared at Cindy and me and exploded into a long, fiery monologue of epithets, exclamations and fractured phrases. Struggling to understand him, I had to interrupt. "Slow down, please! What's bothering you? We don't understand!"

"Is Nazis! Worse! Gestapo!"

Cindy and I looked at each other and shrugged. What was Mr. K talking about?

"Your friend Simpson," Mr. K roared, pointing and shaking his right-hand index finger near my nose, "is a rotten son of bitch. He'd turn us over to authorities. Senator McCarthy will come! Secret police! Oh, poor Poland is doomed."

This venting went on for a full five minutes. The only thing I was sure that Mr. K said from that point on was that we must never take another vacation.

After he left, Cindy and I tried, in vain, to piece together what might have happened while we were in Maine.

"What could he have meant by 'secret police,' Franklin," asked Cindy as she made coffee.

"I don't know – or about Senator McCarthy either. If anything, I would have thought this place was full of Polish revolutionaries, not Polish communists, to listen to him."

I didn't have the faintest idea what Dick had done, but I intended to find out fast. Dick had no phone so I caught up with him between classes the next day.

He had a rather sheepish expression on his face when he saw me.

"You look like you have a Polish tiger by the tail," he grinned. "Can I help?"

"You're damned right you can," I said with such force that I surprised myself. "First you can tell me what in hell happened while Cindy and I were gone! Mr. K exploded all over us last night. What did you do?"

"Franklin," Dick said in a voice higher pitched than usual, "I behaved admirably most of the week. Collected the trash, changed some broad's light bulb – and I don't think that's really what she wanted – and did everything you told me to. Until Thursday."

"Well? Go on!"

"Well, Thursday our torts professor announced we were having our first test the next day. Christ! I hadn't even cracked the book! So I hustled back to your apartment and buried myself in torts."

There was no point in trying to force Dick to get to the point of his explanation. He always felt compelled to give all the details. He lit a cigarette, turned to wave to friends passing nearby, and I waited impatiently for him to get on with his story.

"I got so deep in torts I completely forgot about the goddam trash. Next morning I was still studying when your landlord banged on the door. 'Ven you remove gobbitch?' he kept repeating. I told him I'd do it later, to please go away. He wouldn't. 'Sonny,' he yelled, 'you vill do your vork NOW!' At that point I got so mad I opened the door and gave him the works. I told him it was illegal not to give you a paid vacation and I was going to report him to the National Labor Relations Board. I told him that both buildings were full of suspicious characters, and I told him I was going to report 'everything' to the FBI, the House Un-American Activities Committee and Joe McCarthy. By then I was so warmed up I started throwing in references about the ICC, the FTC, the CAB, the SEC and any other initials I could think of."

He laughed to himself, remembering his tirade.

"Frank, ol' buddy, I scared the living daylights out of him."

Dick did that, all right. And that evening, despite trying for more than an hour to explain to Mr. K the reason for Dick's threats, nothing would placate him or expel his fears. For months afterwards he would quietly take me aside whenever we met and ask in a nervous whisper whether anyone had come to the door asking about him. Great relief washed across his face each time I assured him no one was on his trail.

In spite of the Simpson/Karbowski incident, Cindy and I never had any regrets about having had such a wonderful honeymoon. We hope it didn't delay the Polish revolution.

CHAPTER 25

Walter "Materially" Jackson

"**G**'morning, sir."

"Hi, kid."

"I'm Franklin Noyes. I'm the Super of these two buildings."

"Yeah, I know. Materially, I've known that since you moved in. Enjoyin' it?"

"You bet! I get a big kick out of meeting people, and I'm beginning to get to know some of the tenants fairly well."

"Don't get to know 'em too well, kid. Before you know it, you'll be materially disillusioned. Nobody's perfect and many of 'em are probably rotten."

This Brief exchange had taken place as I was taking in the trash cans several months after Cindy and I moved to 8 West. It was my introduction to Walter Jackson, owner-super of 10 West, next door. Through similar exchanges and occasional conversations in Walter's kitchen, he and I became friends. It seemed as though he welcomed my visits because it gave him an opportunity to talk about himself.

He was in his late 60's and a widower. His wife had died fifteen years earlier from a lingering and financially devastating bout with cancer.

"I was 49 when Janet passed on," Walter recalled. "She was in and out of hospitals and clinics and doctors' offices for materially four years before the Lord took her. Do you have any idea what that costs? And all the time she was sick, our only kid, Tommy, was in medical school in California. Christ, do you know what that costs? Well, to materially make ends meet, I began doing some odd jobs. And now they keep me from thinking about getting materially old myself."

The combination of slicked-back, yellowing white hair, close-cropped moustache, ever-present cigarette dangling from the left corner of his mouth, and a black fedora jauntily cocked on his head gave him a dashing look which belied his years. I told him I thought he didn't look a day over 40, and that seemed to please him.

Walter had spent his entire working career with one firm, a large finance company that moved him through a series of jobs until he was made a branch manager. He had served in this job for 25 years until he retired.

"We bought this house, Janet and me, in the 30's — 1933, to be exact — when things were damn tough, for materially nothing.

Worked like dogs, we did, cleaning and fixing it, and finally turned it into apartments, one on each floor. This first-floor apartment has materially been home ever since."

To provide care for his beloved Janet, and to keep Tommy in medical school, Walter began to do on his own what he did so well for his bosses: He loaned money. To questionable risks. At extremely high interest rates.

"Hell, I had these kids coming in the office all the time who materially had no collateral and no credit rating," he'd recall fondly. "But I knew they weren't bad risks. Some were in the rackets, sure, but most were good, hard-working kids who didn't know how to handle their own money is all. Materially, I helped them get organized. I counseled them and I charged them plenty. Fifteen, maybe twenty percent a month on loans. And materially they all paid me back. I was lucky, too. The company never caught on to my little sideline."

But the "mob" did.

"One day, I had a visit from a coupla mean lookin' guys," Walter ventured over a cup of coffee. "They wanted to know materially what the hell I was doin' in their racket. Told 'em it was my racket and I needed the money to take care of a sick wife and they could go to hell. You know what? They said, 'Okay, okay … you want a little more action?'"

Thus Walter progressed from usury to bookmaking. And a few other things he hinted about but refused to discuss.

"With my little sidelines, I was materially able to get back on my feet financially after Janet died," he went on. "I managed to save this house—at one point I materially had three mortgages on it—and I got Tommy through medical school. Only problem is, he likes California so much he materially won't come home. Says you gotta be nuts to stay in New York City."

Tommy's medical career was a spectacular success while his marital adventures were spectacular failures.

"Damn kid is bright, all right. Gets it from Janet. He went from medical school to all the right places, or so he told me. Now he's a heart doctor and he's teaching part-time at a medical school. When it comes to affairs of the heart, though, he's materially all screwed up. He's on his third wife. Changes 'em almost as often as he changes cars. He's got one kid from his second marriage named Walter after me – and he keeps that poor little bastard in boarding school. He's 10 years old now, and I've only seem him once. Can you believe it? I haven't seen Tommy for five years. Stopped by once for an hour when he was here for a conference. Imagine that. One hour! It was all right, though. We didn't know how to talk to each other."

Not knowing how to talk to each other was not a problem with Walter and me. Mostly he did the talking and I did the listening. Jokes, sometimes; recollections, others; and I enjoyed everything he said. Despite his sometimes tough talk, he came across as a fatherly type, and I believe he thought of me as a kind of surrogate son.

One day Walter telephoned me, instead of waiting until I stopped by later, and asked me to come over right away. 'I feel weird' was all he would say, so I asked Cindy to come along with me for the visit.

The door to Walter's apartment was open and he was sitting on a dining room chair with his hand still on the phone when we arrived. Judging from his pallor and breathing, he was in considerable distress.

Cindy immediately took charge.

"Walter, do you have a family doctor?"

"No, no, Cindy. What do I want with a doctor? We materially got one in the family."

"When was the last time you saw a doctor – not your son, I mean?"

"Twenty, twenty-five years back. It was before Janet died."

"Walter, you're sick, very sick," Cindy said softly. "You need a doctor now. We're going to take you to the emergency room at St. Luke's."

Taking my cue from Cindy, I ran the short distance to Central Park West, hailed a cab, and we got Walter to the hospital within ten minutes. Cindy got an attendant with a stretcher, and in only five minutes more Walter was being worked over in the emergency room.

When Cindy came out, she looked grim. "It's touch-and go," she said softly, knowing I was deeply worried about my old friend.

"He's had a heart attack, a bad one. We'll just have to wait and see."

"Should we wait here?"

"I don't think so. Right now, maybe we'd better go home and try and reach his son and let him know."

At Walter's apartment we found son Tommy's address and phone number, a listing in Palo Alto, California. I tried the number eight or nine times over the next several hours but couldn't get an answer. Finally, desperate, I sent a telegram and urged Tommy to come East immediately.

I did one more thing: I made a sign and fastened it in the entrance of 10 West. It read: "For tenant assistance, or information about Mr. Jackson, see Super at 8 West."

Within minutes, all sorts of people began ringing our doorbell. The first caller, a skinny young man of about 25, insisted that I take an envelope.

"Hey, man, this is tomorrow's action," he said.

"Gotta be worth four or five hundred. Be back with more in the morning."

I tried to refuse, but he wouldn't hear of it.

"You takin' Jackson's place for now, right? You handle his action. 's that easy."

Before I had even closed the door, a second visitor arrived and asked about his radio. "I'm here to pick it up. Here's my money, man. Gimme my radio!"

I told him to come back tomorrow by which time I hoped to know what he was talking about.

By the end of that frantic day more than 30 people had asked me to accept their bets, buy their stolen goods, sell them hot merchandise, lend them money, or give them more time to payoff their loans. To them all I gave the same answer: Come back tomorrow.

I felt like I was being sucked into mobdom's miserable maelstrom and I wanted none of it. But how to get out?

Walter provided the way that night. He died.

Cindy was working the graveyard shift and was with him when he drew his last breath. She called me shortly afterwards. "I'm sorry," was all she said, was all she needed to say.

I had lost a good friend.

Already wide awake from the tumultuous events of this day, her call set my adrenalin pumping and I instantly realized that all my new problems were solved. I wrote another sign and put it in the place of my original notice. This sign read: "Mr. Jackson died last night. Information about his estate should be referred to Dr. Thomas Jackson, Palo Alto, California."

That sign worked well too. Parties to Walter's sidelines never again rang my bell. And within the week, Tommy had returned East, had his father cremated, and placed 10 West in the hands of a real estate agent.

That, "materially," was the end of the Walter Jackson story and my brief, unwitting flirtation with the Mob.

CHAPTER 26

The Uncle and the Niece

Most nights I collected the trash around ten o'clock. The exceptions were when Cindy and I went to a movie or when I was struggling to finish writing a paper. Then the trash ritual didn't get started until eleven o'clock or midnight.

On several of those late nights I was intercepted by one or both of the Saxons, John and Elise, who lived below Cindy and me in No.6. Sometimes we would just swap a few words at the door; other times I would be asked in for a cup of coffee.

John Saxon was a moderately tall, very introspective man of about 45. With thick, silver-framed glasses, a tiny, shiny nose and curly hair, he looked to me like an absent-minded professor. His apartment mate was his niece, Elise, a pretty blonde of about 25.

Thanks to our nighttime coffee breaks, I learned that John was a Princeton graduate, class of 1929. He had quietly but thoroughly enjoyed the madcap 20's and, thanks to his unusual talents, had never missed a paycheck during the economically grim 30's.

He joined an advertising agency in Manhattan upon graduation and soon learned that he had an uncanny knack for preparing and producing successful presentations: new business presentations, sales and promotional presentations for clients, and "prestige" presentations for his bosses to give at professional society meetings and before Congressional committees.

"What I never could do, however," he confessed, "was participate in such presentations myself. Shyness, would you believe?"

Shyness notwithstanding, John's services were so highly valued by his agency that his salary grew steadily even though his title within the agency remained the same: Creative Coordinator. On several occasions he turned down vice presidencies, and on one occasion he flatly rejected an agency offer which would have built a satellite operation around him to permit the merchandising of his considerable talents at even greater profits to him and the agency both.

Every family has a pivotal date in its history, and John and Elise were no exception. The Saxon family, John told me over a drink late one Saturday night, was shattered on June 9, 1939.

"My brother and his wife were returning my parents to their home in Montclair, New Jersey, after a day of fun and shopping in Manhattan," he recalled. "They were nearly there when a drunk driver hit them. The doctors at the hospital said my parents died almost instantly, and my brother and his wife died in the ambulance. The only survivor – she was sitting between my parents in the back seat – was Elise, who was 12 then. She was untouched."

I expressed my sympathy. He nodded to acknowledge it and continued.

"Franklin, I can barely remember the next two years. I moved into the family home with Elise, sold my brother's estate – and I still can't clearly remember doing any of this – and put Elise in a boarding school. I occasionally went to the office to pick up work or to drop off something I had completed. But I was in a fog. The shock was so great that I crawled into my own private world to recuperate."

At this point Elise came in and gently helped her uncle continue the story.

"It was a terrible time in my life, too," she recalled. "I was just entering adolescence; I missed Mom and Dad so much. And then Uncle John would visit me at school with the demeanor of an undertaker. I had always been a happy, bubbly kind of person and I decided that somehow I would be that person again. I needed it. Uncle John needed it. We survived. We had to go on living. And there was no point in living if you couldn't have a little fun."

John picked up the story at this point, looking adoringly at his niece. "She was right, of course, and she gradually brought me out of it. She'd insist that we go swimming or see a movie or invite friends over. 'I'll cook,' she'd say. 'I'm a good cook. Always could fry eggs better than Mom.' She couldn't cook, but she knew I could and liked to do so. So gradually we rejoined the living. In the fall of 1949 we moved into Manhattan and Elise attended a private school nearby. We lived this way while she finished high school and college, right through to the war. They were good years."

Elise was graduated as an English major from Barnard College in 1944 and her uncle helped her get a job as a cub copywriter at his advertising agency. After three successful years in that position, she asked and was permitted to join the agency's media department as an assistant to one of the magazine's space buying specialists.

"Elise was always a popular girl," John said. "The phone never stopped ringing with eager young artists and writers trying to date her. The competition became positively fierce when she moved into media. Suddenly the young artists were replaced by the determined young space and time salesmen."

One of Elise's most ardent suitors those days was Joe Halstead, an advertising space salesman for LIFE Magazine, I learned. Joe, coincidentally, also lived in 8 West. He shared apartment number nine with another LIFE salesman, Sam Browning. Joe met Elise at the agency and, in his words, "I fell head over heels in love with her at first sight. Corny, huh? But true. But she would never tell me where she lived!"

Elise told me this part of the story late one night in Joe's apartment where I had stopped for a brief chat.

"The building Uncle John and I had lived in for about six years was torn down to build some fancy new apartments," she said. "So we found this place and were among the early tenants. Friend Joe here was determined to get my address, but I kept it from him. I really didn't like him much at the time. One night I was getting the mail out of my box when who should be next to me, key poised to extract his mail, than my friend here. We lived in the same building from the moment we had met at the agency and neither of us knew it."

It was thanks to Joe that I became sensitive to the Saxons' changing lifestyle and the altered rhythm and demeanor of their household.

Where once it had been quiet, it now came to life with music which could occasionally be heard throughout 8 West. The trash, usually light, became heavy with empty liquor bottles. And the string of suitors became a veritable stream. The men entered and left the Saxons at frequent and constant intervals.

Then I became aware of a change in Elise's attitude toward Joe. Almost every evening he would try to see her at the apartment, only to be rebuffed at the door by Uncle John. On most evenings after such rebuffs, a very distraught Joe would stop at our apartment to talk it out.

This kept happening for nearly six weeks. In all that time Joe had not once been able to see Elise privately. Besides being turned away at the apartment door every night, his daily efforts at work never got him past the media department's receptionist.

"Franklin," he moaned to me one night, "I don't understand it. Elise and I were having such fun together. We even began to collect things — pots, some linens — that we would use when we were married."

I offered what consolation I could. Maybe this, maybe that? But no. The only thought that Joe would entertain was that if he could find the reason for the change in the Saxons' lifestyle, he'd be able to find a reason for Elise's change of mind — and change it back. Before he could try, however, the Saxons' new lifestyle ended very abruptly one warm spring evening.

Cindy was at St. Luke's on night duty and I was writing a paper on comparative European governments when my Super's bell rang. Thankful for the opportunity to stretch my legs, I decided to walk down to see who was at the door instead of simply buzzing back. Five men were there...policemen! They showed me their credentials then, incredibly, they showed me a warrant to search the residence of John and Elise Saxon!

"I don't understand," I protested. "What could John and Elise possibly do to warrant a search and possible arrest?"

The leader of the detectives handled me gently.

"Look. Here are the words. Prostitution. Narcotics. We have reason to believe the girl is, uh, selling herself and the guy is selling or using dope."

"That can't be true," I pleaded, dazed by it all. "They're fine people! College graduates! He's an executive. She's doing well. It can't be!"

The detective leader moved me aside. "Look, son, we're going up to find out. Tag along behind but please be careful. Stay out of the way."

Uncle John responded to the detective's knock. The other detectives and I were pinned against the wall so we couldn't be seen through the peep hole.

"Who's there?"

"What d'you mean, who's there?" the detective leader shouted. "Me. Me! Hurry up, man. I'm horny as hell."

"Are you Jones? Oliver Jones?"

"Yeh, yeh. I'm Ollie Jones. Now open up before I attract a crowd out here."

"You'll just have a wait a moment, Mr. Jones. You're a little ahead of schedule, you know. Some things can't be rushed."

A moment later the door opened and John was stunned to be frisked and pinned before he could utter a word. Elise was found in bed with a client. Also found in the apartment was a small quantity of heroine.

Joe coincidentally arrived just in time to see Elise and John being led out of the building.

"Elise! What's wrong? What's going on?"

Elise didn't answer.

I took Joe aside, held him till the contingent left and then explained what had happened.

He moaned, "I don't believe it. It couldn't be. My Elise?"

He bolted away from me and ran to his apartment.

At that point I was much too concerned with the other tenants to worry about Joe. I assured them all that it was nothing serious – something to do with Mr. Saxon's secret war-time work I thought – and that the Saxons would soon be returning. I was just beginning to embellish this bit of fiction when Mr. K arrived.

"What has happened?" he demanded.

"I'm really not sure," I lied. I hoped my face didn't betray me. "You knew that Mr. Saxon was involved in something super-secret during the war, didn't you?"

He didn't know, but this information obviously lubricated his imagination.

"Well," I went on, "I think government agents want to hide them a while to keep them safe. They really wouldn't give me any information."

"You think Communists are after them?" Mr. K asked in a very low voice.

"I wouldn't be surprised," I answered, continuing my ruse.

"I think we had better have their lock changed, don't you?"

"Yes, yes, Franklin," he agreed. "You take care of that. Do you think they will return?"

"I think so, Mr. K. Probably in a few weeks. Cindy and I will clean the apartment and I'll have the lock changed. Then everything will be fine when they return. Is their rent paid?"

"Yes, yes. Mr. Saxon pays six months in advance." Mr. K turned to leave.

Later, Cindy and I talked about this Saxon affair late into the night. We were hardly asleep when Joe awakened us with his pounding on our door.

"I can't find them," he moaned. "By the time I got to the police station they had already posted bail and left. Where have they gone? I must find Elise."

By the time Joe had said this much he was awash in his own tears and obviously exhausted and disoriented. As we talked about the night's events, Joe sipped from a glass of bourbon I kept refreshing. After the sixth or seventh ounce, Joe agreed to go to bed provided I promised to help him search for Elise in the morning. At that point I would have made any promise to end that nightmarish night.

CHAPTER 27

The Search

I had barely gotten out of bed the next morning when Joe arrived to organize his search.

"I didn't sleep much," he said. "Did you? I couldn't stop thinking about Elise and John. The whole thing makes no sense. Hell, he makes a lot of money and Elise is doing well ... and she's certainly no nymphomaniac. Why? Why?"

"You know more about them than I do," I told him. "What can I tell you? Let's concentrate on the search. Have you tried the agency? That's the most likely place they'll be found."

"That's the first thing I did this morning," Joe said. "When the receptionist told me they weren't in, I spoke to a friend of mine and told him both John and Elise were called out of town on family business. I said they might not be back for a while. He promised to call me as soon as one shows."

"What about the police, Joe? What did they tell you last night?"

"I got to the station house an hour or so after they were booked. The desk sergeant told me they posted bail and left. He assumed they went home."

"Did you ask him if they left an address or phone number where they could be reached? I would think they'll be arraigned soon so the police will have to know where to reach them."

"Franklin, the desk sergeant just said they left, they went home. I'll talk to him again."

I moved to pour Joe and myself another cup of coffee. As I moved around the kitchen, it occurred to me that it was important Joe feel he was doing as much as he could.

"Where do we go from here?" I asked him. "You've got the agency covered. And you'll check the police. Do you know any of their friends? Do they have any other family? Do they have any special vacation retreats?"

"Elise does have a close friend at the agency," he volunteered. "An artist. Terry. Terry Lang. I'll talk to her. I don't think they have any family. And they did occasionally go to the Adirondacks. But I don't know where."

"Well," I said, "you get started on the search. Cindy and I will clean up the apartment, if it needs it, and I'll have the lock changed so they'll be safe from Communists when they return."

"Safe from Communists? Are you nuts?" Joe laughed when I told him what I had told Mr. K and some of the tenants. "When I find them," he promised, mock-seriously, "I'll give them the new key and tell them to act very mysteriously. Just like they do in all the best 'B' movies."

Later that week Joe reported his progress, or lack of it, on his search.

"Forgive me for not stopping before this," he said. "But my boss insists that I sell space occasionally so I've been run ragged between selling and searching.

"No need to apologize, pal," I answered. "Just give me an update. Have you found them?"

"No, or at least I don't think so. I think Terry Lang knows where Elise is but she claims not to. I've watched Terry's apartment a couple of times but Elise never came out. Anything new here?"

"No. I had the lock changed and Cindy and I did clean the apartment. And their mail is still coming. Joe, did Elise ever mention a doctor to you? I've often wondered if she had psychiatric treatment after her parents were killed."

Joe looked startled for a moment and then snapped his fingers. "White," he said. White. Black. Top. Bottom. No, White. Yeah, I remember her mentioning a doctor with a name like that. But White what? Whitehead? Yes! Dr. Whitehead! He has an office not far from here on Central Park West. I'll try to see him tomorrow. I'm sure he won't tell me anything about her, but at least he should tell her that it's okay to return to the apartment. Give me the new key, okay? I'll leave it with the doctor just in case."

It was four days later, a Friday afternoon, when I became aware that the Saxon apartment was occupied once more. When I stopped to see Joe during trash rounds that night, Sam told me that Joe was with Elise.

"Don't disturb them," he urged. "It's a delicate situation."

When I did finally see Joe some days later he begged off talking about the Saxons. "You hit the nail on the head when you thought of the doctor," he added, though. "That's how I found Elise. When she's ready, we'll both tell you what happened."

I didn't press though I was damned curious to know what happened to both Elise and John.

As the weeks went by, and still no sight of John, Elise and Joe seemed to grow happier and closer. I wasn't sure but I suspected that Joe had taken up residence with Elise.

It was nearly four months after that traumatic night in April that John reappeared on the scene, and almost six months to the day when the three of them invited me in one night while on trash rounds to hear their story.

Joe started.

"You were right, Franklin. Elise had been seeing her psychiatrist all along. I saw him the morning after we talked and left the new key with him. He refused to tell me anything about Elise but I knew, from the way the doctor answered my questions — he hedged — that she was seeing him. I watched his office that entire day. Elise visited him about seven o'clock. I intercepted her as she was leaving the building. At first she was angry and afraid. But she calmed down when I assured her she could come home. I walked her back to Terry Lang's where she was staying."

"You know most of my story," Elise said to me. "How my parents were killed. How I lived with Uncle John. But you didn't know – and why should you – that I have been going to Dr . Whitehead off and on since my parents were killed."

Elise stopped, reflecting on how to continue her story.

"How does a twelve-year-old girl react to the simultaneous loss of her parents and only living grandparents?" she asked, expecting no answer from me. "Dr. Whitehead said it made me three people. One Elise refused to grow any older than she was when her parents died. Another Elise sought to gratify her bashful uncle in every way possible. And the third Elise, the public one, was the bubbling, happy personality."

John cut in. "And I survived that horror myself thanks to Elise – and heroin. During one period while Elise was in boarding school, I admitted myself to a local clinic for treatment. I was given heroin to calm me and from that day until recently I was hooked. The cops were right, Franklin. I was using heroin."

Joe spoke up at this point. "What John did not say," he told me, "is that the heroin had cost him dearly. First his supplier blackmailed him. He kept threatening to tell John's boss if he didn't pay up. And then when this supplier met an untimely end, his successor doubled the charges for the heroin. That's when Elise volunteered to help."

"Franklin," John said with some difficulty, "can you possibly imagine the degrading situation I had developed? To feed my lousy habit I sold my niece! She volunteered to do it, but that's beside the point. It took the arrest to jar me into finding myself. You didn't see me for three months because I arranged with the judge to go to Lexington, Kentucky, to undergo detoxification at the government's center there. I've licked the habit, Franklin. Now all I have to do is lick the guilt for what I've done to Elise.

Elise walked over to her uncle and hugged him.

"Don't worry about us," she beamed. "With Joe and Dr. Whitehead looking after us, we'll make it. We'll get our lives straightened out in no time."

I was happy for their happiness. As I got up to leave, I reminded Joe of one final thing. "Don't forget to tell them about the Communists," I smiled. "And show them how to look mysterious."

A snapshot at that moment would have shown a startled John, a thoroughly bemused Elise and a delighted, laughing Joe slapping his leg with glee.

CHAPTER 28

Civil Servants

The Saxons notwithstanding, our contacts with the police were, happily, limited. Every month or so one or a pair of policemen would ring the Super's bell and ask me to look at some photographs of suspects. Did I recognize anyone? I never did.

Tough though the police were, they were tame in comparison with the trash collectors. But that was part of the drama of being a Super – dealing with Manhattan's civil servants.

The drama with trash collectors always heightened at two specific times. The first was when a strike was brewing. The second was when Christmas was near and the trash collectors wanted gifts.

You could always tell when a strike was brewing by the location of the empty trash cans. Trash cans on the curb or slightly in the street meant that a strike was indeed at hand but that matters were not yet hopeless. Cans separated from their lids – normally they were chained together – and found in the street a half-block away were a sure sign that a strike was imminent.

Christmas was another matter.

The trash collectors, anonymous eleven months of the year but now visible and deliberately friendly, started their visitations about the first week in December to remind you that the holy season was nearly here.

"Surely you will want to remember the dedicated servants in your trash crew," they dared to say.

If you hadn't remembered your 'dedicated servants' by the end of the second week in December, two members of the crew would visit you to reiterate their need for Christmas love and blessings.

"You do have Mr. K's blessings," I told the two-man delegation my first Christmas at 6 and 8 West. "But no cash or anything because it's illegal, isn't it?"

The pair stormed out of the building.

The havoc subsequently wrought on the Karbowski trash cans was incredible to behold.

The first day after the visitation, the chain on one can was cut and the lid had disappeared. By the end of the week, all the lids were gone.

The next week was a period of battering and partial crushing. The cans would be emptied all right, but then they would be slammed into the street or against the back of the trash truck and left in the street to be hit by cars.

By December 23, the destruction was complete.

I was sweeping the sidewalk when the trash crew started down the street toward me. A very fat man, obviously the crew leader, stopped a few steps ahead of the others and pretended to watch me sweeping.

"You like to keep your places clean?" he asked.

I told him yes and tried, nervously, to force a smile.

"Well, those cans are a menace to society," he smirked. "Let's help clean up the city, lads."

Then he and his men proceeded with obvious pleasure to throw all six of my trash cans into the back of their compactor truck.

For Christmas that year, and the next, Mr. K presented me with new trash cans.

CHAPTER 29

Mimi's Art House

One result of the Saxon affair was that I became suspicious about what went on, or what might be going on, in Manhattan apartments.

Consider this example.

I had only a passing acquaintance with the residents of No. 3 in 6 West, Walter and Agatha Muller. I met them at their door a few times when they were putting out their trash, and several times one or the other passed me in the hallway on a Saturday morning while I was cleaning. We always exchanged pleasantries. But that was all. I had never been invited into their apartment for a drink or even asked in to fix anything.

I judged the Mullers to be in their fifties. Walter was a slim dynamo with nearly white hair. He never seemed to be still, at least in my sight. Even when exchanging greetings he was on the move. I guessed him to be about five feet eight inches tall.

Agatha was another matter. Built like a professional football linebacker, she was at least five feet ten barefoot. She had copper colored hair which had to have come from a bottle, yet she was not unattractive.

Shortly after the police arrested the Saxons, I noticed that women, mostly young, seemed to be visiting the Muller apartment at regular intervals.

"What do you suppose is going on there?" I asked Cindy one day.

"How should I know," she replied absentmindedly.

"God, I hope it's not more prostitution."

"I doubt it," Cindy said. "Wouldn't there have to be more men? I think your fears are foolish fancies. Besides, if you're so concerned, why don't you ask Mrs. Muller?"

"Ask? You mean knock on the door and say, 'Mrs. Muller, are you running a cat house?' Just like that?"

Cindy shook her head. "No, stupid. Just say, 'Aggie, are your girls laboring for love or money?'"

"You're no help whatsoever," I snorted.

I dropped the matter at that point but continued to brood.

I was still brooding about the matter when, on a Saturday morning several weeks later, I was confronted by a familiar looking face while I was buffing the mailboxes in the vestibule of 6 West.

"Where is Walter Muller, son?" I was asked.

"I don't know, sir. Did you ring his bell?"

"Yes, but no one answered. I have to see Walter immediately. God," the man boomed, "my show can't go on tonight if I don't get the script!"

Show? Script? Of course! The familiar face, the familiar voice belonged to none other than Basil Rathbone or, loyal fan of Sir Arthur Conan Doyle that I was, to Sherlock Holmes.

"Let me try the bell, Mr. Holmes, uh, Mr. Rathbone," I offered. "Sometimes it only works if you press hard on the right side."

Mr. Rathbone nodded.

I pressed hard on the right side of the Muller's bell, and the response of the buzzer releasing the lock was immediate. Before I could say Dr. Watson, Mr. Rathbone tugged open the door and charged up the stairs.

Sharing coffee with my wife a few minutes later, I fished for her reassurance.

"I don't know whether to be concerned or not," I said. "Do you suppose Mr. Muller really has something to do with scripts? Or is that some kind of front for the classiest whorehouse in town?"

"For heaven's sake, stop it!" Cindy demanded. "I'm sure the

Mullers are not running a ... a house. They're simply enjoying their home. Look, why not talk to the Karbowskis about it. The Mullers are their tenants and neighbors; they must know something about them."

That sounded sensible enough. I decided I'd take my wife's suggestion at the earliest opportunity.

As I was coming home from school a few days later, I heard someone shouting, "Hey, kid!"

I stopped and turned to face a stranger.

"Me? Can I help you?"

"You the Super, kid?"

"Yes ...can I help you?"

"Do you know Aggie Muller?" The man began describing her before I could answer. "Big broad. Red hair straight from a bottle. Knockers ..."

"I ... yes ... I know ..."

The man wouldn't let me finish. "Knockers big enough to smother an elephant. Man, she's the hottest duplicator in all of Manhattan. I can't wait to see her. I gotta see her fast."

So my fears were foolish fancies, eh?

"Let me try the bell, sir," I said. For the second time in only a short while I found myself offering the information that "sometimes it only works if you press hard on the right side."

It worked and the man, about the size of Mr. Muller but much younger, shot up the stairs.

A few days later I could no longer contain my curiosity. I had to know what was going on in the Muller apartment. Off I went to the Karbowskis'.

"Franklin, it is so nice to see you," beamed Mrs. K. "Can I do something for you? As you see, my husband is not home."

"Do you know the Mullers?" I asked right out, not taking any time to small talk and surprising Mrs. K by being that way.

"Of course, my dear," she answered, recovering quickly. "We know them well. Oh, just a moment. Let me give you something."

She rummaged about Mr. K's desk for a moment, found what she was looking for, a card, and handed it to me. It read:

Mimi Renoir and her students
cordially request
your presence at an exhibition
of their work.
Saturday, from 4:00 p.m. to 8:00 p.m.
The Mullers, Apt. 3, 6 West

"Come on Saturday, Franklin," Mrs. K said as I handed back the card to her, "and you will meet the Mullers. What was it you wanted to know about them?"

I thought fast, not daring to explain what it was I really wanted to know, and remembered a little brass plate on the door downstairs which read *Mimi Renoir*.

"Who is Mimi Renoir? Is someone living with the Mullers?"

Mrs. K chuckled. "You and Cindy come Saturday and you will meet Mimi. And Walter and Agatha."

I could hardly wait for the weekend. I would have been the first visitor to the exhibition but Cindy reined me in.

"One never goes to these things on time," she said. "It's not couth, or contrary to protocol or something."

So we arrived at the Mullers' just after five o'clock. Their door was wide open and their apartment was jammed with people ogling and oohing at paintings, which were everywhere. Some were very good, I thought.

Cindy and I were soon separated, she going in the direction of a group of women clustered around Agatha and I joining a group of men.

Shortly after Walter Muller shoved a gin and tonic in my hand I started chatting with a man who was admiring the same painting I was.

"Nice, isn't it?" I said, summoning up all my critical powers. "The primitive style reflects such naiveté."

My fellow art admirer laughed. "My wife painted that," he half-boasted, half-confessed. "Renoir she'll never be. But it's great therapy for her."

Intimidated by this sophomoric attempt at art erudition, I sidled along to another painting and another art admirer.

"Gee," I started, trying to be sophisticated, "what does Walter Muller do anyway? Why is he having an art show?"

The man looked at me with disdain. "Walter duplicates scripts for television shows," he sneered. "This show has nothing to do with Walter. "

I'm not sure whether the look on my face reflected dumbness or dumbfoundedness. I didn't care, though, because I now had part of the answer I had been seeking. Now at least I knew what Walter did — and it had nothing to do with prostitution.

Additional conversation with other guests as I circulated rounded out my intelligence on Walter. I sought out Cindy and guided her out the door and back to the apartment. I could hardly wait to share the news with her.

"I hate to admit it, but you were right," I admitted. "Mr. Muller runs a duplicating business for television shows. The day Basil Rathbone was here Agatha had just finished duplicating the scripts on a ditto machine in their bedroom. They keep the machine at home for just such emergencies. The other man I told you about was a writer for 'Your Show of Shows.' His name is Mel Cooks or Mel Brooks or something like that. He had some last-minute script changes to make before Walter ran the scripts for the show the next day."

Cindy smiled. "And did you find out who Mimi Renoir is?"

"Geez, no, I completely forgot."

"Well, I did."

"And who is it?"

She didn't answer.

"Aren't you going to tell me?"

"Mimi Renoir is just another name for Aggie Muller," Cindy proudly declared. "Would you like to know what Aggie really does?"

"Yeah ... I gather she's not running a cat house."

"Franklin, be serious!" my wife commanded. "It's simple. For years Aggie worked for a psychiatrist as his secretary and assistant. She also paints well. Her boss, who handles mostly women who have had hysterectomies, noticed how interested some of the women were in Aggie's paintings, because some of them were hanging in the office. He asked the women if they'd like to learn how to paint. They all told him yes, and so Aggie, under the name Mimi Renoir, began giving art lessons to the clients. That's why Aggie has so many female visitors."

I was certainly relieved to learn that. And intrigued.

"Cindy, do you suppose she'd let me join her art classes?"

Knowing that I couldn't even draw a crooked line. Cindy just laughed.

CHAPTER 30

LIFE Goes to a Bachelor Party

W hen I collected trash, there were many nights that I felt like an old Princeton grad approaching a lively class reunion.

Both Joe Halstead and his roommate Sam Browning in No. 9 in 8 West were Princeton graduates. From time to time they thoroughly enjoyed collecting old classmates for a round or two or three of school songs and strong drink. When such sessions were happening during my trash rounds, Joe or Sam usually spotted me and could sometimes persuade me to join them. At such times I lingered so long I couldn't remember whether I was a Princeton tiger or a Columbia lion.

Sam and Joe, both in their mid-twenties, had been inseparable buddies for years. After having grown up together on Philadelphia's Main Line, they had both graduated from Princeton. Now both of them had advertising sales positions with LIFE magazine. They were doing so well that until Elise Saxon entered Joe's life, they had been planning to buy an old brownstone on the fashionable East Side. But then Elise had become Joe's obsession, and he refused to budge from 8 West. Sam had merely shrugged and decided not to lose any sleep over it. He was comfortable, so why worry?

Sam always professed to be perplexed about how "The Great Party" started. Joe was convinced this was Browning bull. I had my own opinion.

It was their custom to make flippant comments about "the great bash we had last Saturday night" or the "absolutely fantastic blow-out we're going to have this Saturday night" whenever they stopped in at LIFE for sales meetings or supplies.

As Sam recalled later, a cute young staff artist tried to impress him by preparing a giant poster which announced "LIFE Goes to Sam Browning's Party." When she offered this to him, normal Browning protocol dictated that he date her immediately, bed her at least once and then move on to other, more virginal prospects.

One of these prospects also worked at LIFE as an artist, and she too decided the way to Sam's heart and bed was through a poster. Her effort, in the general design of a LIFE cover, showed copy superimposed over a picture of a Roman orgy. The copy read:

LIFE Goes to a Bachelor Party
ALL Invited
Place: Sam Browning's, 8 West 90th Street
Time: About 8 p.m. …. till end
Date: Saturday!
You bring the booze
and a friend.
Sam will provide the ambience.

This creation, copies of which I later peeled off the walls outside Sam and Joe's apartment, caught the eye of the girl who had created the first poster.

In a fit of rage over being rejected by Sam, she made copies of the new poster and hung them on bulletin boards throughout the LIFE building. That was Thursday afternoon.

Neither Joe nor Sam had needed to go to LIFE the next day, Friday, so they had no idea that the party poster was creating a sensation among the staff. Instead, they were looking forward to something else they had planned for Saturday night: a few couples coming in for a small party. It would start at their apartment with drinks, progress to a buffet supper, develop into singing and games, and climax in different beds and couches in apartments scattered throughout Manhattan.

They still knew nothing about the bulletin board invitation

when their own Saturday night party was just moving into the buffet supper stage. Then other couples began to arrive. The first appeared at 8:15.

"Hi, Sam! This is Jennie, my date. Are we early?"

"Dennis? What ... ?"

"What did we think of your invitation? It was tremendous! Everybody's talking about it. I think everybody's coming, too!"

"Everybody ... ?"

"Well, since you arranged to have your poster plastered on every bulletin board in the building, who could ignore them?"

Sam felt sick, he told me. His vision of waking up tomorrow morning with his newest girl shattered like glass and disappeared. Bill came to the door to see what was keeping him there.

"Hey, Dennis! Great! Come in!"

And while the couple introduced themselves to the waiting dinner guests, Sam and Bill had a quick, quiet conference to find out what was happening. Another couple arrived, and it was from them that they learned the rest of the story. So they decided to make the best of it and gave up their idea of a quiet, intimate Saturday night. Within minutes they had turned up the music, pulled out every size and shape of drinking glass they owned and cleared some floor space.

By nine o'clock 20 more couples had turned up and crammed themselves, shoulder to shoulder, into No.9.

An hour later the party had spilled into the fifth-floor hallway, down the stairs and onto the fourth floor. It had reached this point when Cindy left for work and I tried to make my trash rounds. I couldn't get around the people so I finished my work by ignoring the fifth floor and racing through the remainder of 8 West and then all of 6 West as fast as I could.

By the time I got back to our apartment, the Browning/Halstead guests were filling every possible space from the fifth floor down through the third. Jon Hauser and Bill Brochetti had opened their apartment to the overflow and, getting into the spirit, so had Helen Jason and Dottie Rodgers.

The noise reached unbelievable levels, the temperature soared from body heat, and the smell of alcohol permeated every inch of the building.

Our phone was ringing, and when I answered it, it was difficult to hear who was calling.

"Miss Anastasia is concerned about the growing noise," a voice told me in no uncertain terms. "What is going on?"

I realized it was my boss.

"I'm trying to find out now, Mr. K," I yelled back. "It's a party. Those men who work for LIFE Magazine are having it."

"You must make them be quiet!" he demanded, somehow imagining that a word from me would bring silence. "You tell them!"

"I don't think that's a very good idea, Mr. K," I roared. "We do that, they might write about us in LIFE Magazine."

Maybe that was a below-the-belt swipe for me to take, but it seemed to work. He grunted and hung up. Apparently the thought of being written up in a national magazine so intimidated him, Mrs. K told me later, that he took the phone off the hook and went to bed.

Unfortunately, his action didn't stop our phone from ringing. Neighbors and tenants called throughout the evening. When I got tired of explaining what was happening, I changed my tactics. I simply invited the callers to go and join the party.

At eleven o'clock I was intrigued and delighted with the haunting melody and lyrics of an American folk song which was now emerging from an indeterminate point amidst the increasing cacophony created by the party. I squeezed into the mass of bodies pressed against our apartment door and eased myself down the stairs to the third floor.

There, in the Jason/Rodgers apartment, was a popular recording star performing with his guitar and 60 people singing along with him. Two photographers were busily taking pictures of the folk singer and his admiring audience.

"Do they have parties like this every week?" a man pressed to my shoulder asked me. The crowding pushed him closer.

"I hope not!" I answered. "I'm the Super here."

He grinned. "Better you than me should have the clean-up job afterwards. I don't envy you one bit." I grimaced then pushed my way back upstairs.

By 11:30 the party crowd had reached the first floor. And the police paid their first visit.

"It's the police, let us in," someone yelled when I answered my Super's buzzer. "We're here to investigate a complaint about excessive noise sir."

"Just a moment, officer," I shouted back, and instead of pushing the button to let them in, I grabbed the phone and called Jim Leonard, the current tenant in No.2 downstairs. He, too, was a policeman and I prayed he wasn't at the party.

He wasn't, and I explained what was happening and asked him to intervene with his peers. He did, thank God, successfully, three times that night. The last time – about 2:00 a.m. – he managed to do this only by giving them a shot of his own contribution to the building-wide party.

"You're going to have a lot of explaining to do," he told me on the phone between times. "It's that de Maupeou woman who's called in all the complaints."

"Thanks, Jim," I answered. "I know her, so I think I'll be able to calm her down."

I ventured out of our apartment again just after midnight. In forcing my way slowly down the stairs and across the halls, the human condition appeared to be one of extremes. Most of the guests were very high, either from booze or the atmosphere. Some were very low, very depressed by too much alcohol. And still the chatter and laughter kept the noise at a peak.

I was inching my way toward No. 5 where the folk singer was still holding forth when I bumped into an attractive brunette about Cindy's age.

"Excuse me, please," I yelled, fighting to be heard, "I must get down the stairs."

Before I knew what happened she threw her arms around me.

"Herman, honey," she cooed, "where have you been? I've been looking for you all night. Oh, Herman, I missed you so. Kiss me, Herman, kiss me!"

Obeying her own command, she kissed me and nearly overwhelmed me with alcoholic vapors from her gaping mouth.

With no room to move, it wasn't easy to break the lock she had on most of my body.

"Miss, I'm not Herman," I tried to insist. "I'm Franklin, the Super of this building. If you'll tell me what Herman looks like, I'll look for him for you."

She slipped one hand behind my head and pulled my mouth to hers again. "Herman, shut up and kiss me," she breathed. "I won't let you get away again!"

With her other hand she began to stroke my body. The stroking was accompanied with whispered suggestions that we find a place where we could be alone together.

Still anxious to get to No.5, I tried another tactic.

"Honey," I whispered, "the booze has made me groggy. Please tell forgetful Herman your name."

"Oh, Herman," the drunk woman sighed, "you're too cute for words. How could you forget Maudie? That night at my place two weeks ago? You told me I was sensational. Said you'd never forget me."

I forced a chuckle. "Forgive me, Maudie, it's the booze. You stay right here. I'll find us a place where we can be alone, and I'll come and get you.

My ruse worked. Maudie let me loose and I succeeded in working my way down the stairs to survey the state of the party.

The folk singer and another guitarist, a LIFE writer, proved to be such a talented duet that the noise on the third floor had subsided greatly because everyone had quieted down to listen to them.

Photographers, presumably from LIFE, were still busy taking dozens of pictures.

I took advantage of my freedom from Maudie, and the lull, to have a quick conference with Jim Leonard. At his suggestion I used his phone to call the Browning/Halstead apartment. A female voice answered.

"Is Sam Browning or Joe Halstead there, please?" I pleaded. "This is the Superintendent. I want to know when thy expect the party to end."

"Oh Herman, honey," came a now-familiar voice, "this is your Maudie. Did you find us a place? Please say yes. I'm so hot. Oh, I want you so badly."

I hung up. Adultery was the last thing I had in mind that frantic night.

As I was leaving Jim's apartment, I noticed several delivery people pushing their way up into the building. They were carrying everything from ice and cups and mixers to sandwiches and pastries. Was the party going to go on forever? I was beginning to think so because everything was quickly claimed, someone paid the bills, and the merriment resumed.

I nudged my way back up the stairs, carefully surveying the halls ahead of me to avoid being ensnared by the lustful Maudie. I made it to my apartment without incident.

Through a crack in my door I noticed that the deliveries continued. I couldn't imagine who was paying for everything, and during one of my forays out, I said so.

"See that man up there?" said a red-haired, red-faced partyer, pointing up the stairwell to a plump, nearly bald, bespectacled man. "It's him. He's paying for all this stuff. He's a LIFE editor!" Seeing me looking at him, the editor waved a greeting.

My admiration for editors of LIFE Magazine shot up ten levels, and for this one particularly. He was the logistical genius behind the deliveries, and he had delivery people converging on 8 West almost hourly. To embellish his success even further, he even had an enormous sturgeon packed in ice delivered at 4:00 a.m.!

Eventually, as if in response to an unspoken command, the noise began to die down and I sensed a change in the mood of the party.

The liquor and the hours had taken their toll, and the highs started to give way to boozy weariness and what one LIFE writer described as "spirituous consent," the largely imaginary lustfulness which is inspired by alcohol.

The irate phone calls I had been fielding most of the night from tenants and neighbors stopped and I collapsed on the couch and fell asleep immediately.

All too soon, at 7:30, Cindy roused me from the sleep of the dead by persistently shaking me and holding a cup of very strong coffee close to my nose.

"You'd better get a clean-up party organized," she was insisting, "or you'll lose your job. Right now the whole building could be condemned as a menace to public health."

I groaned. My head hurt.

"Franklin, were you drinking all night?"

"No, 'course not. I didn't get much sleep is all."

"Well, you'll just have to manage with what you got. And get up soon. The place reeks!"

I looked at my wife questioningly. Reeks?

"Yes, indeed," she repeated. "Of booze, wine, smoke, vomit and sex."

Never one to exaggerate, Cindy had under-described the residue of the party. The entire place stunk.

I struggled up to No. 9 and pounded on the door until Sam and Joe answered. In unison, when the door opened, they snarled "Who is it?" staring me full in the face.

"It's your Superintendent, idiots," I smirked, pushing them aside and going in. "Everyone up! On your feet! You've got work to do."

"Argh, coffee!" Joe moaned. "My kingdom for a cup of coffee. Help?"

"I'll put on a pot," said Elise Saxon, coming out of the kitchen, "but then we ALL have to help Frank." Having arrived only moments before me, she looked unbelievably fresh and alert, and I was grateful for her help in getting Sam and Joe moving.

When they were downing their coffee, Elise and I made a quick tour of the building to collect whatever trash we found. This proved to be fairly simple because someone, perhaps the logistical genius, had seen that the worst of the debris had been collected and deposited in the cans in front of the building or in bags next to the cans. Still, from recessed corners our tour garnered several paper cups, a dozen cigarette butts, two liquor bottles, a pair of panties and several partially eaten sandwiches.

Elise chatted the whole time, oblivious of my lack of answers, and gradually my depression at the prospect of the final clean-up turned into optimism.

"Don't you worry yourself one bit," she admonished. "I'll get those guys off their backsides and behind a broom in no time, you'll see. And soon there'll be no more of *these*." She tossed one more empty bottle into a trash can.

"Bet there must be fifty empty bottles there," I sighed, feeling better, though, and warming to her earnestness.

"Fifty?" she challenged, a mischievous twinkle in her eye. "Let's count them!"

I didn't believe what I was hearing. Could Elise possibly be suggesting that we root through all that trash to count the bottles?

"Well, we're going to be filthy from cleaning in a couple of hours anyway," she urged. "Come on, Frank. Let's!"

We counted 92 empty liquor bottles.

When we got back up to No.9, damp from dregs and smeared with wet cigarette ashes, our cleaning crew was ready to start work.

Armed with buckets, rags and scrub brushes provided by Cindy from the basement and with ammonia and detergent from Mr. K, the crew lacked only my instructions to get started.

I started the procession with the vacuum cleaner and had the bucket brigade follow, applying their liquid and sudsy potions wherever they were needed, which was almost everywhere.

Joe suggested "a hair of the dog" while they worked, and soon everyone had a beer to keep him company as he worked. The group became lighthearted and kept making jokes about what might have caused this stain or that one.

"This is probably where Pete wet himself with shock when Marianne said she'd go to bed with him," Sam offered.

"And this is a replay of Jack's anchovy and pickle sandwich, I think," someone else chimed in.

"Hey, you guys, keep it down," Dottie Rodgers yelled, smiling as she stepped from her doorway. "There are respectable people here still trying to sleep!"

"Good morning," everyone said in chorus to her. "Come and join us!"

"Sure, why not?" she said. "Why not? I had a good time last night, too, so it's the least I can do."

In less than a minute she was back out, appropriately dressed, and looking for a sponge and bucket.

The clean-up was completed by lunchtime and 8 West was never cleaner. Every inch of every stair and wall was vacuumed, dusted and washed, and Mr. K was ecstatic.

His nightmare was over and his building was clean. The fact that 8 West still reeked — this time of ammonia — bothered him not one iota.

CHAPTER 31

Thanks for the Memories

I was collecting trash as usual one night about three months after "The Great Party" when Joe and Sam summoned me into their apartment. Elise was with them. "Can you stay a couple of minutes?" Sam asked. "We were sitting here reminiscing about the party – 'The Great Party', that's what they call it at LIFE – so we thought you'd like to join in."

"Sure, Sam," I told him, "I have a minute. I could use a short break."

"You can't imagine the repercussions of that blow-out," Sam told me, recalling the event with a smile. "Elise, you were making notes just now, weren't you? Read some of them to Franklin."

"Let's see," she began. "According to Sam and Joe, the party started at least 18 romances. I won't read the names because you won't know them."

"Make that 19," Joe interjected. "I forgot about Alice and Mike who work in Production. The sad thing is, I think all 19 have busted up by now. I'm proud, though, that Sam and I unintentionally helped a lot of people get to know each other better."

"I'll say," Elise agreed heartily. "Sam and Joe say they know of three pregnancies, all traceable to the heat – pun intended – of that memorable evening. Is that right, men, or am I being too seminal in my calculations?"

"Puns, puns, puns!" Sam complained, although he was smiling. "Enough! Get on with the accounting."

"Well, I think that covers most of the romantic items," Elise said.

"Does anyone care to add to the true confessions ledger?"

I spoke up. "You forgot about George Fink, I think. Is he on your list, Elise?"

"No, he's not."

"Do you all know George?" I asked the three. "He was in number four, under Elise. Short, almost bald, very quiet."

Sam and Joe said they'd seen him but didn't know him. Elise had met him just briefly once on the stairs.

"And is Mona Mecklenberg on your list?" I asked Elise.

"What the hell do you know about that bossy broad?" Joe demanded. "She's clean disappeared. Hasn't been seen since the party."

"Gentlemen and Elise," I announced, "what happened to dear Mona is that she met dear George. At the party. Seems George opened his door a crack to see what was going on and Mona literally fell over into his arms."

Suddenly, I had the total attention of all three. I went on. "She was leaning against the door when he opened it. According to George, he caught her and both fell backwards into the apartment, she almost completely on top of him. She must've been feeling playful because as she rolled off George, she looked him in the eyes and said – and this is according to George – 'First time I ever fell for a man.' What she didn't know was that George was a sexual fuse in search of a match. Before either of them knew what was happening, they were in George's bed!"

A split-second of astonished silence followed, then suddenly and spontaneously my friends Joe, Elise and Sam burst into great peals of surprised laughter. Sam, the first to catch his breath, asked how I knew all this.

"You have to know George to understand," I said. "I'd been his confidante for months. There was nothing he didn't tell me. He also told me that after their first encounter he was determined that Mona wouldn't get away. He proposed to her that very night and they were married within the week. He wouldn't let her go to work or even call work. He was petrified he'd lose her. They moved to a house in White Plains about two weeks after they were married."

"Well, I'll be damned," Joe said, his face pensive. "Wait till they hear about this at LIFE." He smiled, only just realizing the magnitude of what I had just revealed. "Miss Take Charge herself swept off her feet. Wow! I can't believe it. I always thought she was ugly as sin."

"Whoa, Joe," Sam intoned. "Must I remind you that I took her out myself shortly after we started at LIFE? She's bossy all right but as bright as they come. May she and George live in peace."

"Go on with the list, Elise," Joe said. "Pray read the rest of the carnage."

"Well, let's see," she commenced. "Jim Barstow, a picture editor, hit a telephone pole on his way home to Long Island. According to my two sources, his injuries were largely to his dignity. Six good people lost their jobs. Seems some of the junior staffers were too frank with their bosses – or forgot they were present."

"Remember that crack you made about our boss?" Joe cut in. "When I saw he was just behind you when you made it, I thought we were goners."

Sam grinned. "Fortunately he was drunk as usual," he said.

Elise went back to her list. "Three people found new jobs," she read. "One was an unemployed secretary who crashed the party. Couldn't type worth a wooden nickel but apparently does something well. Another was a female runner who barely speaks English. She's now a copywriter. The third ... Joe, who was the third?"

"That cute black girl who kept bugging one of the picture editors to make her a model," Joe answered. "Would you believe she's now a sales clerk? Cute as hell but doesn't know a thing about sales or clerical work. I guess I'll have to teach her."

"Joseph Aloysius Halstead, you'll do no such thing!" Elise declared. "Not if you wish to have peace in this house."

"Hey, Elise," Sam interrupted, "you forgot the biggest news!

Franklin, dear friend, you're about to make your debut in the pages of LIFE! The pictures they took that evening will appear in a story in two weeks. What you didn't know is that our bash was really a fund-raising party for orphaned Korean children. At least, that's what the copy will say."

The expression of disbelief and confusion on my face prompted him to add to his announcement.

"What you also didn't know was that someone took your picture while you were necking with the chick from the editorial department. Cindy will never know, though. You two were so close together you look like a two-headed body."

"Are you kidding, Sam?" I gulped, panic stricken. "My god, Cindy'll never forgive me!"

"You mean you never told her about dear Maudie?" Sam teased. "What's the matter, man? You got no guts?"

"Guts I got, also brains. But I may not have the brains long if that picture ever runs," I answered, my mouth suddenly dry.

Sam laughed. "Relax. Here's the picture. It was too fuzzy for the story. What would you like me to do with it? Give it to Cindy?"

"Bastard!" I half-smiled, "give me that damn thing!" I grabbed the photo, ripped it in half and tossed it in the trash – with a very audible sigh of relief.

Joe and Sam laughed at me. "We wouldn't have shown it to Cindy, you know that," they said.

"Yeah, well you never know," I had to say.

As I was leaving to continue my rounds, I remembered one more thing to add to their list.

"Guess who's having the last word on the party?" I challenged. "He's short, has gray hair, built like a tank, has a slight Polish accent."

"Mr. K?" they called in unison.

"That's right. Mr. K. He showed me some language he's adding to all his leases. Can you guess what it says? It's simple and straightforward."

"Yeah, sure," came the comment from the trio. "What does it say?"

"It says, 'No party or gathering for the purpose of amusement or entertainment shall transcend the boundaries of the apartment occupied by the lessee.'"

Sam roared with delighted laughter. "Hey, we're immortal," he chuckled. "That's the Browning-Halstead amendment to Karbowski's great commandments! Isn't that great! If we're not careful, the Browning-Halstead amendment will become more famous than Murphy's law."

On that not-so-solemn note, and with lustful Maudie's photo remnants safely in my trash bag, I resumed my nightly rounds.

CHAPTER 32

Mr. Milquetoast

"So if by chance we ever did meet again, you wouldn't say anything to my Mona about, uh, that unfortunate incident?"

It was George Fink, here to hand back the keys to his apartment. Newly married to Mona Mecklenberg, the woman he had met at the LIFE party, he was ready to leave for their new home in White Plains.

"If she ever found out, I'd die of mortification."

"Not a word, Mr. Fink," I promised. "You have my word on it."

He left looking much happier than when he had arrived only a minute or two ago, and I mentally wished him well.

The 'unfortunate incident' to which he had been referring had involved such a giant step out of his usual character that I reviewed everything I knew about the man before I permitted myself to recreate a mental picture of the incident itself. Like his meeting with Mona, it had involved a chance meeting with a woman.

I first met George Fink in Number Four 8 West when he called me and suggested that I visit him to investigate what he called "an epidemic of foamy fulminations in the commode." He was referring, of course, to the Plouviers' bathroom-brand shampoo and the resulting suds.

George struck me as being very laconic and introspective at our first meeting. He said little and chose his words and his manner of delivering them very carefully. A short man whom I judged to be about 50, he carefully combed what little hair he had to cover his predominant baldness. He was dressed casually in expensive tweeds and had a book in his hands which, I would learn, he would read by squinting through the tortoiseshell glasses which reposed on the tip of his nose.

George proved to be far from laconic, at least with me. Less than a week after I called to examine the soapsuds, he summoned me to his apartment again, this time to stop the kitchen faucet from dripping. No sooner had I picked up the pipe wrench at his sink than he began asking my advice on a wide range of matters.

What did I think would be the best place to invest five thousand dollars? Given the nearly flat state of the Noyes' savings account, our only asset, I suggested that he might find older and wiser counsel on this matter.

"Well then," he went on, "what about my living room? Do you think I should redecorate it with more contemporary furniture?"

I looked out into his living room.

"No, I think not. Definitely."

He asked why. I told him that the few pieces he had appeared to be fine examples of early American furniture.

"They are, indeed," he agreed. "Each is an authentic antique. The grandfather's clock dates back to about 1750; it really belongs in a museum."

"Then why did you ask me..."

"Whether they should be replaced?" he smiled, finishing my question. "I've recently learned to enjoy having my opinion confirmed, that's why."

And on he went. Where did I think he should go for a vacation this year? To the Islands? To Spain? To the West Coast?

In my stunned state, I muttered I was sure he would find any of these possibilities acceptable.

The questions continued during all the time I worked on the faucet and, inexperienced plumber that I was, it was more than an hour.

Despite his explanation, the reason why George Fink would seek the advice of an unsophisticated college student was still not clear to me. It was only after we began to talk several times a week that it became clear.

Our talks were usually triggered by a call in which George would ask me to come down to "help me" with something. The "help me" sessions usually happened at 8:30 in the evening and seldom lasted more than half an hour.

George was a free lance advertising copywriter and he was also the author of a dozen best-selling children's books, each of which was cherished for its tender re-creation of the imaginary world of children. According to George, the "help me" sessions helped him create some of his best advertising one-liners and headlines. And he said they also helped him decide how the imaginary situations in the minds and lives of the heroes of his latest children's story would evolve.

I was flattered that George considered me a good discussion partner, and he eventually dropped his non-existent repair requests. Instead, he would just call and ask if I could come down. If I had the time and didn't have to study, I went.

I learned that George was the sixth of seven children born to the uneducated but hardworking wife of a truck driver in the Kensington section of Philadelphia. His father died of a heart attack when George was two, and his mother and older sisters and brothers held the family together by taking in washing, peddling baked goods to neighborhood stores, and hiring out for housecleaning and lawn care chores.

The way the Fink family struggled to survive permanently shaped George's life. As a tyke, he was deposited in a play pen or corner and expected to stay quietly. As he grew older, his mother continued to expect him to "keep his place" and remain quiet.

George escaped the boredom of his confined existence by reading and re-reading his limited library of children's books and then re-creating each story with himself as the hero. In George's imaginary world, he and his loyal liberationists – usually camels, giraffes and rabbits – rid the world of all its sins and hardships.

In school, George proved to be a brilliant student. He was graduated near the top of his high school class and used a City of Philadelphia scholarship to study English at the University of Pennsylvania.

When he was graduated in 1932 – again near the top of his class – jobs of any kind were hard to find. With the aid of a professor, he finally secured a job at a Philadelphia insurance company writing materials for insurance agents and occasional articles for the company magazine.

More out of boredom than a desire to earn money through additional writing, George wrote his first children's book in 1937. It was immediately snapped up by a delighted publisher, and George had, with the exception of the war years, written another book every year since.

His first book brought him to the attention of the president of a large Philadelphia advertising agency. The man had bought the book for his son and became so intrigued by it that he arranged to meet George. He offered him a job as a copywriter almost immediately. George and the agency thrived.

Then Pearl Harbor was bombed. George's emotion that day was so intense that he rushed to join the Marines the minute the recruiting office opened its doors on December the Eighth.

Surviving boot training did much to shore up George's self-confidence, and he even hoped he would be assigned to combat duty. It was not to be, however. He was instead assigned to Washington and given a small staff to prepare training manuals on the care and use of small arms.

Immediately after the war, bored with manuals and trying to nurse a dimming spark of self-accomplishment, George headed for New York and another job as a copywriter. Less than six months after his discharge, his sixth children's book was published, and the subdued raves which the literary world reserves for this genre did much to help his opinion of himself.

While George's professional life flourished, his personal life languished. He had no close friends and he seemed to be unable to establish relationships of any kind with women. As a result he was lonely. Desperately lonely.

In his books, George's characters were tender, thoughtful and kind. Fathers lavished generous attention and gifts upon their children, and mothers dealt with those around them with love, selfless concern and care.

In real life George had never known the spontaneous love of a woman. His relationships with the opposite sex were confined solely to prostitutes, and these biologically essential liaisons were becoming less and less frequent. His relationships with real, live children were non-existent.

Then came Grace Johns into the life of George Fink. I learned about her at a Sunday morning "help me" session, and I could see she transformed George's life.

True to his custom, George told me, he slept late "that" particular Sunday morning. He got up about ten, took a shower then put on a bathrobe. After fixing some coffee, he settled down for a couple of hours with the paper. His door buzzer sounded.

George was an excellent storyteller and already he had me anxious to learn what followed.

"And then?" I urged.

George smiled warmly, remembering every moment. "I pushed the buzzer to release the front door and waited for whoever it was to come up and knock."

"And then?"

"'Well, there stood Grace."

Slowly, lovingly, he selected the proper words to tell me about her. I could see it was very important to him that she be properly "introduced" to me and that I not get the wrong impression. So I waited, silently, and listened as his story went on.

Grace, twentyish, frumpy, with dark complexion and hair, was a Jehovah's Witness. Going door to door dispensing copies of "Watch

Tower" and "Awake" was an integral part of her religion. She had started her spiel, intensely, and continued in that manner as she entered George's apartment and went, at his invitation, to sit on the couch. Not wanting to interrupt her train of thought, she had beckoned for George to come and join her.

Entranced and speechless, somehow George had obeyed. For some inexplicable reason which he still could not understand, he found himself being drawn to her. Incredibly, she seemed to be feeling the same attraction.

"It was as if someone had waved a magic wand over us," George said. "We were like the beautiful woman and the prince, destined for each other."

I looked at him to continue.

"Franklin," George suddenly blurted in a completely different tone of voice, "I'm only telling you this now because I think you know me well enough to understand. It's important to me that you don't take this the wrong way."

"I won't, George," I heard myself say in a low, mature voice that I didn't recognize. "Just you see. I'll understand."

He nodded, grateful that I wasn't making light of his tale.

"Grace was, and still is, a profoundly devoted woman. And while I don't share the specific convictions of her religion, I respect what she believes."

Itching to hear more faster, I hoped my face didn't show my growing lack of patience. I knew it was difficult for George to be telling me what had happened, so I forced myself to sit still.

"She is probably the most moral woman born in this century," George declared. "And, because of what she did for me, she is the most revered. By me, at least."

Once more I nodded and, feeling that he had properly prepared the ground for the balance of his narration, he switched back to his nostalgic recounting.

"As I said, I felt like the storybook prince who had finally found his storybook ending – the woman of his dreams. Grace intoxicated me, enthralled me, exhilarated me, I could hear her talking but I no longer heard a word she said. Then she stopped talking."

The balance of George's story came tumbling rapidly out, and I listened in startled, respectful surprise.

Grace's proselytizing had somehow stirred George's manhood into erect form and Grace had noticed. Before either knew what was happening, they were enmeshed in a passionate lock on the couch. Their spontaneous love-making reached its zenith yet never a word had been spoken. Then, spent and breathless, they remained clutched together for several minutes, thinking of their intimacy. Grace spoke only two words more. When George found the courage to ask her name, she said "Grace Johns" and nothing more. Soon afterwards, chagrined but composed, she fled from the apartment and from George's life.

George was so moved by the tender, wonderful moments he had spent with Grace that he became determined to find a wife. My mission, according to George, was to prepare him for this. I must design a campaign that would strengthen his shaky confidence, overcome his intense shyness and make him attractive to women.

Fortunately for me, and probably for George, before I could design such an impossible campaign, the LIFE party happened, delivering to George a storybook-ending package of love and life that went by the name of Mona Mecklenberg.

And now George was married and on his way to a new life in White Plains. I hoped he would be happy and loved for the rest of his life. And certainly he would never have to be afraid that I would pass on the story of his "unfortunate incident." For, in truth, there was nothing unfortunate about what happened between George and Grace. It was the most fortunate thing that had ever happened in George's experience. It gave him the will to find a niche for himself. It gave him determination. It gave him life.

CHAPTER 33

My Explosive Legacy

G eorge Fink telephoned me a week after he moved out.
"I completely forgot to tell you...I left some things in the basement," he said.

"What things?" I asked. "What do you want me to do with them?"

"Remember I told you I was in the Marines?" he said. "Well, I was frustrated that I was never sent overseas to see any action. So I started buying mementos from returning servicemen who needed money more than souvenirs. That's what's in the basement."

"You mean old swords and Nazi flags and that sort of thing?" I probed.

"Uh, not exactly," he said, hesitating. "My mementos are all sort of, uh, deadly."

"Deadly?" I demanded. "What kind of euphemism is that? Will your souvenirs kill people or not?"

"Yes, Franklin, they will," George told me. "But only if improperly used. If you take care of them, they'll be perfectly safe."

"If *I* take care of them?" I challenged. "What are you asking me? What am I supposed to do with them?

George sighed. "Franklin, you misunderstand. They all are really perfectly safe things – a few guns, a shell, some unusual knives. Stuff like that." His tone reminded me of a parent talking to an exasperating child.

I repeated my question. "What am I supposed to do with the stuff?"

"As safe as those things are, the mere thought of them frightens Mona," he said. "So I'm giving them to you."

I didn't know what to say. What was I going to do with his arsenal?
"Franklin?" he ventured.

"Yes, George, I'm here," I sighed. "I'm just trying to think what to do. Look, is it safe to touch those things? Can I handle them without getting killed?"

George chuckled. "Don't be stupid. You were in the Army. I'm sure you must have handled weapons like these."

I groaned. "Please don't do me any favors. You see, I..."

"Now they're all yours," I heard George saying. Before I could say another word, he told me I could dispose of his mementos any way I wished, then hung up.

"Goodbye," I said miserably into an empty phone.

To be sure, I had handled the usual weapons that Army basic training exposed all soldiers to – the M-l, the carbine, the bayonet, the hand grenade, and the anti-tank gun. But I had also been mightily glad to pass them over for a syringe and a microscope. The thought of acquiring a new set of military playthings depressed me.

What does one do with a collection of deadly weapons? I didn't know, and it was only at Cindy's urging that I finally went to the basement storeroom to examine my unwanted legacy.

An old Army footlocker in the far corner of the back room caught my eye. Sure enough, it had George's name, rank and serial number stenciled all over the lid.

It was locked but the key was taped to one side. As I raised the lid, I was surprised to see GI clothing filling the locker. Each item, however, bulged in a most unnatural manner.

I unwound an old olive drab shirt to find the most interesting knife I had ever seen. The handle was enormous, about a foot long, and the blade was several inches wide and made of leaded steel. It had several layers of electrical tape wound around the handle. But the knife was easy to hold and beautifully balanced. Obviously this was an anti-personnel weapon that could be used to split a man's head – with either the blade or the handle. My guess was that it was used by commandos or members of the OSS on clandestine missions in the middle of the night.

Feeling very uncomfortable, I reluctantly continued my probe. Wrapped in another shirt was a fully loaded clip of shells and a magnificent 45-caliber pistol which appeared to be handcrafted. The handle looked like it was made of ivory and it had been carved into an intricate design.

I had hardly made a dent in the contents of the footlocker and already I had the capability of wiping out the tenants in 8 West singlehandedly.

By the time I finished unwrapping George's arsenal, I had one carbine in what looked like new condition, the 45-caliber pistol, a 38-caliber pistol, a rifle which I guessed was Italian and about the same caliber as the American M-I, six knives, all different sizes, and one large brass shell which I guessed would fit an anti-tank gun.

Oh, yes. And I also had a wardrobe of old military clothing, none of which was my size.

I brought Cindy down to see the deadly collection.

"What do you think we should do with all these things?" I asked her.

"Let's give the whole works to our fathers," she answered immediately. "They both love to hunt and fish. Surely they can use these things?"

"Well, if they can't use them, they could sell them," she added. "You can't give everything away, though."

"Why not?" I asked.

"Well, I want that shell," she said, "and that awesome looking knife. When we can afford it, we'll make the shell into a lamp. As for the knife, well, I may need it if you ever get too fresh."

"Get fresh?" I said. "My dear, I am fresh, and I intend to stay that way. So please keep that damned knife out of sight."

I told Cindy that I was proud of her. She had the knack of reducing problems to their basic elements and I didn't. In less than a minute she had reduced my overwhelming arsenal problem to a manageable size and had offered a solution.

Our fathers were delighted with their potentially deadly haul. They so enjoyed playing with their new toys that they began to visit each other frequently. They also promised us an annual supply of venison in exchange for what we had given them.

Cindy placed the shell – it was about a foot long and four inches wide at the base – upright on my commodious desk. She dusted it regularly, occasionally moved it to see how it would look as a lamp in other locations, and regularly tapped it with a knife or fork. She loved to hear the ping of brass.

As Cindy intended it would, the shell became a source of much speculation and conversation. It was not unusual for a friend to lift it high to examine the base or to shake it to hear what might be inside. There was no doubt there was plenty of something in it. It was very heavy.

One evening I was studying for a test in international economics and waiting for my fellow student, Harry Burak, to join me. Harry and I had met in class and had discovered that by studying the subject together we did better on tests.

He was in a great mood when he arrived. "I'm ready for this test like I was never ready for a test before," he declared. "I couldn't sleep last night so I kept studying. By the time I did doze off, I knew this stuff cold. Still do. Why don't I start by asking you questions. Okay, let's see if you understand this Keynesian baloney."

Harry paused to think about the phrasing of his first question. His good humor was contagious, and I waited quite contentedly as he paced the room, his arms clasped behind him.

Suddenly he froze. He seemed to stop breathing. His hands didn't move, nor did his face.

"What's the matter?" I asked, startled at the dramatic change in him. "You feel okay?"

"What's that on your desk?" he whispered, his lips pursed in a thin, white line.

"That? It's a shell. I mean shell casing. A guy who used to live here gave it to me. Cindy wants to make it into a lamp."

Harry frowned but didn't answer. Then slowly, ever so cautiously, he moved towards the desk where the brass piece stood.

"Harry, what the hell's wrong with you?" I demanded, puzzled at his lack of reply. "Look, if you want to examine that thing, just say so! Want me to sling it to you the way they do in the movies?"

"Don't move!" Harry boomed. "Get the hell out of here!"

"Come off it," I smiled, convinced he was joking. "Let's get back to work."

"Listen to me!" Harry ordered. "I was in the Army, too! In the Ordinance Corps. My job was to dismantle bombs and shells just like this one!"

The realization of what was telling me hit home. My stomach clenched into a tight knot of fear. "You mean it's live?" I asked stupidly. "It could explode?"

I felt very weak. All I could see was Cindy tapping it with a knife ... and, oh God! We could all be dead!

Harry moved carefully towards the shell and made a quick visual examination. Then he gently ran his finger along the casing, all the while shaking his head.

"Damn it, Noyes," he said sternly, "why don't you play with *normal* toys? Now look here. This shell is *not* dead. It's loaded and it could go off with the slightest jar."

"How was I supposed to know?" I said weakly. "What should I do?"

"Start at the top floor and get everyone in this building and the adjoining one outside. Quick! I'm going to call the bomb squad and get that damned thing out of here."

His pronouncement all but put me into deep shock. He took me by the arm, shoved me towards the door and assured me that everything would be all right – maybe.

"Look, don't you panic," he commanded. "You have to be calm because people's lives are in danger. Get them out of here …fast!"

I didn't need to be told twice.

I raced through 8 West and 6 West and urged everyone to get outside until the bomb had been removed.

Harry called the police the instant I left. I was still evacuating 6 West when the first contingent of police arrived and blocked off West 90th Street at both Central Park West and Columbia Avenue.

A padded van and four men looking like home plate umpires arrived only moments later.

The commotion of the evacuated tenants on the sidewalk generated more commotion by curiosity seekers. It was a while before I realized that generating much of the to-do was Mr. K in search of me.

Quickly I told him the story of George Fink's armory and of how Cindy and had come into possession of the brass nightmare.

"I nearly have a heart attack every time I think of that shell," I said. "Cindy and I carried it upstairs like it was a loaf of bread. And Cindy has dusted it, rolled it around the desk and once almost let it roll off! Oh God, that thing could have killed us and half the people in the building!"

For once, Mr. K was speechless. He merely turned to watch the bomb squad people setting up for their task.

By the time Cindy returned from work, the bomb had been removed – safely – and Harry Burak and I were back at our studies.

"Hi, guys," she said, corning in and throwing her jacket on the sofa. "Been at it all day?"

Harry looked at me to answer.

"Yes, off and on," I told my wife.

"Great. I'll fix you some coffee."

I looked back at Harry. Neither of us said a word.

"I've decided what I'm going to do with that shell," Cindy suddenly said out of the blue. "I saw the most wonderful article in a magazine, and it shows how to use old shells and other bits of brass to make lamps and candelabras and all sorts of things. Do you know how much brass costs?"

I grimaced. "Harry," I asked, "is she asking a question of economics or metaphysics?"

"Harry stood up and collected his books and papers. "Cindy," he said, "we're done and I think I'd better be getting back. After I'm gone, ask your husband what happened to your brass lamp."

How do you explain a near tragedy to the person who could have been the central figure therein? Very slowly. With a lot of coffee. And a lot more love to control the shock.

CHAPTER 34

Porgy and Mess

I had completely forgotten about the great fishing trip Sam Browning had organized until the buzzer sounded and I was summoned to the sidewalk to "see what we got. You'll be sorry you didn't come with us!"

It was a Sunday night in mid-August, the weather was unbearably hot and humid, and my only regret at the moment was that I had to stir.

The scene on the sidewalk in front of 8 West was straight from the pages of the Harvard Lampoon.

Sam Browning's faded jeans and denim shirt were stiff from salt water and fish scales, and he was only slightly less stiff from the Scotch he must have been sipping between bites all day long. A salt water rod in one hand and a bottle of beer in the other, he was standing between two very soggy and completely stuffed burlap bags.

Clustered around him were the mighty fishermen of 8 West: Joe Halstead, Elise Saxon, Jon Hauser, Bill Brochetti, Helen Jason and Dottie Rodgers. All were filthy, slightly-to-badly sunburned and feeling no pain whatsoever.

"Franklin," Sam shouted at me, "look! These bags are full of fish. Porgies! And we caught 'em all. Must be a hundred and fifty, two hundred of them. Iced and dead fresh. We got enough fish for a year. Ain't you proud of us?"

"Sure, sure, I'm real proud of you," I smiled. "But tell me, what are you going to do with them?"

"Do with them?" he repeated. "Eat them, of course! Freeze some and give the rest away. No problem."

"Have you looked in your freezer, lately, Sam?" I challenged. "It'll hold two or three fish if you're lucky. Four at the most."

"You're a no-good son of a spoilsport," Sam mumbled, deflated. "We'll take care of our little fishies. Don't you worry about us."

I assured my dear friends I had no intention of worrying about their "fishies." But I did suggest, strongly, that they get upstairs into bathtubs before they stunk up the neighborhood.

I returned to my apartment to read a paper on the Arab refugee problem, but the weather-induced torpidity overwhelmed me. I must have been asleep two hours when Cindy nudged me awake. "Look what Sam gave me," she was chirping. She sounded pleased.

I opened my eyes to see my wife, still in her nurse's uniform, waving a pair of porgies before me.

"Hi, sweetheart. When did you get home?"

"Just now," she answered, walking towards the kitchen. "And just as I was coming in, Sam knocked and handed me these. He tried to give me more but I told him I wouldn't know what to do with them. Don't they look good?"

"Yeah, delicious," I said, somewhat sarcastically. "Please get them away from my nose."

"Come on, honey, wake up," she urged. "I want you to clean them. We'll have one for dinner tomorrow and I'll freeze the other."

While I was cleaning the porgies I told Cindy about the fishing trip and the scene that greeted me just before dark that evening. She too then began to wonder what the intrepid boys from LIFE planned to do with a hundred and fifty or so porgies.

About midnight I started my trash rounds, as usual, on the floor above us. Sam and all his fishing friends were still wide awake and jovially drinking and discussing what to do with the next batch of fish.

"Get rid of any yet?" I asked.

"Relax, my friend," Sam said. "We'll get rid of these fish if we have to eat 'em all ourselves. And they're damn good eating. We just ate six for late supper and we're about to clean some more for the pan. We also gave a mess of them away to people in the building, and we've been calling friends to come and get some. No sweat. We'll get rid of them."

Not wanting to cool his enthusiasm, I merely nodded then wished them good night.

The next morning, Monday, Cindy and I took a train for a day trip to visit our families in the Poconos, and Tuesday I was involved with classes until late afternoon. Thus, the affairs of 6 and 8 West were far from my mind the better part of 48 hours.

When I collected trash Tuesday night, I was greeted by Sam so effusively that I immediately became suspicious that something was amiss.

"Franklin, dear friend!" he said. "We've missed you these past two days. Where have you been? It's never the same here, I think, without you. Your very presence adds such class, such élan to this environment that you are immediately missed!"

"Hey, knock it off, Sam," I responded tartly. "You're beautiful, too, but what's this all about?"

No sooner had I voiced my question than I knew the answer.

"What did you do with the fish, Sam?" I asked, not really wanting to hear his answer. And just at that moment I realized that the whole floor stunk. I repeated my question.

"Have you no faith?" Sam purred. "A Princeton man always keeps his word. I told you we would dispose of the fish and we did."

Suspicious, I asked how.

"We Princeton men never divulge our secrets to infidels," came Sam's reply.

The blank expression on Sam's face told me it would be useless to demand specifics.

"Sam, you keep talking like that," I threatened, "you'll soon smell as bad as the fish."

He merely shrugged, grinning mischievously. "See you."

Late the next afternoon after a full day of classes, I returned to our apartment thirsty and hot. After pulling open the doors to the balcony to catch any stray breeze, I poured myself a tall glass of iced tea. Immediately I realized that from somewhere was coming the overwhelming stench of dead fish. Walking back towards the balcony to see if I could figure out the source, I realized something else. Either the building was being invaded by banshees or there was a colossal cat fight in the vicinity. The high-pitched screeching seemed to be coming from the roof of 8 West.

I put down my iced tea and went out into the hallway to go upstairs to investigate. Just then, Mr. K came puffing up behind me. Apparently he had pieced together the same clues as I had and had arrived at the same conclusion: Something was rotten – or dead – in 8 West.

We quickly established that no one was at home on the fifth floor so I used my passkey to gain entrance to both apartments. Both were unusually clean, especially the bathtubs, and both were almost free of fish odor. Yet still the screeching was above us. It was now obvious that both the stench and the cat-like noises were coming from the roof.

Access to the roof from the fifth floor was in a tiny enclosed area in the rear portion of the stairwell. Here a ten-foot ladder led to a roof hatch covered with a heavy trap door.

As I climbed the ladder, which Mr. K steadied, the noise became deafening. I now had no doubt that our roof was indeed the scene of a colossal cat fight. I also suspected that the source of contention was spelled P-O-R-G-Y. I was, however, in no hurry to open the trap door.

I eased it up slowly enough to get an unforgettable view of the event of the century: a porgy orgy! Porgies were spread all over the roof, and it appeared that every fish was being attacked by two or more snarling, scrawny cats. Every castoff in Manhattan must have been there. When one of the more brazen felines sought to make off with some loot, it was immediately attacked by its starving brothers.

Why I kept easing up the trap door I'll never know. I suspect it was sheer fascination with such a gory scene. Whatever, before I knew what happened, I was the painful center in a dispute over one of Sam's beloved porgies.

It happened like this. I lifted the door until it was open about a foot. A leaping gray cat, the remains of a porgy in tow, hit me squarely in the face, lighted on my shoulder long enough to dig me with its claws, then launched itself and the porgy down on a trajectory that caught the craning Mr. K smack in the face.

I dropped the trap door the instant the cat hit me and struggled to keep my balance. Mr. K, in turn, let go of the ladder as he was hit, and he, the cat and the porgy ejected from the enclosure simultaneously, fell to the landing, leaving me to plummet down to fill the space they vacated.

I was stunned and may well have been knocked silly for a few moments. When alertness returned, I was aware of a ruckus in the hallway.

There was Mr. K hotly in pursuit of the cat, wielding the tar-soaked broom we used to patch the roof. Down the stairs they went, Polish invectives on the trail of cat screeches.

By the time I was on my feet and steady, Mr. K had returned with the news that the cat had been driven from the building. The porgy, however, was obviously still nearby. Mr. K picked up the remains of the offending fish, told me to forget about the other cats for now and went off muttering something under his breath about Joe and Sam.

He confronted the producers of the porgy orgy that night.

It was at about eight o'clock, at any rate, that I began to hear the unmistakable sounds of a harsh Polish-English confrontation.

Polish accusations were followed, in Princeton-polished diction, by English protestations of shame and sorrow. The confrontation lasted about 15 minutes before the irate Mr. K stormed down the stairs and out of the building.

As curious as I was to know the details, I decided to wait until my trash collection time before speaking to Joe or Sam about the contretemps. At present I was still so angry at the Princeton pair that I was afraid I might have added physical violence to Mr. K's verbal lashings.

Joe and Sam were waiting for me. Both were the picture of contriteness.

"Jesus, Franklin, we're sorry," they started. "We thought we'd solved the problem. But all we did was nearly kill you. Can you forgive us?"

"I won't charge you for the scratches or bruises," I said, "but I would like the five bucks it cost me for a tetanus shot."

"Yes, yes," they nodded, both reaching for their wallets and each handing me five dollars.

"Here's your money, Franklin. We promise we won't ever pull a stunt like that again."

"Why did you put the fish on the roof anyway?" I demanded. "Why didn't you just put them in the trash?"

"And admit we were damned fools for bringing so many fish home?" Sam groaned. Joe chimed in, "Besides, it seemed like a good way to recycle the fish."

I pocketed the two fives, not feeling the slightest bit bad at having made a profit, and picked up my trash-collecting bag. Nothing I could say would make either of them feel any better or any worse, so I just shrugged and set off down the stairs.

As always, Mr. K had the last word – at the expense of future tenants.

His newest leasing commandment read:

"Tenants shall not dispose of excess foods or food wastes, especially fish, except through the normal disposal methods provided by the landlord.

"Tenants are absolutely forbidden to enter or in any way use the roof of the building in which their apartment is located."

Translated, it all came down to a simple sanction: No more porgy orgies!

CHAPTER 35

Starring the Naked Truth

In my usual two-fingered hunt and peck fashion, I was typing a paper when a knock came at the door.

Facing me as I opened it was a highly agitated Roderick St. John.

"Good morning, Major," I said. "What can I do for you?"

"Franklin, look there;" he blustered, pointing to the upper right corner of my door. "What do you suppose it means? There is one on my door and on every door in the building. Who put them there? What can they mean?"

What the Major was pointing to was a silver paper star, the kind teachers use in kindergartens and grade schools to reward perfect attendance or excellence in tests.

As my mind struggled with the Major's questions, he added more information which only befogged my mental grasp of the situation even more.

"The colors of the stars vary," he went on. "Some are gold, some silver, some a shimmering blue, some purple. Do you suppose there's a pattern of some kind? Do you suppose some maniac is trying to tell us that terrible things are about to happen to us? Gold stars shot on sight? Silver stars to the gallows? Blue stars will be ravished, then poisoned? Purple ..."

"Whoa, Major, whoa!" I settled a hand on his shoulder to try and calm him down. "My god, man, you'll start a riot with your talk of murder and rape. I haven't the foggiest idea how the stars got on the doors. But if I had to guess, I'd say some mischievous kids did it. Calm down, go back to your apartment and let me worry about the stars. Please, Major, go ... and don't talk this way to anyone else.

I'll let you know what I find out."

Reluctantly he nodded and left. Once he was out of sight, I was curious enough about the stars to make a quick survey of the doors on the third, fourth and fifth floors. Sure enough, they were all starred in the same corner. I decided it had to have been a childish prank or game and promptly forgot the whole thing.

I had hardly started my weekly cleaning that Saturday morning when Jon Hauser, shouting to be heard above the vacuum cleaner, summoned me into his apartment. There I was greeted by Joe, Sam, Bill, Dottie and Helen.

Jon shushed everyone.

"We were just comparing notes about our experience with your extraordinary Major," he told me. "My Major?" I asked. "You mean Major St. John?"

"The one and only," they chorused.

"Don't tell me," I said. "He asked you, maybe all of you, what those little stars on your doors meant, right? And he got dramatic? Did he suppose that the residents of all gold-starred apartments would be maced to death in the middle of Broadway? Did he suggest that the gorgeous females in our midst would be ravished before being poisoned? Did he ...?"

I couldn't go on because they were all laughing so loud.

"Franklin," countered Sam, "that's beautiful. Did the Major really say those things to you?"

"Well, not exactly, but close. He was speculating on all sorts of bizarre behavior. "Gold-starred residents would be shot. And so on. What the hell is going on, anyway? Do you suppose he's trying to concoct a plot for his next Brisbane mystery?"

Jon stood up, dramatically held his arms above his head to quiet the raucous bunch and then said softly, "Franklin, Franklin, listen, we have a story. We had some fun with the Major this week. Dottie, you tell him."

Dottie started unfolding the story, smiling all the while. "I was about to start up the stairs a few nights ago," she began, "when the Major suddenly appeared. For some reason, he startled me. I had often seen him peering or leering at me from his doorway, you see, but I didn't really know him and I certainly didn't know why he peered like that. 'Miss,' he said, in a charming English accent,' may I have just a moment? A most peculiar thing has been happening in this building. Have you noticed that there is a little star in the upper right corner of your front door? Every door in the building has one. What in the world do you suppose they portend?!'

"Well, I had had one horrible day so I didn't feel like playing games. I simply said, beats me – why don't you come up some time and we'll talk about it. At that point I left."

She continued. "I told Jon about it later that night and we were chatting about it when Sam and Joe came in. Joe, you take it from there."

Joe grinned.

"We speculated on what the stars might be all about," he began, "and Sam even ran around checking that the doors had them. We reached the same conclusion you did – the Major had to be the culprit. Why? Because who was the first one to notice the stars? Who was the only one asking about the stars? The Major! We decided he had sex problems and wanted to see what the possibilities in the building were."

"We decided that if sex really was his problem, we'd give him something to think about," Joe interrupted. "We concocted stories about what each of us would say when the Major visited us, and we gave each other permission to embellish the basic stories to their tastes. Dottie and Helen were the first to be visited by the Major."

At this point Helen picked up the story. "It was about eight o'clock the other evening. Dottie was washing her hair and I had just finished drying mine when the knock came. The Major was very polite and obviously intrigued by the fact that I had little on under my robe. He stammered, almost like his teeth were chattering. 'What do you think that star means?' he asked me, pointing to the door. I responded as evenly as I could. 'Obviously,' I said, 'it's the work of a sex maniac who has eyes for me and my roommate. He must know we're nymphomaniacs and we need sex every day. We hope that's the case because we've exhausted most of our male friends. We need men, more men! In a hurry!'"

Dottie spoke up next.

"I had just gotten out of the tub," she continued. "Hearing what Helen was saying, I knew the Major was there. So I deliberately left off my robe and walked into the living room stark naked, would you believe. Helen here was pleading for more men and, seeing me, the Major's eyes suddenly bulged out of their sockets. I went into a burlesque routine and slowly did a bump-and-grind toward the door. The Major turned fiery red then sickly pale and had to grip the side of the door, he was so close to collapsing. And judging from the bulge in his pants, well ... Helen eased him backwards from the door and closed it in his face."

Jon picked up the story at this point.

"The next night, about eight again, the Major appeared at our door. I didn't have much on as usual. When I saw it was the Major, I went into my act. 'Mister Sinjun,' I said very slowly, 'I have long wanted you to grace my door! You have such a magnificent body ... such obviously sinuous loins ... such looks ... such character. Please, Major, come in. We must get to know each other better.'

"Just then, Bill came out of the john screaming, "Never! He is mine! You cannot have him! I will defend him unto death! Go away, little man, before I kill you!' The Major never did get to ask his question. He may still be running."

"Franklin," Sam said, "the next act is mine. See this?"

He showed me a photograph of a nude woman. "I'm going to stick it to the upper right corner of the Major's door and then ask him what he thinks it means. Tomorrow is D-Day. It sure will liven up Sunday."

I bit my tongue. Who was I to tell them what they could or could not do? With the balance of my trash rounds still ahead of me, I told them I had to leave. "But keep me posted," I called over my shoulder.

Keep me posted they did.

It was late Sunday afternoon when Sam knocked on the Major's door. The Major answered.

"Yes, young man? Can I help you?"

"Sir, there's a picture on the upper right-hand corner of your door," Sam said, his face expressionless. "What do you suppose it means?"

The Major rose on his toes to stare at what he saw. In an instant he blushed then slammed the door in Sam's face.

Sam and Joe were so disappointed with this reaction that they reluctantly decided to use the ultimate weapon. The ultimate weapon's name was Lauren, a heavenly brunette who had lusted after Sam in his college days. An obliging classmate of Sam's had taken roll upon roll of pictures of Lauren in a wide variety of totally naked and highly suggestive poses. One particular shot which graced the inside wall of Sam's closet – he said he was too proper to offend other female friends by hanging it in the public area – had Lauren on a bed, totally exposed and with hands held out beckoningly to the viewer to join her. The invitation could have only one purpose. The deliciously erotic picture of Lauren was three feet wide by six feet tall and in full color.

Several days later, as I was emptying the daily collection of trash into the cans in front of the apartments, I met the Major as he and his three yipping dogs emerged for the final walk of the day. As I entered the building, I noticed that Sam and Joe were furtively attaching something to the Major's door. Sam held a finger to his lips to warn me to be quiet, let me take an admiring glance at Lauren in her new, very public location and then urgently asked that I open the cellar door. I did so and was quickly jammed behind it with the co-conspirators.

Our wait behind the partially opened door was short. The Major, chattering at the dogs in baby talk as he entered the building, reached for his apartment key, then gasped and froze. He had met Lauren. When he regained his breath, he quickly opened the apartment door and pushed the dogs inside. With a totally stunned look on his face, the Major fell to his knees and began examining Lauren from her toes to her head. He looked like he was about to attack the picture when Mrs. St. John called for him from within. He reacted quickly, pulling tacks from Lauren's far corners and rolling her rapidly. Tucked under the Major's arm, Lauren disappeared into his apartment.

Sam was disconsolate. "Damn!" he hissed, "Do you suppose I'll ever see Lauren again? That body was a part of my life. She was an inspiration for me. She..."

Joe exploded. "Cut it out, Sam," he demanded. "All you'll miss is showing it to your girl friends. He keeps asking his dates if they would like to join Lauren in his pictorial harem," he added for my benefit. "No takers, so far."

The mystery of the starred doors was never fully solved. Whether the stars were a device the Major used to try and develop a plot for an Inspector Brisbane adventure we never did learn. What we did learn, however, was that the Major had a decidedly new attitude toward Dottie and Helen. No longer did he peer and leer from a distance. Rather, he made it a point to suggestively confront them at every opportunity — to their dismay and chagrin.

CHAPTER 36

One of New York's Finest

"Where's the brass polish?"

"Huh?"

"The brass polish. Where is it? Thought I'd pitch in again."

It was Jim Leonard and I couldn't believe my luck. Once more he was actually volunteering to help me with my Saturday morning chores. I happily handed him the polish can and a clean rag, and Jim, not wanting to be idle on his day off, moved away to shine the mailboxes.

Whistling softly to myself as I vacuumed the hall, I thought back to the first time I met him. Like today, it had been a Saturday morning. I had felt a light tap on my shoulder and turned around to find myself facing a giant of a man about my age.

"Where do you keep your polish?" he had said, a broad, friendly smile at once telling me he was the easy-going type.

"Polish? I'm afraid I don't understand," I told him.

"I've finished the chores my wife asked me to do, and now I'm just in her way," the stranger said. "So I thought perhaps you'd like a hand with the mailboxes."

Suddenly it dawned on me. This man was volunteering to help me!

"Oh, you mean the brass polish!" I exclaimed, absolutely delighted at his offer. "It's sitting in the vestibule near the mailboxes. And here's a cloth. Doing those brass fronts was my next chore. Thank you very much!"

The man, still smiling, merely nodded. He held out his hand. "I'm Jim Leonard," he said. "Mary and me, we're next door in Number Two."

"Well, I'm very pleased to meet you, Jim," I told him. "Pardon my astonishment, but you are the first tenant who has ever asked to help me with my work."

After I had told him my name, he strode away, polishing cloth in hand. By the time I got to the mailboxes in Number Six, Jim had finished polishing them and had moved on to polish those in 8 West.

By way of thanks for his help, I invited Jim to bring his wife and join Cindy and me for a cup of coffee.

Cindy and Mary hit it off immediately, and before Jim and I realized they were missing, the two wives were in the bedroom talking about babies. Mary let it quietly slip to Cindy that she was three months pregnant.

It was the most easy and natural thing for Cindy and me to become friends with Jim and Mary. They were the newest tenants in infamous No. 2 in 8 West.

The Leonards were a striking couple.

Jim was a huge, handsome and very calm man. Fully six feet four inches tall, he weighed well over two hundred pounds. Moving with a graceful self-assurance which his size belied, he was a New York City policeman and his beat was lower Manhattan.

Mary, his recent bride, was still a teenager and fully a hundred pounds lighter than Jim. Her complexion like pale porcelain, she was a petite glowing Irish beauty with azure eyes and straw-colored hair.

Jim's one unforgiveable fault was his devotion to the New York Yankees — or such was my perspective as an incurable Philadelphia Athletics fan.

"Want to go to a ball game?" he had once asked me.

"What game do you have in mind?"

"Come on, Franklin," he joked, "a Yankees game, of course. Allie Reynolds is pitching. It's a poor day when he can't beat Bobby Schantz and your floundering Philadelphia friends."

"A poor day?" I hooted. "You've got it all backwards!"

But go to ballgames we did. Naturally, we went to Yankees-Athletics games whenever our schedules and wallets permitted. Jim went to cheer on the Yankees, the perennial world champs, and I went to jeer them, the Bronx bums who all Philadelphia fans were sure were destroying our national pastime.

The friendship of Cindy and Mary grew as rapidly as did that of Jim and me.

Mary did not know how to sew and was eager to learn so she could make things for the baby. No more dedicated sewing teacher than Cindy ever existed. When Mary quit work in the seventh month of her pregnancy, the Noyes' sewing machine was placed in the Leonard's apartment on loan.

I'll never forget the telephone call that brought the tragic news. Mary was then in the final month of her pregnancy.

"Mr. Noyes, this is Captain Ferguson, 25th Precinct," a quiet voice had told me. "Aren't you the Super of 8 West 90th Street?"

"Yes, I am, Captain," I told him. "What can I do for you?"

"Do you know Mary Leonard, Jim Leonard's wife?"

"Of course. We're close friends of the Leonards."

There was a pause on the line.

"Hello?" I asked.

"Mr. Noyes, I have some bad news," Captain Ferguson continued even more softly than before. "Jim Leonard was killed a few moments ago. Some drunk rammed his patrol car broadside. Killed him instantly. Can you go to Mary and help prepare her for the news? I know Jim's parents very well and I want to tell them first. Can you go to Mary? I'll come over as soon as I can."

Stunned, I promised the police captain that I would do what I could.

Tears were streaming down my face when I took my own wife in my arms and explained what had happened.

Cindy's experience as a nurse in dealing with death galvanized her into action.

She called St. Luke's Hospital and told her head nurse there had been a death in the family and that it would probably be two or three days before she could return to work. Then she admonished me to get hold of myself.

"We can't let ourselves go at this point," she insisted. "Once we break the news to Mary we have to be prepared for anything."

"Okay, Cindy, let's go," I answered. "I'll be all right."

Mary was as bright and cheerful as I had ever seen her when she answered our knock. And the apartment was permeated with the odor of ham and cabbage cooking, Jim's favorite dinner.

Mary and Cindy embraced, and Cindy placed her hand on Mary's protruding front. "The baby's lively today," she smiled. "It felt like he just turned."

"Do you think it will be a boy, Cindy?" Mary asked. "I'm torn. I'd like a little Jimmy but I'd also like a little girl."

"I'm sure I don't know, Cindy said, her voice quiet. She pulled Mary over towards the couch. "Mary, I have some news for you. Please come sit down with me."

"Sure," she smiled. "Oh, Franklin, would you please turn down the heat under Jim's ham and cabbage?"

She turned to Cindy. "What's the news? You two going to have a baby, too?"

Cindy took both of Mary's hands and, her face no more than a foot from Mary's, broke the news.

"Mary, Jim is dead. Your Jim. Captain Ferguson called us a few minutes ago. He was killed in a car accident. The Captain asked us to come to you until he could get here. He went to tell Jim's parents."

Mary looked at Cindy in disbelief. Then her eyes became vacant. The tears and words would come in time. For now, Cindy held her close and talked to her softly.

I busied myself with the dinner, which was nearly ready, and then in answering the phone and the door. Captain Ferguson came and went as did other police friends of Jim's. Between the visits and calls, Cindy got Mary to eat a little and even to talk a little.

I slipped out shortly after dinner to tell the K's what had happened. When I returned to the apartment, Mary's older sister had arrived, packed a few things for Mary and prepared to take her to her home. She promised to call us with the details of the wake and the funeral.

The next two weeks were a blur. The wake, the funeral and the birth of young Jimmy all occurred within nine days' time. Cindy insisted on "specialing" Mary at the hospital and stayed with her day and night for three days. She encouraged her friend to nurse Jimmy, a healthy eight-pounder with a lusty cry and a head full of black hair.

At the insistence of her parents, Mary and her baby moved from the hospital to their home. Cindy was in constant touch with her, and it was about two weeks after Mary left the hospital that she told Cindy that she and her brother-in-law would be over that weekend to clean out the apartment.

I was vacuuming the entrance foyer of 6 West when they arrived with an old pickup truck.

Mary and I hugged each other tightly and exchanged greetings. She looked pale and tired.

"Let me know when you need some help with the furniture," I told both of them. "I'll be glad to help you get everything on the truck."

"Thanks," they said. "It will take us only an hour or so to pack everything. Stop by when you finish cleaning next door."

The few items of furniture and clothing that Jim and Mary had took less than half an hour to stow into the truck. As they climbed into the cab, Mary handed me a package.

"It's not much," she said. "Just something I wanted you and Cindy to have. Tell Cindy I'll call her tonight."

I nodded, gave her one more hug, and off they went.

The Leonard's apartment was surprisingly clean and there was little left for me, as the Super, to do. I wiped the baseboards and gave the windows a once-over then used Mary's not-yet-disconnect- ed telephone to call Mr. K. I told him the apartment was ready to rent – again..

Cindy and I opened Mary's package after dinner that night. Mary's gift for Cindy was a frilly, full-front apron that Mary had made herself. Cindy cried. "She sews as well as I do," she smiled through her tears.

My gift was in a small box. I opened it, removed the tissue and was touched to find a baseball – the baseball. The last game Jim and I had gone to together at Yankee Stadium – the Athletics had actu- ally beaten the Yankees – Jim and I both instinctively tried to catch a foul ball hit to our area of the stands by A's pitcher Bobby Shantz. Naturally, Jim outreached me – and he caught the ball. Now here it was.

I cried a little myself. And I was sure I would again – every time I looked at that treasured memento.

CHAPTER 37

Words, Words, Words

"**I** bet you can't think of a homonym for seer."

"Spelled S-E-E-R?"

"Yes."

"C-E-R-E. And S-E-A-R."

"Great! How about dough?"

"As in bread?"

"Uh-huh."

"D-O-E."

"Great again. Most people don't get that one. In fact, most people don't even know what homonyms are."

"Mr., uh, I'm Franklin Noyes, the Super here, and might I ask what's this game we seem to be playing?"

That was how I met Sam Morris one Saturday morning when I was vacuuming the hallway outside apartments 9 and 10 in 6 West.

He chuckled at my question and suggested I visit with him over a cup of coffee.

Ahead of schedule for a change and with a bit of time to spare, I accepted.

He had only just returned from a nearby newsstand and had already completed half of that day's *New York Times* crossword puzzle, from what I could see.

As I went into Sam's apartment, I was stunned by what I saw: Books! Books in bookcases, books on tables and books on chairs. Books on the floor, books on the window sills, in fact books, books, books, literally thousands of them occupying every available niche and inch of his apartment.

Sam was amused at my reaction and, as he cleared the table to make room for the coffee things, he confirmed that he was obsessed with books and words.

"Ever since I can remember I've been surrounded by books," he explained. "My father was a frustrated writer who couldn't make a living writing books so he decided to sell them instead. He started with a small shop in the Bronx and, after my mother died, we moved to Manhattan and opened a shop in the Village. My bibliophile-turned-book-merchant father became increasingly interested in bibliopolism – that's buying and selling rare and curious books of all kinds – and I suppose that's how I got hooked."

"You were 'paged,' you might say?" I ventured.

He shot me an appreciative grin. "'Bound' is closer to the truth. But anyway, one day one of my father's customers, a publisher, asked him if he'd like to try his hand at selling their duds."

"Duds?"

"Books they take a chance on publishing which never sell. They fizzle. The publisher is left with thousands of unsold copies."

"Did your father agree?"

"He sure did. He took on the whole year's duds at a ridiculously low price and set out to resell them wherever and whenever he could. To everyone's surprise, he unloaded them all in two weeks! It turned out he had a remarkable marketing talent, and it enabled him to pursue his bibliopolistic interests all over the map. His business became so large that when he died last year I dropped out of university to run the store in his place, at least until I decide what to do with it."

"Are you finding it a hard decision?" I asked.

"I sure am! I can't bear the thought of parting with everything he accumulated. Maybe that's why I have so much here." His gesture took in everything in sight.

Sam, only a couple of years older than me, then went on to tell me that he had completed most of his course work for his Ph.D. and had had his thesis project approved. He was preparing an etymological dictionary which would trace modern English words back through their origins. He had already accumulated so many reference works and so much information which was related but not germane to the dictionary that he was planning to compile two or three other etymological works too. He became particularly excited when he talked of preparing a dictionary of the vulgar tongue which would trace contemporary man's "dirty" and four-letter words back through the centuries.

Sam's obsession with words was evident wherever I looked. His pleasures — crossword puzzles, double-crostics, anagrams and cryptograms — were scattered throughout the living room, and dictionaries and other word sources were jammed in every bookcase and stacked in every pile.

Even a sampler hung on the wall above Sam's antique roll-top desk reflected his obsession with words. It read:

> Philologists who chase
> A panting syllable through time and space,
> Start it at home, and hunt it in the dark,
> To Gaul, to Greece, and into Noah's Ark.
>
> Cowper, *Retirement*

I told him I should introduce him to Jon Hauser in No. 10 next door.

"Oh? Why?" he asked politely.

"Because, apart from you, he's the only person I've ever met who's confident enough to do crossword puzzles in ink," I told him, standing to leave.

"Maybe I'll invite him over sometime, " Sam answered.

"Well, not too soon," I told him. "Your wife wouldn't like it. He prefers male company over everything else."

"Ah, well then, I see what you mean," Sam answered. "I will wait. But don't you wait long to come over again. I'll introduce you to Jane, my wife, and to Elizabeth, our two-year-old daughter. Right now they're out for a walk in Central Park."

"Thanks, Sam," I said back in the hall to resume my work. "I'd like that."

Sam's path and mine didn't cross again for some time, but during that time I did meet the rest of his family. This was at the Kesslers', the Morrises' neighbors in No. 10.

Cindy and I had met the Kesslers at one of the St. Johns' Theosophy Society meetings earlier on. Ray Kessler had told me how much he liked the neighborhood and the people he had met at the St. Johns', and he hoped I would tell him the minute one of our apartments became available. When No. 10 in 6 West opened up several months later, Mr. K was delighted to rent it to them on my recommendation.

The Kesslers became close friends of the Morrises. Ray and Sam shared common interests in books and words, and Noel and Jane shared interests in classical music, succulent plants and Liza, as Elizabeth was called.

Three distinct and memorable images come to mind whenever I think of my visits with the Morrises and the Kesslers.

The first, of course, is my amazement at Sam's books. After our initial visit and the ensuing hiatus, I saw Sam Morris many times, and almost every time he gave me a volume or two. Thanks to his father's business, he had surplus books in abundance and it gave him great pleasure to present particularly interesting volumes to his friends. Nothing could have pleased me more since I was an avid, albeit broke, book reader and collector.

Cindy, however, viewed my growing collection with mixed feelings. She too loved to read, but she was getting tired of dusting books. The prospect of moving a rapidly growing library once I graduated didn't enchant her either.

"We'll be able to afford a mover by then, I hope," I'd say to soothe her.

My second image is of two-year-old Liza, raven-haired, blue-eyed and pretty beyond belief. She was not only the pride and joy of her parents but also of Ray and Noel Kessler.

When her father was with Liza, he would babble endlessly on, often in baby talk which could probably be traced back many centuries. And when Ray was with her, he sang to her and bounced her on his lap or playfully wrestled her on the rolls of flab which enveloped his middle.

Matters were slightly more serious when the ladies had Liza in tow. Jane and Noel loved to prepare their meals together, and they made it a point to let Liza "help" them. She would roll pastry dough with her own tiny roller, over and over again, until it was gray and tough. But, like the pies her mother and Noel baked, hers went into the oven too, and was dutifully tasted and complimented by her father and Ray.

My most distinct recollection, however, had to do with words.

If Sam wasn't asking me for a homonym for this or an antonym for that, he would playfully badger me for the origin of such words as government or sovereignty. When I couldn't answer to his satisfaction, which was nearly always, I was treated to a lecture, usually lasting five to ten minutes.

One night when I was collecting trash as usual, I was haled into the Morrises' apartment "to make my contribution to the English Language."

Sam had had Ray give him a detailed anatomical explanation of the female reproductive system and then had begun a search through the past and present for words and phrases which described the female's basic sex organ and the sex act itself.

To my surprise and embarrassment, both Jane and Noel were present and paying rapt attention to Sam's discourse on his findings.

"Sam's list has forty words on it already!" Noel laughed.

"Yeah, and I've barely scratched the surface," Sam announced. "Want to help us think of some more?"

"You just go ahead, er...I'm sure I don't know any more than you do," I told him and everyone uncomfortably.

None of them was embarrassed, playing Sam's game in the spirit in which he had presented it. In fact, they were wet-eyed from laughing so much. Ray was holding his ribs they hurt him so.

"So far, we've listed twat, cunt, pussy..." he started.

"And don't forget gold ol' vagina," Jane chimed in.

"Then there's tunnel of love, Mound of Venus, snake pit, honey catcher and cum-catcher," Ray finished. "Sam, what are the others? Tell Frank all the others."

I listened carefully and fully revealed my lack of "culture" and education while Sam gravely enumerated the rest of their list.

They then changed directions and started adding to their list of words for the sex act. Soon Sam had almost fifty words and phrases scribbled on his sheet of paper, and most of the words were unfamiliar to me. Plow, stuff, lay, slam, bang, hump, screw, fornicate, ride, prong, and on and on.

"C'mon, Frank," they all encouraged me. "can't you think of any?"

I sighed, overwhelmed. "I'm just a simple country boy who knows only a few words for man's most basic act," I told them. "But what about making love? And intercourse? And, uh, fuck? I don't believe you put those on your list."

They roared with delighted surprise. Not only had I added three additions to their list, I had given them the three most well-known and well-used terms, and they had omitted them!

"You have just achieved immortality, Franklin Noyes!" declared Sam, wiping his eyes on his sleeve. "When I write my dictionary of the vulgar tongue, I shall cite you as the authority on all three terms."

I was so mortified at the prospect of achieving immortality through three of the world's favorite terms that to this day I have never bought a dictionary of vulgarisms or even looked for the terms in a conventional dictionary — for fear of seeing my name.

CHAPTER 38

Sweet Revelation

"They have the best pastries I ever tasted and Eddie and Margret are delightful people. I'm a frustrated baker so we enjoy picking on each other almost as much as I enjoy Margret's creations. God how I love their pastries."

Jack Ripon was trying to convince Cindy and me to patronize Lengacher's Swiss Pastry Shop in the middle of the block.

"It's worth a visit just for the aroma," Jack said. "In fact, Donna swears it's so rich she gains two pounds just by breathing the air in their shop."

We laughed because Cindy and I had frequently made the same joke about her baking. In my book, her pies were unbeatable.

"Besides, Jack," Cindy said, "our budget wouldn't stand it. It's already stretched to the seams."

"Whose isn't?" Jack responded. "Give 'em a try anyway."

It was close to Thanksgiving before Cindy and I felt we could afford anything store-bought. Then, on a whim, I decided it was time Cindy was pampered with something special. Recalling what Jack Ripon had said, I headed for Lengacher's where everything was reported to be special.

The place was busy when I went in, giving me time before I was served to savor the aroma of fresh-baked, iced pastries and to ogle the decorated cakes and colorful tarts. The goodies were spread out in four cases along the entire length of the first floor of the converted brownstone in which the shop was located.

The first case, the largest, was cake heaven: seven-layer cakes, almond cakes, white cakes, chocolate cakes, fruit cakes, most with artistic toppings of every imaginable kind and all bidding me to buy. Thoughts of robbery started to creep temptingly into my mind. No good, I thought, they probably sell out every day. Nothing left to steal.

The second case reduced me to a drooling fool. Linzer tortes, sacher tortes, napoleons, fruit tarts, butter sponges, all so appealing to sight and smell I was tempted to order a sample of each.

The next case contained nothing but cookies, surely three dozen different kinds, nut-covered, coconut coated, glistening with chocolate or yellow with butter.

The last case was breakfast heaven — doughnuts, plain and fancy; muffins; croissants; Danish-type pastries with fruit glazes; and cheesecakes, either plain or with cherry, blueberry, pineapple or blackberry toppings.

My limited purse and the unlimited array of goodies had reduced me to total indecisiveness.

"I can help you, yah?" The question emanated from a blonde giant of a man with a thick, German-sounding accent.

"I honestly don't know," I shrugged. "I've never seen so many good things in one place. I'm not sure I can make a decision. Are you Mr. Lengacher?"

"Ya, Edvard Lengacher. But my friends call me Eddie. And who are you?

"Franklin Noyes, Mr. ...Eddie. I'm the Super of 6 and 8 West down the street. Jack Ripon said I should come here. He said you have the best pastries in New York."

"Danke," he smiled, bowing slightly. "He is right."

"He also said you were a lousy actor," I finished.

"Ha! Ha! Ha!" he roared, slapping his thigh. "You tell Yack that when he can act as well as I can bake, he will be a rich man."

I laughed too. I liked this place.

My eyes settled on the cheesecakes once more, Cindy's very favorite pastry. Just at that moment Eddie was joined by a beautiful blue-eyed blonde girl of about 20 who was dressed completely in white wraparound dress, oversized apron, stockings, shoes and cap. Eddie put his hand affectionately on her shoulder and steered her around to the front of the cases "Franklin," he said. "No, I will call you Franz, that comes off my tongue better ... are you married? See this beautiful confection? She is Gretel, my youngest, my last unmarried daughter. She lusts for a lover and a husband."

Such forthright talk embarrassed me but only amused Gretel.

"Father, all you think about is sex," she chided gently. "Mama wants to know when the almond paste and the molasses will be delivered. She is just about out of both."

Eddie clucked. "Almond paste, molasses, how can you speak of such things when true love is being discussed? Well, Franz, are you married or not?"

"I have been for some time," I smiled. "In fact, that's why I'm here. I want to buy my wife a surprise – probably some of that cheesecake. May I have a slice for two of that?" I pointed to the blackberry version.

He dismissed Gretel with a gentle slap on her bottom and a wink. "Then perhaps you have a brother?" he persisted, opening the case.

I shook my head, amused at his half-earnest, half-joking question. "No, just me."

"Too bad," he said. "That girl needs a husband."

I met Eddie's wife Margret on my second trip. Introduced to me by Eddie as "my bride and the maker of my four beautiful daughters," she was all of five feet tall and nearly that wide. She had very broadly set blue eyes, a large sensuous mouth and long sandy hair pulled back in a loose, wispy bun.

That Eddie and Margret were devoted to each other there could be no doubt. Whenever he was near her, no matter how crowded the shop, he patted her rear or stroked her arm. She, in turn, would either throw him a kiss or look at his middle region and roll her eyes invitingly. Watching this frequent performance, I wondered why they had only four daughters.

My visits to Lengacher's became a weekly ritual thereafter. I was partial to the cakes and the tortes while Cindy adored the cheese-cakes, cookies and cream buns, and somehow we managed to find the money to occasionally treat ourselves to these luxuries.

I was heading into Lengacher's one lovely spring Sunday morning when I saw a man leaving the shop struggling with a huge and obvi-ously heavy box almost bigger than he could handle.

"Eddie, what in the world was that man carrying in that box?" I asked, waving to Gretel as I came in. "What do you make that large?"

He smiled conspiratorially. "Ach, Franz, you have never seen our special cakes? My Margret is an artist. She can create any scene or sit-uation you want and show it on a cake." He lowered his voice. "Some of them are very *sexy*."

How can a cake be sexy?"

For some reason my question broke Eddie up completely, and this only added to my astonishment. After he managed to stop laughing, he wiped his eyes and said, "Come, let me show you, you poor inno-cent young man."

Eddie called Gretel, who was giggling, to cover the shop while he took me to the lower level where the baking and decorating were done. In a small private room to the rear, the equivalent of the bed-room area in our No. 2 apartments, there was Margret, hard at work carving something out of huge blocks of white cake.

"Ah, Franz," she smiled, beckoning me to come closer, "Eddie has decided to reveal our secret to you, ya?"

I walked up to the crumb-covered work table and gasped at what I now saw. There in front of me, in cake, rested the bodies of two men, positioned to be united.

"They will become even more life-like once Margret has applied flesh-colored icing," Eddie declared.

"Ya," Margret agreed. "They will even have *hair*."

I whistled under my breath. "It's unbelievable."

"It is, isn't it?" said Eddie, taking my comment as a compliment. He was proud of his wife's work. "My Margret can create anything but anything in cake and icing. She is an artist."

Margret grinned but kept on working.

"Who's the cake for, Eddie?" I asked. "Anyone I know?" I meant my question to be a joke.

"Ya, I think so," I was startled to hear. "He's a cake, a fruitcake, himself. Margret, vat's hiss name? Hausman? Nein, Hauser. Yon Hauser. This is the fourth we make for him. Each time the men are in different positions. Someday I show you the photographs we took of those cakes."

I nodded in recognition of Jon Hauser but could say nothing. Eddie moved over to another table.

"Look Franz," he said. "Here is another cake Margret just finished. It is for a funny little man down the street who has some little dogs. He has a hot little sugar bun across the street. She is 25, maybe 30. He buys her a special cake every three or four weeks."

This creation was equally unusual. It featured a Sherlock Holmes-type character, but this one was in the classic position of the flasher with an erect member that was grotesquely large. And not made of cake but of real jade. The missing phallus!

I laughed out loud.

"Don't tell me. Let me guess," I roared. "It's for a man named St. John, right?"

Now it was Eddie's turn to be surprised. "Ya," he nodded. "How did you know?"

"Just a guess," I replied. "Just a guess."

I didn't have the courage to ask Eddie to show me any more of Margret's special cakes. He had already told me more about two of my tenants than I felt I should know.

However, many months later, when I told Eddie that Cindy and I would be moving, he remembered his promise and insisted on showing me his photographs of Margret's unique, frequently erotic creations. Two caught my eye. They weren't sexy but they were very special. One, which Eddie said was ordered every year, featured the Polish flag and Christian cross. Mrs. Karbowski had this created for Mr. K's birthday, he told me.

The other, a one-time order, featured a sailboat carved to scale with the words "Love Always" frosted on the bow. This had been delivered to Mrs. K, Eddie said, but he never knew who had ordered it.

"How come?" I asked, feeling I already knew the answer.

"One day we received a letter containing fifty dollars and a photograph of a boat," he recalled. "The letter asked us to make a cake just like the picture and please deliver it."

"Who signed the letter?" I asked.

"It was not a name," Eddie said. "Wait, I still have the note. I show you. It was some strange letters."

He fumbled among some papers for a few moments and extracted a grease-stained note.

"Here."

I wasn't the least bit surprised to read the same Greek letters that my friend Baldy Baldwin had named the sailboat he had built with Helena Karbowski's help. I recalled "The Master's Helena."

Good old Baldy. Baldy the Boat Builder. He did indeed have a thing for older women. He had been in love with Helena Karbowski after all.

CHAPTER 39

Waldo the Wondrous

The name on the 8 West mailbox read: No.3 - W. Pikulski.

The name on an empty envelope I retrieved after it blew out of the trash bag read: Waldo Pikulski.

According to Mr. K, Mr. Pikulski's first name actually wasn't Waldo, but the real thing had an unpronounceable dozen syllables.

In my early months as Super, Waldo Pikulski was just the name I associated with the smallest, neatest bag of trash in my entire pickup. What Waldo put out each night invariably consisted of a fresh brown lunch bag, barely half full, with the top neatly folded down twice and taped shut. Indeed, there were times when I wondered if someone had mistakenly left his lunch at Waldo's door.

My first encounter with Waldo himself was unnerving. It was a fresh, cool October evening and I was trying to do my nightly rounds at a double-time pace since I was anxious to finish a paper on the Arab refugee problem.

I reached over to pick up Waldo's little brown bag but, as I started to straighten up, I was brought to a complete and startling halt by a hand so large I could feel it blanketing my head. When the gentle pressure on my scalp eased enough to permit me to resume standing, which I quickly did, another hand handed me a small package wrapped in wax paper.

Startled and more than a little apprehensive, I found myself looking at a giant. Waldo! He was six feet eight inches tall, I guessed, fully three hundred pounds in weight, and had shoulders nearly three feet across. Every inch and pound was in magnificent condition. With his shaved head and bare torso, Hollywood could easily have cast him as a harem guard.

"More trash?" I asked, pointing to my bag.

Waldo shook his head. With great difficulty but no lack of clarity, he let me know in what I recognized as Polish and with gestures that what he was holding was a gift for me. Further, I was to taste it. I opened the wax paper and discovered a flattened mound of chopped red meat, raw, with onion minced in.

"Eat it?" I asked, alarmed at the prospect of eating uncooked meat. "Raw?"

He held up a finger and signaled me to watch. Carefully he pinched off a small portion between his massive thumb and forefinger and put it in his mouth. As he chewed he rubbed his belly. Then he pointed to me and to the meat and nodded, his eyebrows raised high. Not wanting to disagree with such a big man, I did as I was bid and tried a small mouthful. It was beef, moist and cleverly seasoned, and it was delicious!

Waldo indicated his pleasure in my first taste of Steak Tartare by flashing a wide grin. Then suddenly he grunted some sort of comment and abruptly closed the door, shutting me out.

From that night on I approached Waldo's apartment with both eyes fixed on his door.

My next encounter with him was close to Christmas. Again, the door opened partially. But this time the one huge hand affectionately patted my shoulder while the other delivered the gift. It was a small cellophane bag of cookies which I needed no urging to taste. Waldo again grunted something – maybe it was Merry Christmas – and again abruptly shut the door.

The pats on the head and shoulders and the gifts of food became almost regular after that. Cindy started kidding me that Waldo had decided I was more fun than a puppy.

"And you cost less to feed and are much easier to housebreak," she would tease.

What completely baffled me was that I never saw Waldo except at trash collection time. Never once did our paths cross while I was cleaning, nor while I was being summoned by Mr. K or to the front door for deliveries. Waldo's life and his apartment were mysteries to me.

Mr. K and I were examining some plumbing when I finally found the right moment to ask my boss to tell me what he knew about Waldo.

"Waldo's parents were, in Poland, our best friends," Mr. K started. "But they decided to stay there when we left for freedom. They begged my Helena and me to take their teenage son — Waldo, that is — with us in our flight. Out of love and respect for his momma and papa, Waldo did as he was told and came away with us."

I listened enraptured while Mr. K told me more about our invisible giant.

He had been an art student in Poland. He started his studies in Krakow, where he became a fine ceramist. Continuing his studies in a monastery outside Warsaw, he developed a considerable talent as a calligrapher and became highly skilled in the use of gold leaf. While with the Karbowskis in Canada, Waldo met three other young Poles. He joined with them in making plans to start a business in New York City where they would produce miniature copies of famous artifacts in museums throughout the world. Their first works would be replicas of ancient Grecian and Egyptian pieces on display in the Metropolitan Museum.

So they came to America, the four young Poles, and started their business with minimum capital and maximum chutzpah. They sold their models, with increasing success, to museums, department stores and gift shops throughout the city. Soon they were negotiating with a marketing consultant to sell their replicas through the mail.

A deeply religious person, Waldo was torn by his inability to decide whether to enter the priesthood. He spent his few leisure hours in prayer at various Catholic churches or in the presence of two Polish priests who had fled from their country in the first few days of the

Nazi invasion of Poland. As wards of the New York Archdiocese, the priests were anxious to find ways to contribute to the church and to their enslaved colleagues in Poland. Because of his calligraphic skills, Waldo provided one possibility.

In the churches, as in everyday life, there are numerous occasions when it is appropriate to honor fellow priests or church members for their devoted service. It is not uncommon at such times to present the honorees with a plaque or an inscribed scroll.

The priests began to solicit information about such occasions then proposed texts for appropriate scrolls. Waldo in turn used his great talent to turn their texts into works of art. The first few examples of Waldo's work were enough to generate assignments to fill his every spare hour.

"That is why you never see him," Mr. K concluded in carefully pronounced English. "Because he is working with ceramics, with his friends, or as a calligrapher, with the priests. He works late into the night to finish his work."

"He must be a deeply dedicated man, Mr. K," I said, standing to leave.

"That he is," he mused. "That he is."

It was close to Christmas again the first time Waldo ever invited me into his apartment. Again I was double-timing my trash rounds and again Waldo's door opened wide. But this time his two enormous arms reached out and enveloped me, playfully crushing me to his chest. Before I was sure what was happening, Waldo lifted me off my feet and into his front room. With obvious pride and delight he invited me to inspect a giant scroll.

It was three feet wide and twice as high and contained quotations from great Popes. A wonder of crimson, green, blue and gold, it was replete with religious symbols and miniature sketches of birds worthy of Audubon. It was magnificent.

"You like?" Waldo asked.

"I love!"

He grinned. Carefully, he started to speak and, with some difficulty, I interpreted Waldo's fractured English and complex sign language. He told me that this piece had been commissioned by the Archbishop of New York as a gift to a fellow American Cardinal now observing his 25th year in that eminent office.

I whistled my admiration then started to look around.

Waldo's tiny apartment was full of unfinished scrolls and clay models of famous artifacts. One wall was covered with paintings. Portraits of his parents were hung in the center, and these were surrounded by religious icons and prints of religious paintings. What struck me about the place, however, was the contrast in scale. Excluding the Cardinal's gift, Waldo literally overwhelmed everything in the apartment, including the tiny apartment itself.

And, very early on Christmas Eve afternoon, Waldo overwhelmed me.

I was making my rounds much earlier than usual so that Cindy and I would have time to trim our Christmas tree. Things were going very slowly, however, because many apartment doors were open, and beside each open door was a tenant waiting for the express purpose of intercepting me and exchanging greetings, usually over a glass of Christmas cheer.

By the time I reached No. 3, I was giddy. Humming "Deck the Halls" I was again intercepted by one of Waldo' s saucer-sized hands. He easily guided me into his apartment where, with his right hand, he presented me a beautifully wrapped package.

In a sensitive display which I will never forget, nor ever fully understand, he reverently pointed in turn to his parents' pictures, to various icons and then to me. His voice rose and fell until suddenly it was stilled by a gush of tears. I accepted the package and tried to start thanking him, but he wouldn't let me continue. Back up to my shoulder came his large left hand and I was gently steered out the door. It closed tight and I finished my early round in a fog.

I put Waldo's gift aside until the next day.

In accordance with our custom, Cindy and I opened our gifts on Christmas morning before going to the Poconos to spend the day with our parents. I opened Waldo's gift last. Inside the wrapping was a magnificent parchment house blessing. The scroll, unwound, was the size of a window pane, and it was decorated with detailed paintings of Cindy's favorite birds – mockingbirds, cardinals, blue jays and Baltimore orioles. Cindy, who had never even seen Waldo, was even more overwhelmed by the gift, an instant family heirloom, than I.

"How did he know I love these birds?" Cindy asked. "Did you tell him?"

"No, I didn't," I answered. "Maybe it was inspiration." And I meant it.

The day following Christmas I stopped at Waldo's apartment and knocked. I wasn't sure what I would say, for surely there was no way to adequately give thanks for such a gift. But no one answered. I knocked again but got no response.

After repeated attempts to reach Waldo over the holidays, I stopped by Mr. K's apartment to ask him how I could reach Waldo to thank him for his priceless gift.

"You don't know?" Mr. K asked, surprised.

"Know what, Mr. K?"

He handed me a piece of paper on which was written the address of a seminary near Philadelphia. "Waldo entered this place on Christmas Day," he said reverently. "He has begun his training for the priesthood."

So, I thought, Waldo got a Christmas present too. He was given the courage to make his decision. I was very happy for him.

CHAPTER 40

The Christmas Party

A Super is never in doubt that Christmas is coming.
The seasonal jousting with Manhattan's trash collectors was one clue. Another was smells. No matter how small the apartments or how alone their occupants, Christmas seemed to stir the occupants' primeval urges to feast, to cook and bake and eat endlessly from the beginning of advent to the birth of the Holy Child.

The surest clue that Christmas was coming, however, was the mail.

The volume of mail started to grow right after Thanksgiving, and the delivery of packages during Christmas week became difficult to keep up with. Fortunately I was free of classes then and could receive and place in apartments the dozens of parcels which arrived at 6 and 8 West the last five or six days before December 25th.

When Walter Jackson next door was alive, he had told me that most Supers looked forward to Christmas with great anticipation because of gifts from tenants. With no hesitation whatsoever he said that on a good year a Super's net worth could increase by half or more.

I wasn't sure how to react to that information.

Cindy and I had both been raised in environments where the Holidays were observed quietly at home with small gifts exchanged among members of the family and only a few close friends. And neither of our fathers had ever had jobs where their employers gave them gifts at Christmas. So our first Christmas at 6 and 8 West was a surprising experience.

Not only did the Karbowskis give us a gift (and a large, buttery babka), so did most of the tenants in both buildings.

They slipped envelopes containing money under our door or personally delivered them, and on Christmas morning when I opened our front door, I was amazed to find ten bottles of liquor, two large cans of cookies, one five-pound box of candy and a three-pound fruitcake. It was enough to make this farm boy believe in Santa Claus again.

Cindy and I were so humbled by this beneficence that the next year, remembering our first Christmas twelve short months ago, we decided we would share this year's gifts with the Karbowskis and the tenants.

A week before Christmas Day I taped an invitation near the mailboxes in both buildings:

> Open House Christmas Eve
> Cindy and Franklin Noyes
> request the pleasure of your company
> on Christmas Eve
> anytime after 7 p.m.
> You are welcome even if you only have time
> to exchange Holiday greetings.

The invitations had been posted barely an hour when our phone and our doorbell began to ring.

"Franklin, what can we bring to your party? Do you need any liquor? Would you like me to bake a cake?" My standard answer became "Bring yourself and your spouse or a friend. The good Lord will provide the rest." I recalled last year's gifts. I found it nearly impossible to collect trash without being intercepted at every apartment. The same questions were repeated and more added. "What shall we wear? Is it dressy?"

"Just be comfortable," was my reply.

When December 24 dawned, Cindy and I began to panic. Last year's gifts had not materialized, and now we faced the prospect of wining and dining thirty to forty people with no food and no drink!

We hurriedly pooled what little cash we had left over from Christmas, and I went off to buy the ingredients for a tea punch and baloney and cream cheese pinwheels. Cindy rearranged the furniture in our apartment and cleaned in desperation.

We needn't have worried.

Soon after lunch Mrs. K arrived with her annual babka, enormous Kielbasa, and a canister of cookies. She was followed in short order by Frances Black bearing three fruitcakes and Donna Ripon with a cold roast of beef, a large container of homemade pâté and several long loaves of crunchy bread. Sam Morris came next with four bottles of wine, followed by Baldy Baldwin with a baked Smithfield ham and candied yams. And so it went, all afternoon, until our apartment was filled with food and drink.

"We've started a tradition," Cindy said, a dreamy, sentimental look in her eyes, as it started getting dark.

"You mean having a tree?" I glanced at the small conifer sitting on my desk.

"No, I meant adding to the decorations on the tree," she said. "Last year all we had was a dozen glass balls and some tinsel."

I smiled. We certainly had made progress. This year we had added eleven crystal icicles and a delicate star. "Maybe our open house will become a tradition, too," I added. "Even though the people will be different, I hope our excitement stays the same."

"If we keep on getting good gifts, it will," she chuckled. "I can't wait to try Baldy's ham."

"Me either," I answered, my mind more on the prospect of greeting good friends than eating.

I placed the gift Waldo had given me that afternoon and two gifts to Cindy from me under the tree, and she joined them with her gifts to me. We stood together, side by side, with our arms linked comfortably, and admired our handiwork for a few moments. It was a tender, close time.

By seven o'clock Cindy and I found ourselves ready to preside over what could have been a banquet for a king. Drink anyone? Would you like eggnog, tea punch (generously laced with rich, mellow brandy), a cocktail, beer, or any of several fine wines? How about food? We have juicy beef, tender ham, assorted cold cuts and sausages, dips for every taste, candied yams, hot canapés, cold hors d'oeuvres, cole slaw, salads of every description and enough cookies, cakes and candies to fill a ditty bag for every tenant.

From what do we eat and drink? These elegant paper plates and cups, of course.

Baldy arrived first. Next came the Ripons, the Dixons and the Blacks, all dressed in their holiday best, and Mr. and Mrs. K, who embraced everyone there as they came through the living room to join us.

The St. Johns came over, followed by Joe Halstead and Sam Browning. Then Cindy let out a surprised, delighted whoop.

"Look who's here! It's Møgens and Carl!"

Sure enough, our two Danish friends, whom we hadn't seen for several weeks, were at the door. Smiling broadly at her welcome, they each handed her a small package wrapped loosely in brown paper.

"More food?" she groaned, gesturing at our already loaded tables.

"I suppose you could call it that," Carl smiled.

"It's food for your beautiful soul," Møgens added.

Cindy blushed.

"Please, open the packages now," they urged her, and she tore away the wrappings to find two more fine pieces of crystal in the same pattern as the one they had introduced her to so many months ago.

Tears appeared in Cindy's eyes. "Oh, you two, you shouldn't have. They're so..."

Hugs from the two Danes stopped her from finishing. "Let's get on with the party," they said. She smiled and turned to see who else had arrived.

By nine o'clock, some twenty people were milling about enjoying the party.

"C'mon, everybody," Jim Dixon suddenly called out, "we're going to sing Christmas carols."

Cindy jumped up. "Let's do 'Silent Night' first."

"No, 'God Rest Ye Merry' is merrier," someone called out.

Baldy made his own choice and began "The First Noel."

Soon everyone was singing in the candlelight in a very reverent, sentimental manner and an atmosphere of intimate brotherhood charged the air. Our Christmas hymns attracted even more visitors and all were welcomed.

At ten o'clock I slipped out to clean the halls of trash for that holy night and to urge those tenants who had not yet come to our party to stop around.

As I hoped it would be, the trash was very light. Nonetheless, my rounds gave me the chance to remind the Kesslers and the Morrises that our open house was still going strong.

The party had changed into a sit-down affair when I returned. The carol singing was still going on, but the dozen or so couples had all found places to sit, mostly on the floor.

Near midnight almost all of the tenants had come to our party and gone. Nine people – the Ripons, Dixons, Kesslers, and Baldy and our two Danish friends – decided to stay longer, and Jim Dixon was still leading the caroling, now not much louder than a whisper and a hum.

I interrupted the singing to make an announcement.

"Cindy and I have to leave you for a little while. Please don't be insulted, but there's something we want to do."

Carl, thinking the party was over, looked distressed. "So soon?" he asked.

"No, no, not at all," I assured him. "It's just that we like to attend a midnight candlelight service on Christmas Eve, and we're going to the Presbyterian Church at 86th Street and Columbus Avenue. Would anyone like to come with us?"

Carl said he would; so did Møgens and Baldy. They went for their coats.

"Okay," I laughed to the others still sitting, "you keep the home fires burning until we get back. See you in an hour."

And our friends went with us to church.

When we got home there were even more people than when we left. Jon Hauser, Helen Jason and Dottie Rodgers had come down. The party got its second wind, and Cindy started serving food again. I put on a pot of coffee.

The caroling and easy conversation went on until dawn. I had drifted in and out of sleep several times, stretched out on a chair, and was awakened at six o'clock by Cindy. More food. She and Dottie had prepared a huge breakfast of ham and eggs and Christmas pastries and yet another pot of coffee, glorious coffee, for our remaining friends, who were now exchanging sentimental stories of their Christmases past.

Jon, enchanted by the simple pleasure of it all, was as pleasant as I had ever seen him.

"We should do this every weekend!" he declared.

"Yes, oh do let's," Helen bubbled. "It's all so absolutely delightful!"

"Well, maybe every weekend," Cindy said, starting to clear the table, "but not ALL weekend!"

Everyone laughed at her mock severity.

"And I'm sorry to tell you," Cindy went on, "that that means this weekend, too. We have a train to catch."

Everyone groaned. Even after twelve hours they hadn't had enough of the party.

"We're spending the day with our parents," I told Baldy when he asked why we needed to catch a train. "But, you know what? I have an idea. Everyone, you don't have to leave. You can spend Christmas

Day here if you want. Or take some food if you decide to leave or it will spoil."

In two seconds flat the guests decided to stay on without us. Møgens and Carl were delighted to have a surrogate family for the day, and Jim started a new round of carols.

Cindy and I put our gifts for our parents into a shopping bag and caught the eight o'clock train. Tired, we slept all the way to Cresco in the Poconos where Cindy's father met us.

We had lunch with Cindy's parents and an early dinner with mine, and the day passed rapidly. Loaded with gifts and baked goods to bring home, we caught the six p.m. train out of Cresco and got back to 8 West about eight o'clock as expected. Both of us were dead on our feet and longing to get to bed.

"My eyes feel like they're full of tinsel," I yawned. "I..."

Just as I was about to insert the key into our door I realized it was open. We entered to find the party we had left that morning still going strong! We couldn't believe our eyes. Jim Dixon was still leading Sally Dixon, the Ripons and Baldy in carols, Jon was sentimentally embracing Helen and Dottie, and Carl and Møgens were playing hosts. It looked as though they had been preparing and delivering food and drink all day.

To our astonishment, the apartment was spotless.

"Welcome home," everyone called out warmly. "Look, we straightened up for you."

Cindy was enchanted. "That's probably the best Christmas present of all," she declared. "We were dreading the dishes."

Someone handed us each a cup of coffee, and then everyone started to tell us what a wonderful day they had had. We sat down with our guests and somehow our fatigue simply disappeared.

The party finally broke up about ten o'clock, some 27 hours after it had started. Baldy was the last to leave, and he wouldn't budge until the last piece of food was put away and the last coffee mug washed and dried.

"Merry Christmas!" he called down the hall as he left. "And to all a good, uh, day!"

While the trash I collected that night was heavy, it wasn't nearly as heavy as the sentiments I collected as well. Eight or nine people stopped me to say thank you, and everyone else either made a point of opening their door to shake my hand or say a few words.

I stopped at the Dixons to thank them for the music and for cleaning up but was amazed to receive an apology from Jim.

"I know I monopolized the singing," he said, "but 1 haven't enjoyed Christmas so much since I was a choirboy."

"Me either, Jim," I assured him. He grinned, forgiven, and I went happily on my way.

The most astonishing sentiment, however, came from Jon.

"Whether you know it or not," he announced, "you have become a father of sorts for everyone here."

"Even you?"

"Could be," he grinned, "but if you tell anyone, I'll deny it. Anyway, what I was saying was that to most of your tenant-neighbors your party couldn't have been more meaningful. It represented a return home for Christmas."

With that mind-boggling sentiment in mind, plus the remembrance of our friends' enjoyment, I wasn't sure I ever wanted that Christmas – or my days as the Super of 6 and 8 West 90th Street – to end.

CHAPTER 41

Ring Out The Old, Ring In The New

From the spring day when the University of Pennsylvania accepted me for graduate work in the fall, my days as the Super of 6 and 8 West were numbered. The only question that remained was how many.

Cindy and I were torn between staying in New York City until the last possible moment or leaving as soon as I was graduated from Columbia. We finally decided, in late April, that the, latter course was the most rational. The sooner we moved to Philadelphia and settled in, the easier my transition to graduate school would be.

The K's, expecting the news, were nonetheless sad to hear it. Helena started to dab at her eyes.

"Franklin," she sniffed softly and daintily, "we have grown very fond of both of you during these past two years. You have kept the buildings clean, you have dealt well with the authorities, and you have been kind and helpful to the tenants."

She came closer and touched my face then Cindy's. She became pensive.

"But now that you are graduating from the University, you must do more important work. You, too, dear Cindy."

Mr. K concurred in all that his wife said. "Will you help us find another Super before you leave?" he inquired anxiously.

He looked so worried he made me laugh. "Of course I will," I told him. "That's the least I can do."

He nodded, relieved.

When I visited Columbia's Placement Office the next day – my first visit there in nearly two years – I was enchanted to find my favorite clerk, Matilda, still working there. She was delighted to learn that the Super's job at 6 and 8 West would remain a Columbia tradition.

"If you give me a minute, I think I can find the exact same notice that got you the job," she said, opening a file drawer and beginning to flip expertly through masses of paper. "Yes, here it is, exactly as David Weiss wrote it."

Once again I read:

NEED AN APARTMENT AND A JOB?
Get both as a package.
I'm part-time Super of 20 apartments
and get my apartment rent-free in return.
Am finishing school about Labor Day
and need replacement soon.
Contact David Weiss
through the Placement Office.

"Let's not argue with success, Matilda," I told my friend. "Change Labor Day to Memorial Day and David's name to mine, and let's see what happens."

"So be it, Franklin," she smiled. "I hope it works as well for you as it did for David."

It did.

The phone was ringing when I got home later that day. Soon it was arranged that the caller, a Walter Speck, would visit me at five o'clock to discuss the Super's job and talk to the K's.

Right on time the Super's bell rang and I went down to meet my potential successor.

Walter was a Korean War veteran who was just completing his second year of work in archeology in Columbia's School of General

Studies. He planned to marry in June and was as desperate for an apartment as I had been two years earlier.

"You have no idea how confusing everything is," he blurted. "My fiancée and I have no place to be alone together, and I'm sick and tired of living hand-to-mouth on measly part-time jobs."

"Yes I do," I told him, feeling almost smug.

He looked startled. "You do…what?"

"I do have every idea how it feels. What you're saying is almost verbatim what I told my predecessor. And let me tell you, everything will work out fine, better than you could imagine."

That broke the ice. He grinned, took a deep breath and started asking questions about the job.

I briefly described the Super's duties and promised to spend a half-day or so with him showing him the buildings and describing the tenants if he got the job.

He asked me about the landlord. "You'll find out soon enough," I told him. "I'm taking you to meet him now."

The interview went very smoothly, and Mr. K was warm and cordial. He offered Walter the job within five minutes of our arrival.

"You come back next week," Mr. K suggested, "and our Franklin will show you everything."

Walter didn't miss the 'our' reference and knew at once that he had found a new home.

But before he returned, I wondered how much to tell him about the tenants and their irrepressible landlord. Should I tell him that Mr. K was plotting to overthrow the government of Poland? Should I tell him about Jon Hauser and his ménage? And what about Felicia St. John and her Theosophical Society? Or the Blacks and their baking and their predictions? Should I repeat Baldy's colorful comments about the tenants in 6 and 8 West?

"Franklin," he had said to me one day when he was sanding the tiller on his boat, "I can't decide whether the fauna who inhabit these two buildings belong up the street at the Museum of Natural History or across Central Park in the Zoo. Whichever, you deserve a medal for preserving and protecting some damned fine species!"

And should I titillate him with tales of Sam and Smudge and soapsuds?

I decided on absolute discretion.

I told him that the tenants were a fine, affable, cooperative group who would no doubt try to ply him with as much booze as they had me.

"Control your liquor intake and you'll have no troubles, particularly with your bride," I sagely observed. Then I let my observations on the tenants end at that.

Cindy and I were exceptionally busy almost to moving day, which was to be the day before Memorial Day. I had tests to complete, including a rugged three-hour oral exam, and Cindy was left with the myriad details involved with moving. One thing was certain: we could no longer move our earthly belongings in only a car. Indeed, a full third of a moving van would be needed.

The K's stopped by early our last night to give us a "gift for our new house, may it be blessed," and to wish us well in Philadelphia. Mr. K took me aside.

"Make some babies soon," he urged. "You must make many babies."

For the first time in all the time I had known him, I shared a sly wink. "I shall be pleased to comply with your advice," I grinned. "If that's your last order, it's the best you've ever given us."

He winked back. No longer was he my boss; he was my friend.

After much hugging and hand-shaking, he took his wife's hand in his and together they took their leave.

"It's sad, isn't it?" Cindy commented. "It's almost like leaving another set of parents."

"Or gaining them," I answered.

Baldy stopped by soon after for a last visit. He brought two bottles of wine and enough cheese and French bread to feed everyone in both 6 and 8 West. Indeed, most of the tenants did stop by during that long night of reminiscences.

Jon Hauser came to say goodbye. Cindy gave him the usual glacial treatment, icy stares and frosty responses only when answers were absolutely necessary. Jon, however, at long last, was determined to melt that glacier.

"Cindy, I must beg your forgiveness," he said in a sincere, formal voice, one I had never heard before. "You sew beautifully, certainly as well as I do. You cook masterfully. And to keep Franklin as contented as you do — sexually, I mean, because he has never accepted any of my invitations — you most obviously know a great deal about sex."

Cindy spluttered and started to protest, but Jon insisted on finishing.

"As a city boy, I greatly envy Franklin. In finding a country girl like you, he found the best of all worlds."

I decided to save a thoroughly tongue-tied Cindy the necessity of a response to that lyrical monologue by guiding Jon to the door with protestations of lifelong friendship. I heard him chuckling loudly when he reached the stairs.

The moving van arrived at seven the next morning and by eight our belongings were aboard it. Cindy and I then scrubbed our apartment's floors and baseboards and carefully hung the rags in the bathroom to dry.

By nine we had bags in hand and were ready to leave for Pennsylvania Station and the train to Philadelphia.

I left Cindy in front of 8 West with our bags while I went to leave our keys with Mr. K. He greeted me at the door with a warm embrace and pulled me inside. There sat Walter Speck with a document in his hand and a rather puzzled look on his face.

"Hey, good luck," I smiled. "I hope your years here are as good as mine were."

He pursed his lips.

"Thanks," he said. "I think I'll need it. We were just going over the lease and...my god, do you know it has 56 'thou shalt not' clauses?"

I nodded but kept quiet. This was no time to start him worrying .

"There must be as many as there are in the Old Testament," he persisted. What in the world is the reason for them all?" .

Exchanging knowing glances with Mr. K, I decided to enlighten him just a bit.

"You'll find that Mr. K is both a moralist and a capitalist, with the latter strongly supporting the former," I told him.

Mr. K nodded his agreement, even though I knew he had not understood half of what I had said.

"By the time you leave," I went on, "the 'thou shalt nots' will probably be up to 75 — and you will be able to annotate every one of them."

Walter put a wry expression on his face. "That's all you're going to tell me?"

"That's all you need."

Mr. K roared his delight at my cryptic response. "And now you go?" he asked. I nodded.

With a hug for Mrs. K, a warm handshake with Mr. K and a nod of confidence to Walter, I departed 6 and 8 West and met my wife out front.

My days as a New York City Super had come to an end.

ABOUT THE AUTHOR

Frank W. Dressler, a retired association executive, has volunteered since 1995 with two international organizations in Russia, the Ukraine, Azerbaijan, Romania and Bosnia and the Republic of Georgia, and through his church, in Zimbabwe, Nepal and the Republic of Georgia. He lives with his wife Winifred in Susquehanna County, Pennsylvania.

CPSIA information can be obtained
at www.ICGtesting.com
Printed in the USA
BVHW081053120321
602301BV00005B/398